Night Music

Night Music

A FICTION BY
SVEN STOLPE

TRANSLATED BY
JOHN DEVLIN

SHEED AND WARD - New York

Night Music was originally published in Sweden by Albert Bonniers Förlag under the title *Spel i kulisser*.

Contents

Night Music

The Three Wise Men
O here and now our endless journey stops.

First Shepherd
We never left the place where we were born,

Second Shepherd
Have only lived one day, but every day,

Third Shepherd
Have walked a thousand miles yet only worn
The grass between our work and home away.

First Shepherd
Lonely we were though never left alone.

Second Shepherd
The solitude familiar to the poor
Is feeling that the family next door,
The way it talks, eats, dresses, loves, and hates,
Is indistinguishable from one's own.

Third Shepherd
Tonight for the first time the prison gates
Have opened.

First Shepherd
Music and sudden light

Second Shepherd
Have interrupted our routine tonight,

Third Shepherd
And swept the filth of habit from our hearts. '

The Three Shepherds
O here and now our endless journey starts.

Wise Men
Our arrogant longing to attain the tomb,

Shepherds
Our sullen wish to go back to the womb,

Wise Men
To have no past,

Shepherds
No future,

Tutti
Is refused.
And yet, without our knowledge, Love has used
Our weakness as a guard and guide.
We bless

Wise Men
Our lives' impatience.

Shepherds
Our lives' laziness,

Tutti
And bless each other's sin, exchanging here

Wise Men
Exceptional conceit

    Shepherds
With average fear.

     —W. H. AUDEN
     For the Time Being
     A CHRISTMAS ORATORIO

PART I

Aubade

1

Roofs sooty and black, white pigeon traces which the dirty city breath has not yet had time to soil, feeble panting from six chimney pipes. Is there no wind that can tear asunder these coverings of haze and fog?

People live beneath the roofs and chimneys—beehives of them cooped up in small compartments. The street is still hidden; only tree tops can be glimpsed. In the distance at the main railroad terminal train whistles are snarling. Nearby is a flagpole, where one lone, wind-tattered flag hangs without life. Someone forgot to take it in.

The city begins to stir beneath its dirty blanket. Cars line up and big trucks clatter from the country with loads of vegetables and carcasses. The beast must be fed once he throws off his sooty covers. On the river's opposite side the huge drums of the gas works stand fat and bloated; one can make out the mass if not the silhouette. Their heavy pressure forces poison gas through countless small pipes into every cubicle. A twist of the wrist and a friendly stealth would blot out the poor souls lying behind drawn curtains, regathering their scattered energies in wretched sleep.

Now comes the clattering of pans and coffee pots. Water pipes begin to grumble. Sleepy faces have to be scoured. A new day is waiting! The garbage trucks have taken away their loads and housekeepers drag rusty barrels back into the yards. A wind is shoving against the smog and somewhere on the horizon behind the barracks the sun lurks, its rays still unable to cut a path.

The street can be seen now. There are small buds on the trees; spring will soon be here if it gets a chance. A grotesque turtle of a streetcar thumps by and blindly slugs along in its predestined pattern.

The city awakes, hesitantly and without joy. Puffs of wind come from various directions. The dirty flag makes a final attempt to unfurl, then falls back limp and wraps itself around the black staff. Only a torn rag on one corner continues a feeble flapping.

In the cells of this huge, smoke-filled beehive human beings are supposed to flourish. Souls are supposed to unfold into life like graceful flowers. Down inside there, man is supposed to stand erect and alert to his destiny, man who was created to inhabit a paradise refreshed by cool springs and gentle breezes.

Farther out in the suburbs the foul ugliness is slowly oozing. It encompasses the few trees and thickets and forces them to wither. It shoves its sewers and gas pipes through the soil and undermines the substratum. Slowly a circle expands, a pregnancy of smoke, fumes and the exhalations of a cooped-up humanity.

Blackened church spires emerge from the thinning fog. They are copies, parodies of proud cathedrals which a thousand years ago were hurled up over the small grey cities of the Ile de France and Bourgogne. In the midst of this nightmare the children of men are supposed to meet Him who caused the heavens to arch over, the springs to gush forth, and the song of birds to fill the heavens.

Fat smoke puffs from an unbanked stack, and when it is blown aside the factory district is revealed. This band is the river, the receptacle for the thousand sewers with the garbage, refuse and excrement of all that has been the delight of tired bodies. Here are the staunchly fighting parks, a cracked mirror of nature. Here lies that giant invertebrate, the Parlia-

ment and Palace, in tame Empire décor. Then the narrow streets broaden out into avenues where now and again construction holes yawn.

A young man is walking through the "ant-hill city, city full of dreams/where the specter in broad daylight accosts the passerby." His head is sunk forward and his pace uncertain.

He is twenty, perhaps. A light, even tan. Not a wrinkle, except those that crop out when he raises his glance in a distracted, somewhat nervous reflex. A shock of hair falls over the left side of his forehead and now and again he has to throw it back with a quick pass of the hand or jerk of the head. A confident man has confident hair that knows its rightful place; this hair has not yet made up its mind how it will lie.

He stops in front of a bookstore. How could he pass it by? His eye runs over the list of offerings—lyric poetry, sociology, new philosophical works; he is accustomed to digesting book titles.

The first days of deceitful April. Spring's charm is still promised, but even now summer is lurking nearby and soon the great heat will bring torment. A thousand voices rustle, whisper and chatter in the foliage. Nervous showers chase darkly-frilled fields over the shining surface of the water. Then all becomes quiet. The scudding clouds disappear, the last bush trembles into silence. Everything becomes an expectancy, a suspension of time, a release that never arrives.

It is then that the young heart feels its first pain. Youth looks into himself astonished. Do I really have all this within me? What is it deep inside that causes me so much pain? His hand reaches toward his heart; his eyes become vague and his mouth set. Life, life that had been morning freshness, life that had been a whispering promise and a secret courtship suddenly becomes a battle. Leaning forward he looks down uneasily into an abyss opening behind a deceptively soothing trellis of lyricism. The ground under him is crumbling. What unknown awaits me? Is it life itself that fills me so full of dread?

He shakes his head, as if such a gesture could shake off his fate. He slicks back his hair as if his thoughts could be made clear by the gentle motion of a slender hand. Slowly he turns into a walk leading up to an imposing residence. The house he is about to enter is massive and forbidding. Built of dark stone, it is heavy with ponderous heroic adornment in the Florentine style, with fenestration designed to keep light from penetrating. A maid opens the door and the young man steps into a stone-paved hall the ceiling of which echoes back footfalls in feudal fashion. Unlikely Tritons blink down from walls lined with Baroque chairs. This is indeed a dwelling suited to the Prime Minister of the country.

"Have you eaten, Georg?"

"No, I forgot to."

"Well, that won't do! People have to eat."

"Louise, you ought to know by this time that we are not allowed to eat directly before Communion."

"Have you been to church?" The maid was puzzled, almost shocked. This sounded like the nineteenth century. Church and religion were to help people when things were not going well, in times of sickness, death, or an unexpected flunk at school. If Georg had been to church, something unpleasant must have happened to the boy.

Georg paid small attention to her questions.

"Shall I bring up a tray?"

"Thanks, Louise, I'll wait until lunch."

22

The maid stared at him. If the scion of the family went to a bar or a brothel, well—that was natural. They all did it. But Mass . . . and on a weekday? Something must have happened to him. Shaking her head she retreated behind the drapery after letting him into the library. Despite the stone floor her movements were noiseless. The Prime Minister had ordered the servants to wear rubber heels.

Georg entered the library, a square room fitted all around with low bookcases housing series of legal periodicals, domestic economy matters and Parliament records, all in impeccable order. Another young man was standing at the desk, his back to the door. Lean and spare, with slightly sloping shoulders, he was examining mail and sorting the letters and documents into separate piles. Though a thick carpet covered the floor he noticed Georg's step and turned.

"Don't be startled, Wendt! It's only me. Has Father left yet?"

"No, he wants to stay home to hear his speech."

A bored grin flitted across the boy's face. "Does he have to stay home for that?"

An alert glance on the part of the Secretary. He was aware of the irony, perhaps shared it, but he was accustomed to handling himself nimbly. A secretary is not supposed to have private reactions.

"The Prime Minister's address is going to be broadcast at nine o'clock, then twice again during the day."

"How bombastic! Don't you agree, Wendt?"

A quiet, searching glance: "Have you been out?"

"Yes."

"To Mass?"

Georg nodded and sank into one of the leather armchairs. Why had he answered the question with a mere nod? Before him were the cigar box, the huge lighter and the equally outsized ivory-handled cigar cutter. Why was everything so grandiose? Why couldn't there be delicate, elegant, comfortable, even useless objects in this house?

Wendt had finished sorting the letters and documents. He moved the ashtray slightly closer to the center of the table and set the chair back several inches. Georg smiled at him.

"Wendt, you're comical!"

"Thanks. Do you think it's funny if a man does what he is paid to do?"

"There are various ways to do things. Do you plan to listen to Father's talk?"

"It touches on many important matters . . ."

"So, you're the one who wrote the speech!"

"I would never attempt such a thing. But I did write the outline."

Georg rose quickly and measured the room with rapid steps, his left hand in his pocket, the right dangling. Suddenly he stopped and looked down at the street. Except for two police officers at the intersection it was deserted, but he knew that more were stationed in the house across the way. The Prime Minister's residence was under guard. Perhaps there were even machine guns behind those curtains.

"Wendt," he said quietly; "Wendt, tell me. Have you always been like—like this?"

"Yes," came the dry clear voice from behind him, "yes, always."

Georg turned, his quizzical smile almost a pained grimace. Slowly he walked toward the secretary. Wendt, as spare as himself, was ten years his senior, his face tense and recollected, his lips a straight line. His hair had begun to thin out somewhat.

"Haven't you ever wanted to take a post yourself? Have you always been so damned objective?"

"I am non-political. Because of the nature of my profession

24

I am concerned with politics, but from a personal point of view it does not interest me at all."

"I can't understand how anyone can be like that."

"I can see the justice of most points of view. When you're built that way, you can't act. You can hardly live. I am completely satisfied to be your father's secretary. People like me are necessary."

"But you're not really living!"

Wendt's glance was unwavering: "Do you consider yourself alive?"

Georg did not answer but began to pace back and forth again.

"So far as I'm concerned it's a mystery. You're highly gifted. At times I almost think that you are the one who feeds my father most of his ideas . . ."

"Nonsense!"

". . . and yet you're so detached, so 'objective.' It's beyond me. You don't write anything, you don't even have your own home, you're not married . . ."

Wendt looked up quickly.

"Don't make fun of me, Georg."

Georg stood still, turned slowly and suddenly seemed embarrassed.

"Pardon me . . . I'm an idiot . . . I didn't have that particular affair in mind at all . . ."

"That's all right," Wendt answered briskly.

Georg stepped closer to him and thoughtfully laid his hand on the other's shoulder.

"I mean that business about my sister—that's all forgotten, isn't it? You can tell me the truth. It's not bothering you any more, is it?"

Wendt shrugged slightly and moved away a step so that Georg's hand slipped from his shoulder.

Georg looked into his eyes. "I've got to tell you something. Be happy that you are rid of her. I had to say it."

Wendt's lips became more severe: "We won't talk about that now. His Excellency was quite right at the time."

Georg didn't move; his face darkened.

"No, he was not right! His reasons were based on pride. Inhuman, as always. But I don't pity you a bit because my sister is a. . . ."

"I continue to maintain the same high respect for Miss Regina as before," Wendt answered professionally.

Georg looked after him as Wendt crossed to the door leading to the dining hall. He stopped and spoke without turning.

"His Excellency is coming," he said dryly.

2

GEORG remained standing and stared toward the door. Then he threw himself comfortably into the armchair, reached mechanically for a cigar, put it back and lit a cigarette with the enormous apparatus that required both hands. Across the ascending haze he seemed to feel the whole atmosphere of the house rise up against him: dark, smoke-stained draperies, massive furniture at once static and sterile—a room created to reverberate with phrases.

Prime Minister Falk entered.

" 'Morning, Wendt. Anything new?"

He glanced at his son.

"You could at least look up, Georg! Smoking so early? That's not like you, if I'm not mistaken. No, don't put it out. It's not dangerous for moderate smokers like you."

He can't stop offering advice. He's forever talking about this relationship, that relationship. If he could only really hear himself for once. Georg shifted in his chair.

Falk walked to the desk and threw down a newspaper that he had been reading at breakfast.

"Have you seen the *Morning Post,* Wendt? They're still writing that stuff! They have the nerve to keep it up!"

"You don't have to worry about it, Excellency."

"But, my good man! Everybody reads it! I heard yesterday from the Field Marshal that His Majesty guffawed at the latest gossip."

"I did too, Father."

Falk turned slowly towards his son; he was somewhat hurt and surprised. As his eyes fell on the shock of hair and the tall slender form, his features lightened. He loved this young man and was determined to do everything in his power to make his life happy or successful, and if possible, both. He allowed a smile of self-indulgence to play over his features and it was only then, when the official, the First Minister, the juridical thinker had disappeared, that he became himself, a powerful, bear-like Germanic type, with beetling grey brows and American black-horned glasses which little suited him.

"You laughed? Weren't you a bit ashamed of yourself, my boy?"

His glance continued to be cheerful and mild. Of course a boy should be able to laugh at his father if he wanted to.

"It was funny, Father! Admit it. Of course it was disgraceful nonsense, but so is all journalism."

Falk's smile faded, to be slowly replaced by his habitual mask. At first he spoke hesitantly, then with increasing conviction and finally with pathos of tone and gesture as if on the speaker's rostrum.

"I don't understand you, Georg. Somehow you have become cynical. Your father's name is dragged through the mud, outrageous charges are laid against my personal integrity, reports are made—altogether false ones—about my stock holdings and it is asserted that the National Bank is leading me about on a leash. They don't know when to stop! And this paper is supposed to hold decent, middle-class, Catholic views. In the same issue there are two articles on religion. Behind this campaign is Dr. Graber's personal hate. Nothing else. You laughed! And His Majesty laughed! The Field Marshal told me that the King had this gossip read to him while he was taking his coffee, minutes before I arrived. The others were embarrassed and uncomfortable, but the King laughed himself half dead."

"Really? He's tremendous!"

Georg pushed himself deep into the chair, his left hand dangling limply over the armrest so that his cigarette almost touched the carpet.

"Watch out for that rug, Son. You'll burn a hole in it! So! It's tremendous if they laugh like young puppies when the name of the country's Prime Minister is wiped in dung!"

Georg got up and stepped forward, his eyes still twinkling.

"Yes, Father, it's tremendous. I put no stock in monarchial dignity and all that stuff. You know that. But the King is one person who is loyal to you. He thinks a lot of you and he will never betray you as so many others have done, even if he does happen to have a sense of humor. And he can't be shocked."

Falk nodded ironically several times. He sat down by the desk, thumbed briefly through some letters and then looked up again. His face was drawn.

"Yes, that's true. But he is also reckless and hotheaded. I can never get anything out of him. I've never heard him speak an intelligent word. Sometimes he laughs right in the middle of a vital discussion. At the last Council of State he was watching a bird on the window sill. Suddenly he jumped up and wanted to get a closer look. Just like a child!"

Georg had gone again to the window. He raised the photograph of the crowned King, looked at the slender smiling face and nodded.

"He's a free man; that's his secret."

Falk glanced at his son. Was that an innuendo? The youngster had good qualities but was inclined to be brash and indifferent.

"You can talk like that if you want. But let me tell you: it is lucky for this country and for you that there are people who are prosaic, uncomplicated, practical . . . people who don't shrink from performing difficult tasks."

Georg had turned toward his father and was aware of the secretary standing motionless and impassive. He didn't quite know how much irony to put into his voice. As a result he said hesitatingly:

"You mean people like yourself, Father?"

"Yes," Falk answered stiffly. "Think what you like; reproach me for my pride—I've been reading about it for four years in the newspapers, so it doesn't hurt me any more."

Circling the desk he grabbed a cigar; the thick heavy hands fumbled with the heavy lighter. Finally he caught the light, took a few puffs and said with rising professional pathos:

"I don't know whether you understand this affair or care to understand it. But in your interest there exists an invisible chain that runs all around this ancient land. A human chain, made up of men who stick to the job they are called upon to perform. And I don't mean the military. I mean upright, dedicated human beings, each one of whom is a source of strength in his own right. These people bear the burden that others have thrust upon them. They remain loyal while others become traitors. They offer their heads as sacrifice . . ."

He had completely forgotten where he was and stood at the

29

desk as if on a speaker's rostum addressing an invisible audience.

Elbows propped on the armrests Georg watched, his half-closed eyes hidden behind interlocking fingers in a sort of instinctive act of protection. "Old Boy," he thought, "whom I like and perhaps even love. Don't you know you are speaking to yourself, trying to convince yourself? That metallic clang comes only when a person is uneasy and insecure."

But his father droned on, switching unconsciously to the diction of formal address:

"I assure you that it is only because of such a ring of will and character that this country still holds her ancient liberties. Everyone admires the virtuosos, the great connoisseurs, the master spirits, the poets who proclaim treason the highest good and burn incense unto themselves. But who thanks the watchers on the frontiers in their anonymity? No one!"

Georg's glance fell upon his mother's picture, ritualistically placed on his father's desk. His father's hand pounded the top of the desk, inches from the frame. Why couldn't he aim a little better? Why was his mother living out at the country house and so seldom here? Why was she now a wraith, a broken woman simply living out her years? He was almost shocked when the next second he heard his own voice—trembling:

"And do you number yourself among these anonymous heroes, Father?"

Falk looked steadily at his son.

"Yes," he said. "But perhaps I am not anonymous. I belong —unfortunately—to the public. There has been laid upon me a heavy burden, namely to be the First Minister of this country. Do you think it's a game, a pleasure? No, it's a sacrifice."

Georg closed his eyes. Now the boundary had been crossed. "Sacrifice" was a big word. Sacrifice meant to be nailed to a cross, to stand quietly while being spat upon, to lay down one's life for one's friends. Sacrifice meant to surrender one's self, to take on the injustices and terror of life without complaint.

"Just a few minutes before the broadcast," he heard Wendt say.

The secretary had stood detached the whole time.

"The thought occurred to me that Your Excellency would prefer to listen in the drawing room. The radio there is better and if an important telephone call should come in Your Excellency can sit there undisturbed."

Falk nodded in cheerful anticipation of hearing his own voice.

"Very well—Georg, tell your sister that I will be speaking on the radio in a few minutes. She didn't come down to breakfast—as usual. I want her to hear me even though I know that her views and mine do not often tally."

Wendt had gone to the desk. Without looking at Georg he said quietly to Falk:

"I have here some material that I have been wanting to show you, your Excellency. I mean about Dr. Graber and the *Morning Post*."

Falk's features brightened; he couldn't control his obvious pleasure: "What's that? Really?"

Becoming again aware of Georg, he checked himself.

"Yes. So then . . . we will discuss this later. I have no desire to become in any way linked with this man. When you touch him you get your fingers dirty, and that's unpleasant."

He motioned to his son: "Georg. Please try to find your sister. I insist that she hear my speech."

Georg nodded, snuffed out his cigarette and went slowly toward the door.

His expression fresh and youthful, Falk turned toward his secretary. Hate has a rejuvenating quality.

"Did you really dig up something about Dr. Graber?"

He was full of enthusiasm but he did not forget to pull up his trouser creases as he sank down at the desk. Agility lay in those meaty hands!

"I have a series of investigations underway," said Wendt. "One set of facts or the other can be used—more than we dreamed."

With soft passion Falk answered, "You don't say! You don't say!"

As he leafed through the dossier which his secretary had placed before him he began to exclaim:

"So he *was* mixed up in the Gloria affair. He *did* take meals with Edvardsen and Rubow. Can you actually prove that?"

"Yesterday evening I had the Attorney General look through the papers. The picture is crystal clear. Your Excellency, I have never been so completely sure of any situation as I am of this one. If our material is put to use—in the right way—Dr. Graber is politically a dead man. Furthermore, the situation is such that from a moral point of view he . . ."

Falk looked up and raised his clenched fist:

"Moral!" he shouted, "what are you saying, Wendt?"

Wendt had crossed his arms and was looking out through the window; the morning fog had lifted a bit and the sun seemed about to break through. Really, it was no longer necessary to use the light. He walked to the door-jamb and turned off the electricity. Falk followed every movement and nodded approvingly: the fanatic for order was keeping the electric bill down. Wendt was unsurpassed; nothing escaped him.

"Well?"

The secretary walked slowly back to the center of the room:

"I dislike condemning him. But my investigations show that he has lived with another woman. Under an assumed name he took a flat for her at Constitution Place. He rented it furnished, through a strawman. I have seen the lease and talked with the superintendant, who is quite upset to learn about it."

Falk's fist smashed down on the desk.

"A whoremonger and a hypocrite! And he has the nerve to moralize about my private life, which the breath of scandal never . . . Who is this woman?"

Wendt shrugged.

"I don't know too much about her. The name is Helene Gritz. Apparently she once studied medicine and now lives very quietly and withdrawn. Evidently he got to know her two years ago during that world cruise."

Falk realized that his display of interest was perhaps too great. He caught himself and nodded, brows still frowning. Then he relighted the cigar which had gone out during his display of righteous zeal.

"Well, now. All this is very interesting and it confirms my suspicion—or at least my intuition, because I certainly anticipated something of this sort. But when all is said and done it may well be his own private business. If he wants to be the chief penman of the Conservative Party, defending morality, tradition and religion and, at the same time, live like a pig . . . But the Gloria affair—that should be brought out into the daylight."

"If Your Excellency agrees, perhaps this other matter could be released—carefully."

Falk looked at him. Now he was completely himself, the calm clever head of the government.

"No. I will have nothing to do with that. I don't want to use his own weapons. He can write scandal stories if he wants to. By the way, what time is it?"

Wendt looked at his watch and checked it with a glance out toward the church steeple.

"Your address begins in exactly forty-five seconds."

33

He stepped forward and opened the door to the drawing room. Falk followed him, then stopped, a troubled expression crossing his face.

"We really should phone my wife in the country and tell her to listen. And the children? Where are they? Where the hell are they? They're unbelievably indifferent recently."

With a heavy step he walked through the doorway.

3

THE PRIME MINISTER's voice rang from the library:

"My fellow citizens! This is a time of unspeakable confusion and unleashed passions. It is a time when even the most hallowed laws for the conduct both of nations and of individuals are not merely placed in jeopardy but appear lost for generations to come. In this awful hour, I, as Prime Minister of this country, want to direct to each individual an earnest cry of warning. I choose the words of the poet: 'In the name of God, act bravely!' "

Georg and his sister entered the room. The girl paused to listen, held her hands over her ears and said in her deep, passionate voice:

"For God's sake, close that door! Or better yet, pull out the plug!"

With his finger on his lips Georg crossed to the drawing room door and closed it silently. He went to the library radio, fiddled with the knobs and lowered the volume. Then he sat down opposite his sister, who had thrown herself on the couch.

"We must act as if we are listening . . . in case he should come in."

The girl laughed scornfully and blew a cloud of cigarette smoke towards him as he gazed pensively at her, chin propped in his hand, elbow on the arm of his chair.

There had been a time when he was still a small boy and she was already a young woman. Then his admiration for her had been infinite, but now he was beginning to see her through older eyes. She was just as beautiful now as she had been when he first became aware of her: blond hair and naturally dark eyebrows, a clean-cut, intellectual profile plus the intense vibrations of a sensitive disposition—it was as if she had been created from finer material than other women; as if her reactions were more sensitive, quick and incisive; as if she could feel nuances and be influenced and tortured by what merely passed over the others.

Often he had thought: Regina has been created to suffer. One could never imagine that she had the power to carve out a secure niche in an ordinary existence. She belonged, rather, to another plane of reality: imported cigarettes, tense Russian composers, breakneck horseback rides in the early morning. Above all, she belonged to the dance.

Her entire body expressed her feelings as effectively as did her sensitive features. He was twelve when he first saw her dance, and she was twenty. It was also the first time that he saw a woman all but nude. The recital was a benefit performance at the Polish embassy. Permission had been granted him to attend since it was his sister who was to perform. Her grace had penetrated his consciousness so painfully that ever since that time all his experiences of beauty had been associated to some extent with feelings of anxiety and anguish. Was she real? He was staggered by the thought that mankind could actually live the miserable life that ordinary existence seemed to be! Gadgets, technical skills, streetcars, factories, money! How could people stand it when this other reality existed within their reach? A strong feeling of revulsion had gripped him when he noticed how coolly the audience appraised her limbs. He heard someone remark that she was still tan—actually her skin was naturally dark. He became aware of the existence of sensuous power, although he didn't realize precisely what it was. He had looked upon the dance as a sort of sanctuary rite, a great, disciplined, chaste artform. When applause greeted the close of her performance and he saw her impassive face, he was convinced that he had been the only one who had really seen her. He was proud of such a sister and he longed one day to be able to penetrate into her world. He soon realized, however, that if he were to share her world, he would have to become an artist himself —and that he could not be.

Now he watched her tenderly and uneasily. This beautiful face—how long had it been since he had seen it in repose? She lived her own life; she practised her dancing but gave few recitals. She had her own circle of friends who seldom or never came to the house. Often she would visit her mother out in the country and pass weeks there with her books and her music. She composed dance music but always burned the manuscripts. Peace surrounded her only when she danced. And this peace was so complete that it seemed not far removed from the peace of death. Beyond the realm of her art, her self-created second reality, the remaining quotient of her life seemed to be pain and nothing else. In recent years her bitterness and cynicism had increased. He had compared other women to her—and all without exception suffered in contrast. If only he could help her in some way! But he knew that she saw nothing more in him than a clumsy boy. There had been times when she had tried to teach him, of all things, how to walk, but he could never follow her instructions and she had given up her efforts with a tired laugh.

Regina winced as she listened, but said nothing. She drew her lips into a straight line, snuffed the cigarette and sank

36

back into the cushions, letting the last of the smoke drift away. In her dusky voice she remarked:

"It's not very pleasant to have a big bluff for a father, is it. I find it . . . oppressive."

He had heard her say similar things before yet a feeling of unrest swept over him as he caught the hatred in his sister's voice that found him at a loss for an answer. His own relationship with his father was ambivalent: he continued to respect him; he was still impressed by the concentrated drive and the importance of his person. At the same time he could see his naivete, his inability to make distinctions, his pigheadedness. As for the situation regarding his mother . . .

"I agree that it's hard to take a father that you can never understand," he ventured hesitantly. "But I often wonder if anybody understands him. Maybe nobody understands his own father."

Regina lay with closed eyes, her head propped against the sofa pillows. He noticed the rise and fall of her breast.

"No," she said after a while. "So far as I am concerned I have never even been introduced to him. It's as though I had never even heard rumors spoken about him. So far as he's concerned I simply don't exist."

Georg looked up. How could their father not love her, not be proud of a daughter who embodied sensitive breeding and beauty? As so often happened he shrank at the sound of his own voice.

"At any rate he knows what you've been up to lately!"

It was as if for a moment his subconscious had taken over his speech mechanism and turned off the switch leading to his intellect.

Regina bit her lip.

"Naturally," she said. "Everything that is not pertinent to my individuality he knows perfectly. But myself! No contact, not even a vibration!"

The sun was now pushing through the center French window. A stream of light fell upon her figure, but her face continued to lie in shadow. In a few moments her features would also be distilled in light. He sat quietly; the buzzing of the muffled radio was faint. Or was the noise coming from the other room?

Regina, he thought to himself, do you know how much I love you? Isn't a brother's love something to be cherished? You have never caressed me, have never helped me but you have dug yourself so deep into my subconscious that I can never see other women except through you. Oh, Regina, Regina . . .

"Regina," he said, his voice stumbling, "may I ask you something?"

"Certainly," she replied, eyes still closed. "Only you won't get any answer if it's an unpleasant question."

Georg, cheeks flushed, fixed his eyes on the carpet, then looked up. He wanted to grasp her hand but didn't quite dare. It wasn't right for her to go around with bare arms. She should be more careful about putting those beautiful lines on exhibition. Every time he had seen her dancing with a young man he had actually become upset. She should dance alone, not with a lustful, earthy male.

"It's a very interesting question—for you as well as for me."

Once more he hesitated, then tore himself free of his cowardice:

"Regina, are you satisfied with your life—the way you are living it?"

She raised herself languidly. What lay in that expression? Boredom, aversion, scorn? It was a dark well of melancholy upon whose surface all of these nuances played like the lustre of a sun-spangled inlet. Again she made an effort to speak but closed her mouth instead. Why did she do that so often? Was it self-control, her desire not to hurt? Or was it merely because it was so useless to say anything. People speak so that they can be understood; yet one human consciousness had never yet succeeded in making another understand itself. Nevertheless at that moment a friendly light came into her eyes; she tilted her head pensively and said slowly:

"Satisfied? That's really a dull, bourgeois word you're using. There's no such thing as satisfaction—at least not in the world of reality. To be a human being means to be never satisfied."

She got up without the aid of her hands. How he loved that sovereign dominion over her body and its nimble charm! If only he himself possessed this superiority, this ability to win easily such quick little victories!

She tossed her hair back and took a cigarette, but let the match go out as she was about to light it. Her figure was now half into the cone of light and he could see her profile as she parted her lips; her head rose as she answered, eyes fixed on a distant point:

" 'As I live it,' you said. I have the impression that I don't really live my life or determine what it is. Something brutal outside of me pulls the strings, sometimes for good, sometimes for bad."

She receded into the semi-darkness of the opposite side of the room, walked to the window that still lay in the shade and said so softly that he could hardly hear:

"I don't know whether a grand piano has so much to say. After all, it's the alien, brutal pianist who does the deciding."

That was just like her, just her way of talking! She and she alone spoke like that. Now Georg stood up, for he realized that an anxious moment was coming. How would he be able to offer anything to this unusual mind that would not be brushed off with a gesture of her hand? What made him imagine that he could even graze her world? But he must try. As truly as he loved her he could not be an idle spectator

to what was happening within her. He could not close his eyes
to what everyone else was noticing. He went toward her and
paused half way, his hand mechanically grasping a book in the
case between the windows, his eyes fixed on her back. Her
blond, Grecian hair was silhouetted against the dark blue
curtains. Almost groaning with fear he said:

"Regina, I am younger than you and I understand what
you mean when you say that I don't know what I'm talking
about. But you know that I am very fond of you. We've
always stuck together and been friends."

She turned towards him and though he couldn't see her
face he sensed the expression of smiling compassion, even
sympathy that was playing on it.

Vehemently he continued:

"You have changed. You're nervous, spiteful, off-balance."

There was a moment of silence.

"Yes, anything else?" she asked, softly and clearly.

He made a motion with his left hand; the right still held
the book half drawn out of the case.

"But don't you understand . . . that . . . that it hurts me?
Regina, you have troubles . . ."

Let it sound as naive as possible, he had to get it out!

"Can I help you?"

Quickly Regina moved toward him. Though she was
shorter it was he who felt small—and he could hardly bear
her gentle smile, for behind it lurked that sadness continually playing across her eyes and over her high forehead. She
stood before him, pushed the book back and almost with the
same motion ran her hand across his cheek.

"No," she said, "You can't—but you're nice."

She moved across the room and then stood with her back
against their father's desk, arms framing the outline of her
body, hands propped on the edge.

"I live exactly as I must live," she said. "No one can do

40

anything about it—neither Father with his commands and his goddamned morality, nor Mother with her prayers and liturgy, nor you with yours—and that's it."

Georg stepped up to her, arms dangling:

"Regina, may I say something—without your getting mad?"

Again she inclined her head a little, and he could not tell if her eyes were tender or scornful.

"Say it."

He pulled out his handkerchief and awkwardly blew his nose.

"Regina, I really know so little about you . . ."

He sensed that her features were becoming more stern.

"You see," he continued quickly, "you say that I can say what I want to . . . but . . ."

Though his eyes were glued to the rug he was completely aware that she raised her head and grinned. And he heard her mocking voice:

"But what is it? What do you want to say?"

He risked looking directly into her eyes and saw his sister standing there, wretched and disturbed. His heart overflowed with pity and he said strongly:

"You are unhappy and upset and that makes me very sad."

Silence again. He didn't venture another look but went back to the table and lit a cigarette.

"That is nice of you," he heard her answer, as if she were stifling a yawn. "But in a few years you'll be just as distraught. To be a human means to be distraught and tormented."

With a quick gesture she continued:

"At any rate you've never heard me complain!"

He turned violently:

"I wish you had complained! Regina, you're not living any more, you're drifting without a rudder. Deep down inside you don't want to be a bohemian. You don't even like that

41

sort of people. You were created for another type of life, and you are throwing it away."

When she spoke her voice was furious. "Pardon me. Did you close the door a moment ago or not? I almost thought that I could hear the moralizing basso of the 'father of his country.' It gets on my nerves! Haven't I already told you to let me alone?"

She had been hurt but that could not be helped.

"It's all the same to me if you get mad. I've watched you for the last year. You've grown old. Yes, it's the truth, even though you are still beautiful. You don't sleep well; you take sleeping pills. You've stopped having fun and learning. You worry me, Regina."

She moved toward him again and before she was even close he experienced her being, a wave of frigidity. Again she allowed her cool hand to glide over his cheek; lightly she touched his hair and tousled it. Then she passed on to the sofa and sat down where she had been before.

"All that you can leave for Father," she said, becoming friendly again. "He knows no greater pleasure than to be uneasy about others and sure of himself. Furthermore, I assume that you understand that any life is better than the way he would have it: conform to the pattern, obey laws you don't believe in—become a pharisee, a moral automaton."

"You know," he said, "that I don't believe in his morality any more than you do, Regina. That's exactly why I can't understand how anyone can go on drifting the way you are."

This was dangerous ground again, and again he knew that her brief, deliberate pause meant both that she understood him fully and that she would spare him the pain of a slashing answer.

"I have never done what you say. I have never stopped trying to live up to worthwhile ideas. About the other matter,

I don't bother at all. I don't pretent to be better than I am. That is at least one thing that Christer taught me before Father closed in."

"Yes, Wendt. What really happened between you two?" He used the opportunity to slip over to neutral territory. "Who can understand Wendt? He must be able to see through Father. And yet he is so loyal to him that he gave up his love for you. He must have been really in love with you."

Regina lay back on the pillows and closed her eyes.

"I don't know," she said quietly. "I never understood him. I was young then, too, and he is not like other people. He leads his life as if he didn't belong to it, as if he were serving other purposes. Somehow he seems like a monk—not your variety."

"Regina," Georg said forcefully, "I want to escape from Father's clutch too, but I don't want to be wrecked in the process. That would be worse than remaining bourgeois. I want to follow another standard, another morality that can be judged by both instinct and reason to be good."

Regina smiled.

"We all do. But there is no morality which can satisfy the instincts. It's as simple as that."

Georg bent over and grasped her hand.

"I'm not so sure about that," he said softly but with passion. "I believe that I'm beginning to become aware of something. Regina, you would never guess what I've discovered. The only correct way to live is to put one's self at the service of a holy thing, of a great and demanding idea . . ."

Irritated and weary, Regina stood up; her tenderness toward him was passed.

"Now I'm the one who's getting uneasy," she said, "Have you got religion? So long as your Christianity was aesthetic, your church-going could be tolerated. But this smells of incense from a long way off!"

43

He smiled.

"No. On the contrary. Do you know what I think? The only solution is to be . . ."

Regina passed her hand over her mouth as if to stifle a yawn. At the same moment they heard steps coming from the salon. Georg lunged at the radio and turned up the volume. Applause greeted the Prime Minister's speech, which had just ended.

Christer Wendt, who opened the door, had seen Georg's stratagem but his face remained blank. He bowed to Regina, who did not appear to notice him. Herbert Falk entered. He was somewhat flushed, his movements quicker than usual. His eyes flew around the room.

"So this is where you have been, children? Well, it was probably better so. Well—what do you think, now? What do you think?"

Rubbing his hands together he circled the room, stopped, stretched. Before anyone could answer—brother and sister were looking at each other hesitantly and cynically—he continued in the exact tone he had used upon the radio:

"If the people could only see that we must hang together if we are going to get out of this difficult situation. A small sacrifice is always worth the effort, isn't it? If each and every one of us would sacrifice a little—would contribute some personal dedication!"

"What will his party sacrifice, might I ask?" Regina said, so softly that only Georg could hear.

But the father noticed that she had turned toward her brother and walked up to the girl.

"What did you say, Regina? In this matter you and I may perhaps be on the same side." He flashed a friendly, twinkling smile. When he is dictatorial and patriarchal, thought his daughter, he's sinister. But when he becomes the tender father—he's really awful! When he claps me on the shoulder I'd like to scream and bite his finger.

44

"Yes, personal dedication is truly wonderful," she said icily.

He looked at her awhile—without seeing her, completely absorbed in his own train of thought. Just keep looking, she thought. I'll say what I want to. You've never learned to listen to anyone but yourself. It keeps you going.

"I assure you, children, that I would give up my post tomorrow if I did not believe that I have a task to accomplish."

"What is your task?" Georg asked bluntly.

His father looked at him with his unseeing stare.

"To unite! To integrate!"

He turned to Wendt.

"I would like to know whether His Majesty listened."

Then again to the children.

"And your mother, have you heard from her?"

"Not since yesterday," Regina answered dully. "I was out there. She stayed in bed all day."

Falk frowned and nodded with concern, but it was evident that his thoughts were elsewhere.

"Yes, I called this morning and heard that she . . . the poor woman! It's wonderful that she doesn't have to be here in the city during this trouble. But it is a bit dangerous to have her alone out there in the country when something might break loose any moment. Remind me, Wendt, to give her a call before I go."

Remind me I have a wife, Regina thought.

She and Georg had arrived at the door together. Falk looked after them and said suddenly:

"Children. Pardon me—may I say one more thing to you?"

They turned, Regina in the sunbeams, Georg in the half shadow. Falk walked toward them, raised his hands to put one on the shoulder of each, but checked himself when he noticed Regina's protective frost.

"You are so ravishingly pretty today, Regina," he said; then, a little uncertain of himself, "yes, ravishing . . ."

45

He stood a moment motionless, then continued:

"The vulgar self-seeking don't realize that they're taking existence for granted, that they're burning and squandering the common wealth of the land. They don't realize that other men offer sacrifice freely given."

His earnest glance pierced into her.

Before Georg could say anything he heard Regina's torrid voice:

"So you're sacrificing yourself, Father?"

Falk stood motionless as if he had suddenly grown old and full of grief.

"I see that you are cynical, my child," he said slowly. "But my answer is yes. That is what I am doing. And let my witness be my entire political career, with all that it has brought me in hate and lack of understanding. It is a sacrifice—a sacrifice of time and energy. It is even a sacrifice of harmony within my own home."

He nodded vigorously, clapped Georg on the back but did not risk touching his daughter, who had moved away from him, and quickly stepped to the door.

"Thanks, Father," Georg said boyishly.

But at the door Regina turned her handsome head and said clearly and distinctly:

"Be careful, Father, that you don't sacrifice too much!"

4

I HAVE just come back from the monastery. Thank God I still have enough strength to get there. Stephan is very kind. Though he is not a Catholic he faithfully pushes my wheel-chair the considerable distance every morning, even in the rain. Sometimes I can hardly get up. I sleep poorly and the pain is always there. It gets worse when I bathe, put on my clothes and come downstairs to get into that horrible chair. I have received permission to eat a little before starting for Mass, but I can't help feeling ashamed of myself when I take advantage of it. I feel ashamed not to be able to bear the slight dizziness caused by fasting. What a paradox, when I once thought I could give up my whole life for Him Who sacrificed everything without complaining.

(*Inserted later and in different ink:* Apparently He did complain! He sweated blood; He begged that the chalice might pass from Him and on the Cross He quoted those terrible words from the Old Testament. It's hard to believe, but I guess it gives us permission to weep and complain a little.)

I wonder if the fathers at the monastery with their cloister-white faces realize that they could all be martyrs by tomorrow. They are a poor community and can barely spare the money to subscribe to one paper, a Catholic weekly. I doubt if they all read it. But they're ready. They would consider it an honor to be killed. "They consider themselves fortunate to be able to suffer for His name's sake."

Of course, I realize that feelings and emotional experiences are of no importance when a person is striving for interior perfection. But I couldn't help noticing what a beautiful morning it was as I rolled on the silent tires along the short path through the woods. At the spot where the beech grove begins and our own path branches off to the left I asked Stephan to stop. We always stop at least once anyway so he can catch his breath. The first green has already begun to appear. The beech grove, my secret Shakespearean forest, is beginning to spring into life. When it reaches its full maturity the horizontal leaves will catch the pale sunlight and refract it with indescribable beauty. Then one seems to be rambling in a deep green sea with the sun breaking on the surface above. It is one of nature's miracles and every year I look for it with renewed anticipation. The foreshadowing was there this morning. How lovely!

My poor Herbert! So many years have passed and I have constantly hoped someday to be able to awaken him to spiritual reality. If only someday he could glimpse the reality of the spiritual life, just as this morning I became aware of the coming of spring to my forest. I spoke about it again and again with Father Bruno and we prayed together for his spiritual welfare. Nothing happened. Year after year passed until finally I realized that it was the very waiting itself that made up the substance of my life. I had to learn patience; I had to realize that I could do nothing myself and that my greatest efforts to be selfless made not the slightest impression on him. He didn't even notice them; he assumed that I was like all other women—perhaps a bit more boring—because I was always trying to bring him into contact with churchmen and always wanted us to help religious causes.

Suddenly I realized that if I was ever going to win him I had to be ready to give up everything I loved most. I guess is was precisely this pious, devout life that I loved most. I forced myself to put an end to most of my charities and Father Bruno strengthened my resolve. To live with my husband, to be his wife, to share his interests and to help him—that was my most important task. It wasn't always easy, especially when he turned more and more from the scholarly life to politics. Our house became peopled with partisans and their give-and-take over political tactics and seats in Parliament. For years it brought me to the brink of despair. I saw how ideals were vanishing; how the conversations no longer touched upon essentials. I longed for the time when we were young, when we lived in Salzburg in summer while my husband was studying philosophy and had friends among creative writers and musicians. How strange to realize that Nietzsche and Klagge and Heidegger once concerned him so deeply! Now all the books stand in their cases out here in the country, untouched except for Georg's occasional browsing. I guess my son's interests lie in other philosophers.

Then the great trial came. Despite his principles, he became unfaithful. I know that I really carried on miserably. I knew that I should have kept silent, held my sorrow to myself, prayed to God, and showed not the slightest trace of jealousy. But I couldn't measure up to it at all. In the end I was able to wear the mask, but the effort stretched my nerves so that I became and remain a wreck. Through all this Father Bruno was both kind and skillful. He handled me carefully and taught me step by step that pain was a burden that God had laid upon me. Perhaps I could win my husband for God if I could show him in a concrete way that my injured pride was not the most important thing in my life. If I could show him that I would not insist upon my "rights" above all else. What rights did I have anyway? Maybe I was not guilty of his particular sin, but there were other defects in my life equally serious in God's eyes. During both years of his love affair— when I never saw him more unhappy—I never said the slightest thing that touched upon that topic. I believe that to the end he did not realize that I was aware of it. Something worse, however, was yet to come . . .

As I write my birds are singing. Achilles is a strong tenor. He knows spring is coming because warm sunlight floods through the ever-open windows facing the park. Outside Stephan is puttering about the garden. He keeps talking about four or five new vines that he wants to put up on the wall.

An Arcadian silence reigns. How far removed I am from everything that is being reported in the papers, which is supposed to be so vital. Silent it may be here, yet Stephan says he would have difficulty stopping a mob at the garden. They seem to be all Communists and they hate us because of my husband's policies.

One fine day I knew my husband's affair was a thing of the past. I heard the details with my own ears—from the "other woman" herself.

I understood her thoroughly but I couldn't help trembling the moment she appeared. It's quite an experience to meet a person who has hurt you as much as she had. She had been crying—and was looking quite pretty. Somehow I got the idea that she had come to apologize and as a result I was quite touched and received her graciously.

I soon grasped the real purpose of her visit, however. My husband had informed her that they must part—because of his political career; not that he loved her any the less, she asserted.

I thought to myself that this last might not be quite true. My husband has a remarkable talent for combining very distinct motives in such a way that the most decent—relatively speaking—comes out on top. I don't possess this talent at all.

Then I asked what she really wanted of me. She put her teacup aside—it was from the service which I inherited from my mother. If she had ever seen who was holding that daintily wrought masterpiece! It seemed that she expected my help to "win back" my husband. She was working on the supposition that everything had ended between us—obviously he had led her to believe this. And now I was to make him realize that political affairs should never interfere with the course of true love.

I don't anger easily and sarcasm is not a part of my disposition. Nevertheless, I believe that I said a few words that were not very friendly. At any rate, I had Georg sent for to show her what sort of home it was that she was destroying. She left and I felt quite happy. At last! Now a new life could begin. Now my husband would see what I had given him by my loyal silence and subjection.

I believe that the most difficult problem of all was his indifference after that break. He seemed to have forgotten everything. Even me! Neither of us existed so far as he was concerned. He plunged even deeper into his political career. The degree candidates stopped coming. They had always been a pleasure because they recalled the academic atmosphere of my own father's household. My father used to say, even in his advanced years, that intellectuals, artists and women are the only people worth associating with.

So I had to begin again. More long years passed and slowly the images of remembrance were repressed; my subconscious was purified and the association of ideas didn't slide so easily back into the painful wounds. My soul became purged but my attitude was not the less troubled and insecure. Did the situation indicate that I should get out of his life entirely? As the years went on, my sickness gradually became worse until I finally became as I am today, spending most of my time out here removed from the world and surrounded by a protective ring. I rarely have visitors. I am an almost eccentric person, useless to my family, unable to help. All I can do is go to church.

As my children grew older I was unable to influence them. Louise looked after the town household—she was always very loyal and competent. When my husband became Prime Minister and had to move to the Residence I could not go with him. I attended the first great official receptions but couldn't keep it up. Now I believe that he has quite forgotten that he has a wife. He thinks of me no more than he remembers the one great love of his life. From now on I can pity her without hypocrisy. She has a son Regina's age who is going to be a doctor. Perhaps she is as lonesome as I.

My life is wasted; it becomes continually drier; it is losing its substance. The other world is continually pressing upon my soul behind the stage-props with which nature surrounds us. I am fit for one thing only—a holy life, a life of the spirit. *But I have not yet attained it.* I have almost abandoned so-called reality and am living in an in-between area. Far off I hear the rushing of the world: in the newspapers, in Georg's chatter, in every speech my husband makes. And equally far off I hear an echo from another world. Sometimes it's not very easy.

On days like today things seem to go more smoothly. I become ever smaller while Christ becomes greater. This is how it should be. I can see that my life is nothing but a slow death and a stealthily progressing release. I am not insane, even though there are many who think that I am. My nervous system is delicate but I am in complete possession of my senses. On this point I have no doubts, even though I am cut off from the regeneration and the renewed energies that life gives to others. I live from a small inheritance which I cannot increase. The end is approaching.

Sometimes I imagine that when my time comes I shall dissolve unnoticed amid the things that I love: fluttering motion, reflexes of light, the quiet and friendly wind that moves the leaves in my forest, the secretive interplay of the lights that I long for in the beech grove.

Near me Achilles is shrilling wanton trills, uninhibited in the joy of living.

Father Leo is my confessor now and has been since Father Bruno's death. You have to have someone and I was not in a position to make a selection, so I determined to take the priest who was easiest to reach. His confessional was nearest the church door. It can't be the way it was with my friend Father Bruno; I will simply have to learn to live without his

paternal friendship. That too is as it should be. My tie with
Father Bruno was an earthly bond, the rather selfish joy of
being numbered among his special penitents—his children.
But Father Leo is also very good, although admittedly I do
not listen nearly as attentively as I should to the advice he
whispers after confession.

Oddly enough my husband asked about him. Last Sunday
he wanted to know to whom I now "belong" and I looked
at him in amazement when he mentioned the subject. Of what
interest could it be to him? I soon received an explanation
and if I had believed for a moment—and I didn't—that he
finally felt the need of a spiritual director I would have
seriously deceived myself. No, it wasn't that. My husband
is the leader of a party and he must take the Catholics into
consideration. I note in his current speeches that he continually speaks of the Church and tradition. Most likely
these are the matters that he wishes to discuss with Father
Leo. They meet when I am not present and I realize that I
would be in no condition to sit in on their conversation. I
am firmly convinced that Father Leo is very familiar with all
that is happening. It is said that the Dominicans in our
monastery always have one father who is skilled in political
affairs, for they have much to fear and have to be continually
on guard. Someday the Red majority will be upon us and
all their property will be taken from them. Perhaps there is
truth in the rumor that in such an event they would leave the
country immediately.

At any rate, all that is probably in the future. I imagine
that I will not witness this catastrophe, for I will have long
since departed. A good gust of wind some spring morning
would be about all I need to cut me down. I can imagine
that one day I will be sitting in my conservatory by the white
curtains that flutter with the slightest breeze. The breath of
the gentle wind will carry me forth and I will float away and

unite with the reflections, the rustling of the groves, and glistening of the sun—with everything that I am still capable of loving upon this earth.

5

REGINA was twelve when she attended a Swiss convent school in Pensier, not far from Freibourg. One day she was summoned to the presence of *la mère générale,* a venerable woman of some seventy years who was finishing out her active career by airplane visitations throughout the world to the various houses and schools of the Order. The cause for this confrontation had been a slight misunderstanding: one of the rules stated that there was to be no talking in the washroom and the dormitories. One day Regina found that her soap had disappeared—a classmate must have taken it. She attempted, with signs and contortions, both to explain the situation and demand the return of her soap, but her efforts only caused the other girls to start giggling. A battle royal broke out and suddenly one of the nuns was standing in their midst. Regina was pointed out as the one who had caused the others to laugh and was thus responsible for the scene. Her conduct mark for the week went down considerably—a fact which was advertised by a system of beads, similar to an abacus, posted in the corridor. All were witnesses of her shame.

Regina gritted her teeth in defiance. She had not spoken; she had been unjustly punished. She carried on a series of animated debates with her teachers and when they would not yield she demanded to be allowed to speak with *la mère générale.* She insisted with such determination that finally the permission was granted.

Trembling, she was ushered into the presence of the old lady, whose upper lip was adorned by a fine but visible mustache. The other "Madames" at Pensier were ceremonious, regal, and affected and laid great stress upon their own dignity. *La mère générale,* on the contrary, was a slight, vigorous woman who more than anything else reminded one of a French peasant. She knew everything that should have concerned her, knew everyone personally, and was never haughty. Once, when the new General of the Dominicans, a Spaniard, came for a visit and proved that his French was not exactly fluent, the old lady conversed with him in perfect Latin.

"What do you have on your mind, my child?" she asked in a friendly fashion.

Regina, in school-girl French, explained the situation while the old nun listened attentively.

"In other words," she said, "you think that you were unjustly punished."

"Yes," Regina answered, "I didn't say a single word in the washroom."

"I fully believe you," the old lady answered, "but in this case I am going to have to congratulate you."

Regina stared back in astonishment.

"Don't you understand? The opinions which we form about you girls, my child, are not so important. You could probably earn ones that are just as good or better somewhere else. But if you have learned to bear an injustice without bitterness you have won a great victory. Nothing is more useful or necessary."

"But my conduct mark . . . ?"

"Your mark is higher in God's eyes. You realize that in your heart, if you have told the truth, as I believe you have. Our mark in this matter is of no importance. Next week you will have your regular mark back again and you ought not to bother yourself any more about it. Just imagine how it would be if Jesus demanded that he be paid according to service rendered! Or if His Apostles did, or all the martyrs of the Church!"

Regina was unable to answer. She reflected a moment and then blurted out:

"We have learned that a martyr is a person who freely chooses the path of suffering."

"Quite correct."

"I think that the rule is foolish. Why shouldn't we be permitted to talk in the washroom?"

The old lady's eyes twinkled as she answered.

"You don't think that I am of the opinion that the rule is particularly sensible?"

"Then why does it continue in force if even *la mère* believes that it . . ."

"It is maintained precisely because it is stupid! Oh, I see that you are confused but I want you to understand me. One day when you have grown up you will go out into a world that has been built by *les messieurs*. Everything in this world from beginning to end is stupid. Almost without exception it recognizes only stupid prohibitions and the orders which you will receive and the pressures to which you will be subjected are at least equally senseless. Thus, it can only be to our good if we get used to such things while young and obey stupid prescriptions without offering resistance, as for example: There will be no talking in the washroom. Do you understand me?"

Regina understood. Crushed and confused, she left *la mère*'s office. When her roommates asked how the interview had gone she merely shook her head. This was something that she had to think over. Was it through such means that one gained the inner composure and self-mastery that the best of the nuns displayed?

Everything came to an abrupt end. There were forces

within her which she could not control, or which she did not understand why she should control. One day the convent informed her parents that it would perhaps be better if she were transferred to another institution of learning. Beginning with that date she changed schools rapidly. Quickly she discovered that her deepest yearnings and strivings were precisely the cause of her conflict with convent schools. She wanted to dance. When the nuns suddenly discovered that she had introduced her friends to dance melodies of her own composition and to clothes of her own design, they were shocked and looked upon these occupations as somehow immoral. Nor did it help matters when Regina showed precocious signs of exhibitionism. She suffered irresistible impulses to throw off her clothes and dance in front of her roommates. Despite considerable objections on the part of her parents she succeeded in obtaining formal instruction in ballet. After her student years in Switzerland she began to teach ballet in her native city. She wasn't particularly happy doing so, but how else should she keep herself busy? To live in the gloomy Residence of the Prime Minister, as a support to a father whom she had never understood, required a stamina that she didn't have. She did not have the slightest personal desire to remain at home anyway, certainly not on Christer Wendt's account—the affair with him was past, once and for all—it had been nothing more than that. But she could not return to Switzerland because of Isabelle.

Isabelle was not a member of the Institute for the Dance. She had come there with her sister, one of Regina's former schoolmates. This sister was a strong, gangly girl who was preparing herself with great energy and no talent for a career as a ballerina. One would not have guessed that they were sisters.

The first time that Regina came in contact with Isabelle was on the street in front of the villa which housed the Institute. She sprang from a streetcar with such delicate grace that Regina stopped and gaped. When the sixteen-year-old noticed Regina's embarrassed admiration, she smiled and her face was so winning that Regina was utterly fascinated. Isabelle seemed first to close her eyes or to half close them; then after the long black lashes swept back again her eyes were already on Regina while her mouth took on the contours of a maidenly but melancholy smile. She was the Italian brunette type, not particularly beautiful, with a rounded profile and a nose not proportioned to it. Her face and arms were tanned.

In her smile they recognized each other but passed each other by. For the remainder of the morning Regina was in a state of excitement as if she had read a superb poem or listened to a piano composition by one of the supreme masters. What dazzling freshness surrounded that young girl! How fine the sensuous magic of her motions! The sister soon brought them together and Regina insisted that the younger girl must learn to dance too. Oh! She would like nothing better. Her family, however, was of the opinion that one folly in the house was enough. She had finished school and was supposed to go to England during the summer. She often sailed on Lake Zurich in her father's open sailboat and Regina was asked to accompany her. Finally they became inseparable and for the first time in her life Regina felt that she meant something to another human being, that somebody trusted her and confided in her.

For her part Isabelle admired Regina. Wide-eyed, she followed the dancing lessons which she frequently attended and blushingly asked her new friend for an autographed picture. This she enclosed in an expensive frame, but dared not display it in her room in town. She kept it in her little room in the pavilion of the country house.

The two made excursions to this house. They would sail awhile on Lake Zurich, then take a brief stroll from the dock to the parents' summer residence. Some fifty meters higher, near the flagstaff, was the pavilion and the Alps in their glistening whiteness could be seen from this vantage point. Down below lay the lake, with its scattering of white sails. It became their custom to take their meals in the little village inn, after which they would wander through the forest, climb the steep slopes, or bathe in the lake, still cool from the waters of the Alpine brooks.

Stormily Isabelle refused to obey her parents and go to England, pleading that she wanted to stay quietly in the country to read. Young men from the Gymnasium in the city and from the University vainly courted her, invited her for motorboat or automobile rides. Once on a street in Zurich a young man greeted her in Regina's presence. Isabelle blushed violently and Regina, to her own amazement, experienced a strong feeling of distaste toward the boy. Isabelle was quick to sense Regina's reaction; she answered the boy brusquely and dismissed him.

"Why were you so unfriendly to him?" Regina asked.

Isabelle walked on silently for awhile, her step light.

"It is you whom I love," she said softly.

Regina walked along as if she had not heard but inwardly she rejoiced. Damn those hungry, sweaty men! Let them have their drab world for themselves. Another world full of meaning and pure beauty exists and they can never even become aware of it. When Isabelle was about to kiss Regina goodbye as was her custom—two swift pecks on each cheek—she clung to her and did not let her go.

"What's the matter, Isabelle?" Regina whispered.

The girl, her head lowered, pressed closer to her friend and did not answer. Then she tore herself away, a tender, worried expression on her face. In a flash she was at the garden gate, then gracefully up the steps. Above she turned and waved, the sleeve of her white dress catching the sunlight, her arm tanned against the white of the door which framed behind her an older woman dressed in black. Then she was gone.

Father was accustomed to waft the fragrance of tobacco about—except on Sundays when he smelled of leather.

Christer Wendt was cool, neutral, unsubstantial—ice. Yet strangely challenging.

Georg was always in a hurry and in a sweat.

Regina's other young associates were awkward, noisy scatterers of cigarette ash, accurately represented by their cheap manner of speaking.

Young Isabelle, however, was cadence, purity and repose— and beneath the surface she glowed. This was true love, real possession of another human being.

They read lyric poetry together, took auto trips through the passes, rambled about in the sunny snow areas, spent nights in lovely little inns where peasants sang at evening around clean-scoured tables.

They never spoke about men nor did they mention their families. When they read lyric love poetry composed by men they understood it as if it had been written both for and about themselves. Unconcerned they wandered ever deeper into a world situated above the realm of men. They were glad to reveal and possess intimacies about which no one else knew anything. They strolled on the beach at Montreux and smiled when they saw a young pair pass arm in arm. Chaste in their relationship, they were ofttimes silent, filled with reciprocal gratitude and the same quiet joy. Both had shaken off the social *milieu* of their childhood which now seemed insipid and debasing and to which they could not possibly conceive of returning. Of the future they thought little, although at times they played with the idea of dancing together as a career, or co-founding a school for the dance. After a few moments, however, they grew bored by such future plans, so filled were they with the golden present. They didn't want to miss a moment of their sunny splendor.

Far from naive, they were aware of the deformations which love can take. They would exchange sarcastic comments about a close-cropped, masculine looking woman or a hip-swinging, effeminate man. Such things impressed them by their terrible lack of proportion. Once, in the square before Baur au Lac in Zurich they heard a man break out into a girlish, high-pitched laugh. Disagreeably impressed they turned to see a fat youth in the company of an elderly gentleman. Without saying a word they got up and moved away.

Regina recognized clearly that there was a large layer of sexuality in the substratum of her feelings for Isabelle. Well, so what? Why be afraid of such a delightful element in their relationship? She had no doubts about her own basic normality, for she had flirted with and desired young men. This, however, was something different. This was beyond understanding, a poetry and magic transcending reality.

When Regina was with her young pupils in the dancing school, improving their carriage, demonstrating movement and searching for ways to convince them of the elements of rhythm and meaning, there were times when she felt actually sick at the sight of the heavy mass of incorrigible flesh topped by the subservient and stupid faces. How could she infuse spirit into this sluggish matter? How were these awkward forms to be filled with the magic of poetry and hammered so that they could express it? Occasionally she would break off a lesson in despair, leave the room and stand facing the wall of her private office, fists clenched, eyes shut tight. At such times Isabelle would appear before her mind's eye—Isabelle who had nothing to learn, since her very essence was grace, meaning and lambent beauty.

Slender white boats cutting Lake Zurich.

Birds by-passing the laws of gravity, majestically unpreoccupied, resting on their wings in flight.

Villas blinding-white along a stretch of shore.

Snow-capped Alp-chains glistening in the sun, *alpe in neve senza vento.*

A dreamland where no word need be spoken, where no desires were satiated, where no conflicts threatened gloomy torment.

Apple trees in bloom, motionless on steep green slopes; a gust of wind and petal-snowflakes on the ground.

Green water of mountain brooks.

Mighty glaciers, blueing with shade.

Interwoven with all: one light, chaste, supreme line—a young woman with step more delicately beautiful than the first-born images pressing into a young poet's imagination.

Eyelids slowly sweeping back to reveal those deep-set eyes, innocently unashamed yet glowing with deep fire . . .

She would return to the class, angry and stern. Some of her pupils would burst into tears. Still others would stare in amazement and terror. Then, in desperation, she herself would dance for them, blinding them with her genius. Finally, with a scornful gesture, she would dismiss them to shower and change, a hopeless, unwieldy herd. For a long time she would stand motionless, arms crossed. At last she would start pressing her nails deeply into her upper arm until she moaned in pain.

Thus, day by day her emotions grew increasingly taut until she had a constant dose of sick nerves. In Switzerland her expression had been open, receptive and full of wonderment. Now it was hard; her mouth took on bitter contours. Always slender, she was now almost emaciated. She skipped many meals because eating often disgusted her, but above all because she loathed the inevitable chatter and counter-chatter with unwelcome, awkward, stupid members of the human race. What had been a cool Olympian dream became in time transformed by longing and abstinence into painful warmth, then passonate desire and finally despair.

When Regina arrived at home Christer Wendt was in the hall. She threw her coat on a chair, nerves tight as bow strings. As always he bowed slightly, silently. When she moved without speaking toward the private apartments he asked:

"Would you care to take breakfast, Miss Falk? They have just begun."

"No."

"You ate out?"

The girl was astonished.

"No."

She went on her way, then turned impetuously on the first step:

"I would rather pass up breakfast than listen to Father's painful questions as to why I have come home so late."

He nodded and reached for his hat.

She glared at him with scorn:

"Furthermore, I meant it when I said that you were to call me 'Regina,' as before."

He raised his eyes:

"His Excellency does not want me to."

"I know of few things that mean less to me than what His Excellency is pleased to want or believe. I want you to address me familiarly! Understand?"

Wendt bowed again.

"I think that would be improper. When we are alone, however, I shall of course follow your instructions."

She grimaced in disgust, sprang down to the hall floor and stood before him, pale and trembling.

"Follow!" she stormed. "Follow, Christer! What is wrong

with you? A man like you has followed enough. Can't you grasp that? Why don't you rebel? You have brains, talents, determination—everything. And yet you debase yourself. I can't understand it."

Quietly he put his hat back on the shelf; under his arm was the inevitable attaché-case. He looked at her.

"What do you want me to do?"

Regina shook her head in confusion:

"That I can't say. That's your affair. But I know what you should have done."

She grasped his arm spasmodically and quickly let him go.

"You should have *taken* me, of course! Don't you realize that?"

His face remained impassive—couldn't he even blush or blanch? Did he have no blood in that dried-up body?

"I am not so sure I agree," he said, and again reached for his hat.

She laughed and once more the smile contorted her face.

"Oh, that's it. 'Not so convinced.' You're never convinced. It's hard for me to figure out a man who always bows, gives in, conforms! And what does he bow to? To a whole heap of prejudices and pomposity—like the father-of-the-people inside there! Don't you see that it would be a pleasure, even a duty to scorn him? Don't you see that you were created a human being and a man?"

As her voice rose he warned her into silence by pointing to the door of the dining room. She saw the gesture and shrugged. Suddenly she was ashamed. What was the point? Why should she try to breathe life into an emotion which had long since died? And of what concern to her was this corpse-like man?

(White ascending profile . . . , a face turning slowly toward her . . . , a glance full of anxiety and passion . . . , coldness, resistance . . . , burning snow . . .)

64

Scornfully he shook his head.

"One can be a man in various ways. It was perhaps not only out of respect for my superior that I conformed at that time."

She awoke. What was he saying? What was he daring to hint? She dug her fingers into his shoulders.

"You mean that it was because of me? That you didn't want me?"

He carefully evaded her hand.

"I would be grateful if we could reach an agreement and could look upon it all as stricken from the record."

Again she was trembling. What made her probe ever deeper into the agony of this old wound?

"Nothing can be stricken out," she said softy. "Suppress it, cover it up; it thrives and gnaws from within. And it poisons. Push it away, turn yourself away—it bobs up again as soon as you are alone."

Her words seemed not to have reached him.

(Oh, the young agile mind that understood everything without recourse to words. The body that was nimble as thought! The easy, gentle good humor . . . and the snow. White snow that smarted and burned . . .)

"Furthermore I have the impression that it is very good for you that you have . . ."

Again she awoke from her reverie. "Very good for me? What is?"

"You know what I mean," he said, looking into her eyes with utter calm.

She shrugged once more.

"That I have consoled myself, found another, and so forth? Yes, I understand. But I do not forget you. I don't forget defeats. And you don't forget me either."

"Excuse me," he answered. "I don't wish to hurt you, but

I must tell you the truth. I have forgotten. I no longer have my earlier arrogance and illusions."

Regina's smile masked her discomfort. He was both insulting and insolent. Next came the pangs, the familiar boring pangs.

"You have forgotten?"

He nodded. "Yes, Regina, I have forgotten and I'm glad that I have."

She turned her back on him, stepped away, whirled around the first pillar and leaned against it. Her eyes were fixed on no point in the cold whiteness of the room.

"You are diabolic! I never could quite get behind your facade. You never speak quite the whole truth. You're either too confused or hurt—but you always have yourself well in hand. You're so much in command that you never give yourself away. Perhaps it was just this that attracted me. I wanted to be the one woman you would be completely open with. But you didn't want it."

He stood motionless, the attaché-case dangling from his right hand.

"I have never tried to wear a mask."

She advanced a few steps, then checked herself.

"No," she said vehemently. "Because you were born with one. I wanted to rip it off. Who are you really—deep inside?"

"I am a very ordinary human being. I have become resigned in a not especially pathetic fashion. And I don't want to burden anyone in the future with my feelings and illusions. That's the whole story."

"Thanks. That's the mask that everyone can see. Behind it is something different."

"Well, what is it, Regina?"

She stood up to him and to her own astonishment said:

"I believe that you are passionate, hard-headed, vicious and implacable. I believe that you have secret ambitions, only I can't figure out what they are."

Christer Wendt smiled for the first time. It was a quick, painful smile that he seemed ashamed of. Instantly he was again master of himself.

"No, no," he said. "I know my limitations and I am much too vulnerable to try to exceed them. That's the sum total of it. Be careful. His Excellency is coming."

From the direction of the dining room the rumble of chairs and the confusion of voices. The meal was over. Regina wheeled, poised on the point of flight.

"The father-of-the-people has filled his belly. The father-of-the-people is in a peaceful and mild frame of mind. God deliver me from it! I'm going. Don't say that I was here. Please."

Nimble, noiseless steps. Christer Wendt didn't look after her, but she turned again despairingly, almost out of her mind. In a flash she was down again. She edged in front of him and kissed him. A second later she was again at the stairs and up.

This time Wendt's glance followed her. It was full of pale hatred.

As the door of the dining salon opened he turned around so that he offered his back to those entering. He acted as if he had just arrived and were on the point of putting his hat on the shelf. The Prime Minister stepped up to him in order to allow his guest to pass. It was a Dominican priest in the garb of his Order.

6

I AM NOT going home. Oh yes, the name "Hans Graber" is over my door, but I have no home there. Let her wait; I have waited a whole lifetime. I am as much at home here, in this dirty rain-soaked suburb with filthy slime squirking under my shoes, surrounded by grey-spattered houses, as I am in my study, my prison.

I can't stand it any longer; I give up.

When it comes to the Last Great Things I can imagine that they might well take place in a district just like this—rainy and foul-smelling. Then the whole world will be converted into the dirty suburbs of bombed-out capitals, with the jaw-bone of a ruin jutting into the wind now and again. We will be ordered to crawl out of our holes and get in line. Then we'll have to pass one by one, pallid, faint and wet, before the Great Judge. Even he will be there. Then I'll pull myself together and say:

I accuse; I accuse *you!*

They can do with me what they want but they won't be able to keep me from thinking and speaking and telling the truth.

I do not claim to be perfect. I am not particularly out of the ordinary. But in this affair that wrecked my life I conducted myself with a clean heart, without guilt and without self-interest.

I met her just as I had completed my examinations and was beginning my career. Naturally, like all others, I was beseiged by a hormone attack which quite unsettled my reason. But I am a man of no great passion and disenchantment followed fast. I discovered that she had been seduced by her employer—I overlooked it; it didn't seem unnatural. I knew that she had also had another liaison—all right; I had had one too. I sensed a certain instability, but again I could say as much for myself. Perhaps everyone is unstable. And I thought: Let me love you and you will become strong. Then you will find the identity you have dreamed of! You were not so much to blame as your parents, who didn't care about you but threw you out defenseless into the world. They were too involved in their own divorce problems.

When we became engaged I discovered that she had not even told me half of the story. I began to get a fuller idea of who she was. There was still another man in her life—a Spaniard. I knew him and it was I myself who had introduced her to him. They had a brief dalliance from which a child was born. Just before she came to me and asked me to be her protector, she gave the child for adoption abroad.

I could have let her go; I hesitated. Then I gritted my teeth and thought: This is my vocation. Certainly it burns and hurts but I have the duty to take this burden upon myself. No one else will do it. In my simplicity I thought further: I am following the path that God has prepared for me; it is His way of nurturing and maturing me. His Creating Hand is at this very moment re-shaping my whole being, especially where it suffers from the wounds of pride and anxiety. Thus, I feel myself compelled to take a wife with whom other men have played, then scorned. I was mortally afraid, though certain of victory in my interior life. At any rate the die had been cast; if I could survive the moment I would gain peace and security later. So I plunged in. We married and I took the job of foreign editor in Lenz—I wanted to bring her far from the amosphere that had poisoned her.

There Herbert Falk was professor of law—Herbert Falk who is persecuting me now and who has become a respected political leader in this country. He was always the same: ruthless, cold, egotistical, power-hungry. I suspected nothing. I built a little house for the two of us. Once, when I was away, he lured her to a little excursionists' lodge in the vicinity. She hinted about it. She reported—with an almost proud smile—that he had visited her and proposed the possibility of marriage. I allowed myself to be deceived and wrote him a polite, friendly letter telling him that many happy as well as all too many sad things had bound us together and I was not in a position to let her go. I regretted that I might have offended him. What fun he must have had when he read my letter. I can imagine the way he laughed.

Once again I began anew. Our child had already been conceived when she went through this affair. I convinced myself that there could be no doubt as to the paternity; also, that the child could not have been physically affected by its mother's betrayal of me during the first months of her pregnancy. Even the doctor gave me definite assurances that there was no medical possibility that the child could have suffered the slightest influence from this misfortune. I shudder when I remember with what composure she affirmed that I didn't have to worry for she had already been pregnant at that time. Indeed, I found that the whole affair had left her untouched; it was a mistake, she confessed, that would not be repeated. I knew that man is weak for I am weak myself.

Difficult years followed. I couldn't sleep and suffered from hallucinations. I left Lenz and we went back to the capital. During a few of the succeeding years I imagined that I had won a victory from the incident. The hallucinations disappeared and there was a time when I could sleep several nights in a row without my misfortune hovering in my imagination. I avoided Falk and attempted—although not always successfully—never to mention his name.

It was at this time that I began to come closer to the Church. The priest strengthened me in my faith: it was God's hand at work. My magnanimity and patience had paid off. I could be sure that God's love was at work among my woes and I accepted this love in the spirit of the martyrs. I knew but little of the history of Christianity but had leafed through the writings of the saints and knew that to all of them God was silence and emptiness; not closeness, benevolence and love. Why should my experiences be different? I had a long road to travel and I found myself in a tunnel. I had left light behind me and I was unable to glimpse the other reality far, far ahead of me. But at least I was on the road toward it even though heavy-hearted and sad.

Our boy . . . From the first moment he was marked. I know that doctors would claim that he was affected by my sorrow and the high tension between me and my wife. This I reject; I am certain that he was injured within his mother's body. I cannot imagine that a mother could go unpunished when she betrays her husband while carrying the seed of a new human being in her body. It would be impossible for her not to shatter her emotions and consequently look forward with horror to the day she will bear. I did my best to keep Thomas from suspecting. Yet he grasped everything while still a little boy. He scorned his mother almost from infancy. Under these circumstances it was natural that I did not want more children. Yet another came. Once, when we were living in a hotel, she made passionate advances. I was touched, perhaps also a little flattered, and consented, taking it at once as a good omen. Perhaps after all these years we would yet find peace, slough off our anxiety and shape a new common identity. I remember thanking God in the quiet of my soul as I withdrew from her and noted the expression of happiness on her face as she whispered how wonderful it had been.

She hadn't changed a bit. She had had a new and completely unsuccessful adventure with one of my friends, a student whom I had always regarded as a man of character and loyalty. Fearful of the possibilities she had thrown herself at me. Again she became pregnant and bore a son who arrived nine months after her affair with my friend. Whose son was he?

And always I was continually involved in great political battles. I was sick and nervous but I threw myself into one struggle after another. There was not a moment when I dared

71

be alone or unoccupied. My physical health was all but shattered and there was no salvation for my nights. I was amazed at how poorly my body was functioning. Books, plays, persons —everything reminded me of my own misery and called forth the painful associations that I was constantly trying to avoid. Yet every discomfort, or the slightest bodily pain, or a kink in one of my limbs, or a chance ache, all evoked the same searing images. Without exaggeration I can say that year after year I have been waked up three or four times a night by the same anxieties cropping out in my dreams.

Here is the harbor. I can hardly make out the ships' sterns in the fog. I'm freezing in the drizzle.

I remember that once I lived in another world. I know now that I would find it poisoned and evil-smelling even if it were a spring day with the sun shining. In the garden in front of our little villa I can hear my wife singing. She hums happily as she stands there bent over her rock garden. So far as I am concerned, I don't care whether the sun shines or not. Why should I care if there are flowers in my prison window?

I must also confess to you, double-faced Judge, that at the time of my disillusionment I came close to ruin. Chance would have it that I did not become addicted to drink, although I certainly wanted to. No one could have taken more noble steps to destroy himself with brandy and wine than I did, but my physique refused to break down completely. Thus, in despair I was naturally drawn toward other women, most of whom I don't even remember any more. For some years I lived with a woman and shared her with many other men. In spite of her depravity she was affectionate, friendly and gave me a sort of peace. My own wife was tremendously egotistical in sexual matters. She wanted her physical love to be a command performance, a paying of homage. Yet she was always passive and always left me with the feeling that every gesture of affection was made at the cost of a victory over herself. But this other light-headed, careless woman was tender, good and generous. Even in the act she was by nature on the giving side. She gave me so much pleasure that for a time I was able to banish my ghosts. Without being very articulate she understood and offered me the beauty of her body so that I could forget.

But grief cannot be killed by lust. And she had other friends. I didn't dare let our relationship become too close for fear that the old game would be repeated. Her body cooled my passions and opened up the violent realms of lust about which I had known but little up to that time. But despite my pleasure I knew that sooner or later a new catastrophe would be sure to break upon me.

Before this could happen I broke with her, disappeared. I went to a priest—the first good one I could find—and went to confession. He took it all very quietly and became my friend. He told me that my case was one in a dozen, that thousands of men in the same city were in similar straits. I should not despair because Christ had suffered and died for people exactly like me.

I could see that at home my wife lived in her own world and had no regrets. She was filled with her home and her children, and I admit she took care of both extremely well. She was kind and friendly to me and treated me like a poor psychopath who had to be handled with special care. From time to time I would catch snatches of her conversation with friends: It was too bad about me; I had certain stupid complexes, certain compulsive imaginings that made life difficult for her but with which she put up because deep down I was really quite a lovable person.

I don't know how I was ever able to make any professional progress while carrying this load. But I did. I did what I was required to do and considered it a matter of pride not to let my ruined life show on the surface.

Now, in retrospect, I recognize another fact: beneath my reasonably quiet facade, behind my self-control, lurked my hate. I detested her happiness, her peace of mind, her thoughtful motherliness, her ability to look upon my pain as a psycopathic phenomenon. I never tried to take her with me to church because it seemed more natural for a person like her to stay away.

I admit readily that these tensions eventually killed what small political and journalistic talent I possessed. Often I would lose command of the general view and tone of things. I made undisciplined attacks and went off-balance frequently. How could it be otherwise?

During these years I was still playing with my old thoughts, convinced that God was concealed behind my misfortunes. It was my fate to suffer. My contemporaries in similar circumstances all got divorces, but not I. I wouldn't even be tempted with the thought. I wonder what was the real reason for that? Perhaps I didn't want to put my unhappiness on exhibition? No, it wasn't pride but rather the will to conquer, to put us both back on the right path, to defeat the demons that filled our little house and who, I soon realized, now pursued our sons with the same ravenous hunger.

Little Joseph died. I hardly remember him. He had come into the world to conceal adultery and perhaps was not even my own. But Thomas grew up. He was defiant, distrustful, gifted, implacable. He clung to me with an almost hysterical love and scorned his mother so thoroughly that her every word sent him into boiling rages. He couldn't remain at home and had to be sent to my half-brother who ran a boarding school. I won't mention his antics there.

One day I met Herbert Falk, the man I had constantly avoided. I had never written anything about him, though I often felt tempted to comment on his new political career. I was afraid of myself for it would have been easy for me to lose my mind in his presence. This meeting was unexpected. I was coming from the vesper service at the Dominicans' and I was supposed afterwards to go to the banquet at the Journalists' Club. I had no knowledge as to who had been invited. He was there in his new political role. I circled the room greeting the tuxedoed gentlemen, most of whom were friends; there were but few whom I did not know. Suddenly he was standing before me.

We were surrounded by people. My head whirled. I don't know whether I blushed or grew pale but I was hit by a wave of disgust. When we shook hands I felt as if I were touching a toad. I dropped his hand with a jerk and moved on without looking at him. Perhaps he hadn't recognized me.

But chance would have it that we were seated together. I could feel his thigh against mine beneath the table cloth and I quickly withdrew a little. We didn't converse and my thinking was muddled. I could hear myself talking agitatedly, directing the conversation diagonally across the table away from him. Maybe he spoke to me but if he did I didn't answer. I was crippled with hate and don't know what I would have given to see him punished.

I avoided drinking too much and kept trying to say the Hail Mary. At dessert an idea hit me like a blow: it is possible that all these years he hasn't given the affair a single thought. Or perhaps he looks upon it as an insignificant episode—maybe he even regrets it, although he has no idea that he has all but destroyed my life, and that I have lain sleepless every night for twenty years, or that day by day he has submitted my family to torture and is still doing so, and that the fate of my son is to be put to his account down to the last dollar. Maybe he is really a very ordinary person and it's only my imagination that pictures him as massively egotistical. Maybe he is a very ordinary person—like myself.

Now the wet has oozed through the soles of my shoes.

75

Listen to the steamer bellowing out there in the roadstead—it won't be able to come in through the narrows today. The downpour won't let up. I think an unpitying, murderous rain rilled over Him as He hung on His Cross, stiff, bloody, wracked with pain. It's the picture that always comes to mind when I think of the Passion of Christ. If He knew the sorrow of the whole world He must have known this pitiless, cold rain.

But He never experienced the cold-blooded betrayal of a wife. It is said that He took every human misfortune upon Himself. How many of us would gladly submit to bodily torture if only we could escape mental anguish? There are no angry martyrs.

I left the table; I didn't dare stay longer. I went to the vestibule for my coat and hat. The host followed me, concerned, as I told him I was sick and disappeared. That night I didn't go home. I went to Helene Gritz, whom I had not seen in many years. She was at home and greeted me with the old, warm friendship. I wanted her and she was ready. She was too tactful to ask me any questions. Rather she replied—with her body.

Since that day I have not gone to confession, nor have I set foot inside a church. Father Leo can wait; I won't look for him any longer. I can't.

But there's something else I can do. I feel the strength within me to battle Herbert Falk. I know that his regime is grotesque, his policies madness. I know he is trying to unite the nation in some sort of a conciliatory movement. I shall not allow myself to be influenced by personal hate. I consider it objective fact that he is vicious—a moral hypocrite. Don't I have decades of living proof on my own body? I hate that man—and I know I have the right to.

I'm not saying all this to You, cold Judge surrounded by fog and streaming rain. I don't need Your grace and I don't want any grace. I demand justice. You can beat me down to the ground just as Falk has. You can sharpen my pains, for You are indeed a past master at the art. But You cannot smother my last cry, my cry for justice, Demon!

The bells are ringing at St. Stephen's. I have to go to the editorial office.

7

THE PRIME MINISTER crossed the hall diagonally toward the library where he again stepped back, permitting the Dominican to enter ahead of him. Wendt bowed and as the two passed the Prime Minister said casually:

"My secretary, Christer Wendt."

The monk bowed but did not shake hands. Wendt's eyes searched after him. He had been startled when he noticed the habit and the blood drained from his face for the second time that afternoon. Where had he seen this monk before? Round face, sparkling eyes, an awkward rolling gait—a caricature of his profession and a parody of all vows of self-denial and scorn of earthly things. Wendt already knew that he was Mrs. Falk's new confessor. Thus, he must be from the monastery near the Prime Minister's summer residence. But why should His Excellency bother with this roly-poly monk?

At the doorway the Prime Minister pulled back the curtain and called out into the hall:

"You can come in, Wendt!"

He disappeared as the drapery fell heavily back into place. Wendt stood a moment motionless, shook his head, walked across to the large mirror above the marble-topped table resting upon lion's feet, and closely examined his face. He noticed his disturbed expression. But why?

When he entered the library Wendt was again his calm, confident self. Falk had taken his place at the desk while the Dominican was seated opposite him in the high-backed easy chair. The priest was not leaning back, but rather sitting bolt upright, gently puffing from the exertion of the walk from the dining room. Oh, what a servant of the Lord!

"I must thank you, Father, for this morning," said Falk. "You have thrown light on a lot of problems. According to what I see now of the determination of the Catholic elite to sacrifice and struggle, I venture—for the first time in a long time—to believe that we may yet avert a catastrophe."

The Dominican nodded. Wendt's casual eyes watched him.

Falk went on:

"But what continues to worry me is the intellectuals and the headway that Marxism has made among them. I have conducted a little survey: approximately a third of our professors are crypto-Communists and you know how impressionable students are. They can't imagine that truth is found anywhere else than at the feet of the teacher whom they are idolizing at the moment. I can even remember when I was that way myself.—How do you think my wife is?"

Father Leo turned his head toward the Prime Minister. His neck lay in deep folds and a heavy gesture of his fat hands accompanied his answer:

"She is physically somewhat weak. Spiritually and intellectually, on the contrary, she is . . . alert."

His hands described a broader gesture as if to indicate that at the moment he had no more to say. Falk nodded, troubled.

"I think you're right," he said. "We both need your advice . . ."

The Dominican broke out into a short boyish laugh, so completely unexpected that Wendt turned in astonishment.

"Oh, my counsels—they're thirteen to the dozen . . . mere talk . . . nothing more. . . . But I'm your friend!"

Falk nodded.

"I know that," he said. "And I am grateful for it. You should also get to know my son."

"I know him already."

"Yes, but you must become his friend too, his confidant. He worries me. You will soon understand why. And Regina?"

"I have met her several times. She is utterly charming."

"She's very beautiful. Too beautiful. It takes a strong personality to carry off such extreme beauty."

"You're right."

Falk reached for his morning cigar and Wendt, without officiousness, was there with the lighter. After several puffs Falk said:

"Thanks. The foreign newspapers should be here by now, don't you think?"

The secretary nodded and went to get them.

"If you only knew, Father, what a prize I have in that man, honest, discreet, loyal. With a remarkable talent for political improvization."

"That's good. Where did he come from?"

Carelessly leaning back in the chair, cigar in the corner of his mouth, thumbs under the watch-chain on his old-fashioned dotted vest, the Prime Minister answered:

"Well, you might say . . . well, he was a young homeless intellectual who has found stability here working with me. He has put down roots and developed character—I am quite proud of the formation I have given him, if I do say so myself. One day I hope to be able to open his eyes to the truth of religion. Then you will be called in. He's really remarkable. As I was saying, he has really brilliant political—I might even say politico-strategic insights. Of course I never told him so."

"In what way?" the Dominican asked a little suspiciously. "Are you thinking about anything specific?"

Falk was on the point of an immediate reply but blushed heavily instead. He thought of *"l 'affaire Graber"* and felt a little uneasy. It would not be particularly pleasant if the Dominican were to see through his motives at this point. But he certainly had nothing to fear. Quietly the priest sat there, a harmless smile on his face. He was an innocuous man who could be circumvented easily. It was pleasant to chat with him.

"No, nothing specific," he answered after he had blown forth a cloud of smoke. "What I mean is that Wendt can find escape hatches."

Placing his hands on the desk he leaned forward:

"Understand me. When one has been as hard pressed as I have been, one needs friends, true friends. I have at least two: you and him. And that means a great deal. Moreover, there is also Regina . . ."

He meditated a moment. The way he employed the word "moreover" suggested an element of doubt. The word "friends" caused his thought to sift out all those who were not his friends. Regina was not his friend.

He continued:

"I don't understand why my daughter never comes to breakfast. Actually, her day doesn't begin until ten o'clock and she is really worrying me. I am beginning to believe . . ."

At that moment Wendt returned with a packet of newspapers.

"Well, Wendt, what does the press say?"

Without waiting for an answer he turned again to the Dominican and said cheerfully, continuing in his nonchalant mood:

"Would you believe it? I didn't see a single newspaper all day yesterday! If the public ever knew that! It was wonderful to be able to stroll with my rifle in God's good countryside, like a normal, civilized human being. You don't get anything for nothing and you have to recover what you have spent!"

While he was speaking the Dominican was closely scrutinizing Wendt, who had placed on the desk a small dossier over which he was bending. The secretary read the domestic press privately at home early each morning so that later he could give the Prime Minister a preliminary briefing of their contents.

"I have underlined the columns dealing with foreign policy as usual," he said. "There is nothing sensational. Some strikes in the coal mines in Wales. A little variation on the stock market in America. Nothing outstanding."

Falk had barely heard. He was relaxing into a sort of ineffable peace. It had been a long time since he had had a heart-to-heart talk with a churchman. The higher Church dignitaries he met only on formal occasions. And he was afraid of the Nuncio. Much time had passed since he had seen priestly acquaintances of his wife in his home. She must bring them together now out at the country house— he had not been out there himself all week. Moreover, this cheerful priest communicated a certain feeling of confidence. He was very mild, not particularly gifted, but also not in the least irritating or arrogant. From him one could expect no professional advice, no tactless clerical intervention.

"Well. What about internal politics?" he asked, somewhat distractedly.

Without looking up Wendt answered:

"I am sorry to say it, but the entire press is talking about the Graber situation."

Falk pulled himself together, visibly delighted, but at the same time quite anxious not to reveal his feelings to the Dominican.

"What a mess," he said in a regretful tone.

He turned to Father Leo:

"You undoubtedly know that this Doctor Graber has attacked me most irresponsibly, even to the point of dragging in religion. He wants to warn the Catholic Party not to form an alliance with me—for moral reasons. I have not answered the charge—I wouldn't soil myself doing it. But now I hear from Wendt how hopelessly he himself seems to be mixed up in scandals. First, there is the Gloria story in which the police may soon become interested—although I am not certain, such things are outside my sphere. And now these sad disclosures about his private life."

He turned a troubled face to Wendt and asked softly:

"Any more news about that?"

"The story has been treated for a whole week," the secretary answered. "*Figaro* and *Augenblick* have brought out further details. They have photographs of his place of dalliance and of his mistress. It seems that this affair has been going on for some time. Helene Gritz carries on, if I may say so, an almost professional career.

Falk shook his head and made a gesture of disgust.

"Shocking. And a man like that thinks he can put himself forth as a moral authority. A man who doesn't even go home to his own house. If I only knew how the newspapers got hold of all this . . ."

He glanced uneasily at the Dominican who was sitting, the harmless smile playing quietly across his face, studying Wendt closely. He didn't act at all shocked. Oh, these monks are clever. They know everything, understand everything, and never let themselves seem scandalized.

Suddenly the Dominican spoke:

"Can you remember where we met for the first time, Mr. Wendt—that was the name, wasn't it?"

The secretary looked up slowly; he had had time to prepare for this and his features registered polite astonishment.

Falk removed the cigar from his mouth; his eyes played back and forth between the two.

"You two have met?" he said. "You are already acquainted, knew each other some time ago? You never mentioned this, Wendt?"

The latter turned to his chief:

"No. In the first place I have hardly had the opportunity to meet Father Leo since it was only recently that Your Excellency made his acquaintance. And secondly, we have simply never met!"

He turned to the Dominican:

"Forgive me if I am mistaken. Could I have forgotten? Where could it have been?"

Slowly the Dominican began to rise—he had to apply both hands to the task—and gradually eased his heavy bulk to an upright position. The blood rushed to his head with the exertion and his rosary clattered heavily against the arm of the chair despite his efforts to secure it.

"Well," he said easily, "just now as I was sitting there watching you it seemed to me that I had seen you once on a lecture platform."

"On a lecture platform?" Wendt repeated, in full command of himself. "Impossible."

From the direction of the chair in front of the desk a resounding laugh was heard. It was followed by an even louder cough. The Prime minister had inhaled his cigar smoke the wrong way.

"Well . . . ," he said snorting and coughing. "Well, that is simply . . . impossible, isn't it?"

The Dominican turned toward Falk—he was now deliberately close to Wendt.

"Perhaps I'm mistaken," he said. "I'm often wrong."

From the distance of only a few paces he looked Wendt in the eyes:

83

"You look exactly like a young man whom I once saw at very close quarters, who interested me extremely."

Wendt melted back a few steps and began to apply the letter opener to the foreign newspapers.

"An accidental similarity . . ."

The Prime Minister had recovered from his coughing spell:

"Perhaps you met each other when you were both in the lovely bloom of youth—at the University—or during some academic debate."

"No," the Dominican said quickly. "I studied in Rome and I doubt this was the case with Mr. Wendt. I have an event in mind which does not go too far back."

Wendt shook his head smiling:

"An error, unfortunately." He turned to the statesman: "Your Excellency, if you don't need me here any longer, perhaps I should go ahead to the Executive Offices and prepare a few matters."

"Yes. Do that," Falk answered. "Do that, and I'll come along shortly. I'll just take a look at the papers and try to digest a few things."

Wendt departed, first bowing to the Prime Minister, then with equal correctness to the Dominican, who responded with a smile.

"No, Father," said Falk after the drapery had fallen back into place. "There you are mistaken. The young man has never in his life risked showing himself on a lecture platform and he won't do so in the future either."

The Dominican sank slowly and carefully into his chair.

"Perhaps. I must really have been mistaken. But I hope that you are very sure of him."

Falk threw his head back and shrugged.

"I am completely sure of him. As sure as I am of my own self. He knows me from inside out."

"And *you* know *him* inside out?"

Falk coughed and dried his mouth ceremoniously on his handkerchief.

"No . . . no, that would perhaps be saying too much. His private life, moreover, is not particularly interesting. But I ought to tell you this side of it. A few years ago he fell in love with my daughter just before she went to Switzerland to study dancing. I put a quick stop to it."

"Why?"

"Oh, he comes from a very different . . . And she was too young, and too overstimulated. I am thoroughly fond of him but don't think he would have made a suitable husband for my daughter. She inherited more than a bit of her mother's eccentricity. Well, you are already familiar with this. But ever since that time he has been superb—brilliant. I have a high opinion of him and I can tell you that he owes a lot to me."

"Splendid, splendid," the Dominican said, distracted. "I'm glad to hear it."

At this moment a maid stepped in from the hall.

"Pardon me, Your Excellency. Your Excellency has a caller."

A change in Falk's countenance. He became angry, almost brutal.

"Didn't I tell you I'm not receiving anybody now?" he asked heatedly.

"I said that," the girl answered in dismay. "But she wouldn't go away. She gave me her card and said that she was quite sure that Your Excellency would receive her if you knew who she was."

"They all say that. All of them! You should be familiar with that dodge."

"Perhaps it really is something important," the Dominican

85

suggested. "Wouldn't there be a point in looking at the card?"

Falk stood by the desk and crushed the cigar on the bottom of the ash tray.

"Give it to me."

The girl stepped forward with a small engraved card and Falk snatched it.

"Mrs. Graber," he read.

The Dominican slowly turned his head.

"What in the world does she want?" said Falk. "No. I will have absolutely nothing to do with that family."

The Dominican stood without moving.

"Why not? You were just saying that her husband is attacking you. If the wife of your enemy is calling on you she is sure to be in trouble. You have nothing to fear. In your place I would certainly receive her. You have the time, don't you?"

Falk stood indecisively, breathing heavily.

"Time? Certainly I have time. But what good will it do? What will I say to her?"

"That depends on what she says to you," replied the Dominican, with a smile.

Falk turned to the uneasy maid. "Ask Mrs. Graber to come in."

Relieved, the girl departed, and Falk took a few steps toward the window. "I hate women's tears," he said. "I've had enough of them—especially in my own family. Pardon me for being so blunt."

He stopped before the Dominican and looked at him, full of concern. "I really don't know what good this will do, Father."

Father Leo's smile was now quite open, almost prophetic. "I do," he said. "Trust me this once."

Both turned toward the door. The Dominican, panting

lightly, raised himself slowly from his chair; the rosary clattered again. A woman of fifty entered. She was small, unmistakably pale as she stepped from behind the curtain which the maid held for her. She stood quietly a moment as the heavy material rustled back into place.

8

IT'S A FUNNY thing, but whenever I take a walk I can't keep from laughing to myself. There's another one stopping in his tracks to stare at me. What sort of crazy Dominican is that, with his big belly, walking around snickering to himself in the sunshine. He can't possibly be a real man of the spirit. That's all too evident. But really, I am not laughing from self-satisfaction—although things are going quite well with me. In all reverence I am laughing at the Lord God. All real leaders, talented people, and saints He does away with through sickness, accidents, or concentration camps, leaving boobies like myself to survive. He leaves the embattled Church to people like me, and I find that almost funny.

That fragrance coming from the lower windows in the bakery. Fresh bread! Some people speak about the fragrance of spring; others dwell on the scent of a woman. Just what is there in the fragrance of fresh bread? At the monastery we often eat stale bread and it is, no doubt, more practical. But, like everything practical, it doesn't taste good.

No. I must move along. I can't stand here all day looking in a bakery window.

How people lie! How difficult it is for them to stop play-acting! If I myself were not so great a sinner I would get angry as I did in my youth, God help me, when I wanted to "fight sin." Since that time I have had no inclination to criticize others. I know from experience how it is when the Devil gains power over man's body: in the midst of the pious words and all the proper liturgical formulas one suddenly finds himself caught hand and foot in his snares.

Look at that wood-carver behind the window. I always have to stop and secretly watch old craftsmen. Their features are properly chiseled, not expressionless lumps of dough like mine and the rest of the bourgeoisie. Is it because they build, construct, *create?* We are in God's likeness and He is a Creator. *Ergo:* man's task consists not in tearing down and destroying, but in creating. What do I create? Disorder! Goodbye, bearded integral man inside there. You probably don't worry much about the state of the world, but what you do you do well. That's not the case with me. Is there another priest anywhere who can honestly confess that everything he ever did in his whole life has turned out badly. Whenever I begin to bend an affair straight it immediately becomes more snarled and I put a horrible strain on the Holy Ghost. And yet they continue to leave me at large! Ridiculous!

Children, children—how pale they look! Whoa there, stop the rough-housing! Leave the little one alone! And watch out for the bus, you scamps!

At any rate, I have just come from a prison where I find myself involved in the affairs of seven pathetic people. Three of them are particularly nice and good; the others are rather intractable, and the whole thing is going to be difficult to unravel. Now let's see:

First there is Regina. She didn't look at me. I might as well have been elsewhere. She slowly inclined her head as she went past me and that gesture signifies the following: "Another one, fat and full of unction. Please don't touch me with your sweaty hands." How well I understand her. It must be difficult for these beautiful human animals of slender limb and noble features; it must be difficult for them to understand that God loves them exactly as He loves the ugly and miserable.

Regina impresses me as a real human being. She has an elemental impact. Her sisters are not the telluric females with heavy haunches and sweaty strands on their foreheads. No, her home is with the creatures of the air, spring breezes, sea winds, sea gulls. And behind all the beauty and pride is a heart screaming in need. And now I am placed across her path so that she may come to know her Redeemer. It's funny. My thick bulk will hinder you from seeing Him, Regina. He was a young man in the fullness of His beauty and strength and He chose His fate Himself.

I have seen but a single person who perhaps reminded me a little of Him—a Protestant minister in the concentration camp. We were friends and when we stood in the quadrangle for roll-call he would help me to smuggle through the lines my mouldering lumps of bread, our poor *oblata* and the only species under which we possessed the Body of Christ. He used members of his own religion to pass the bread lumps along the line from one dirty hand to another, and the line was a kilometer long. At the far end one of my Catholic boys stood quivering and secretly put the lump of bread in his mouth. He didn't hear me say the words of consecration because I stood a good way back and the music shrilled during the executions that the whole camp was forced to watch. But he knew that it was valid. That was reality. I will never forget the smile on my Protestant brother's face when he helped me. His turn came to be yanked up on the gallows because he had given help to a sick Jew. He was a tall, spare dark man with wasted features and a great diagonal scar on one cheek. His teeth had been knocked out during a beating. They hanged him. Me? They merely chased my fat bulk around. It was probably entertaining to kick me a bit, but what harm did it do my flesh?

You should have seen *him,* Regina! There is other beauty

besides that of noble motion, well-turned limbs, pure skin, and sparkling eyes. My God, my Friend and Redeemer, help me not make everything worse. I can do nothing on my own strength—that You know.

Here are the stairs; now its a question of really going slowly so my heart can rest a bit.

So on to number two—Georg. Fine material. Less dissipated but already somewhat chewed in that direction. He still goes to church and confession, I know, but never to me. How right he is. But what a collection of wild birds are flapping around under the shock of hair! It horrifies me when I see the way he looks at his father. But when he kisses his sick old mother's hand or talks with Regina—oh, I'm not blind, those are warm springs. But I wonder what is bothering him. What is keeping him from thinking clearly? I really don't know him too well and we have only discussed theology, which never interested me too much. When he asked me what Christ actually did in the abode of the dead I was unable to give him a correct answer—I can never remember the proper answer in such instances. I think I answered that at any rate Christ did not do anything wrong. I don't think the Prior would have appreciated this reply.

Here's the top of the stairs. Better stop awhile and catch my breath on the stone bench. It would be more ascetic to keep going, but if I did that I could become quite snobbish about my piety. Let's choose the middle way: I'll rest but I won't sit down. I'll stand, and furthermore I don't believe that stone benches are good for rheumatism.

Number three is the old lady out there in the country. At first I thought it was the same old pattern: sentimental pretense and external, gurgling self-indulgence, with pride well camouflaged in the background. Then I began to think that the old lady was not quite right in the head. (Try to imagine what a retinue of such poultry the Redeemer must have had wherever he went. And He put up with it!) Then I began to find her. Yes, she's a little bit crazy but not too much. She is also a bit sentimental, but not to a dangerous degree. But above all she is beginning to see herself. I can reach her. She must be handled with tact. But how can I learn tact? "You should become a blacksmith," my old mother used to say, back home in our Alpine village. Perhaps. But it is not even wise to put a hammer and solid matter into the hands of a person like me.

The old lady with her wheelchair and birdcages we can forget for a while. And now on to number five, or is it number four? Four it is.

So then, the Prime Minister. What a scene he put on when he received little Mrs. Graber. What shameful make-believe! He had no idea that I was Dr. Graber's confessor at a time when he still had a need to go to church; nor that I am the occasion of his having thrown it all over. Poor Graber. Twenty long years, complaining and unwilling, to be sure. Doing the right thing in spite of it all; convinced that it was his task to try to love his wife, even though she had betrayed him twice and his fatherhood was uncertain to say the least. I was the one who convinced him that it was sufficient to want to forgive. "You should *want to want to* forgive." Under no conditions did he have to feel anything. The Church didn't demand that he have kind feelings for his executioner. His heart didn't need to overflow. I know that for twenty years he daily said his stubborn "I will" without hope, without a glimmer of comfort, without the tiniest ray of light entering his darkness.

I have prayed more for him than for most men I know because I recognize myself in him. How often I've wished he could feel a faint breath of warmth. Never. He forced himself to go to church; he forced himself to pray for the forgiving heart that he did not possess. I told him that that was sufficient, but he complained that he was performing the externals of love without possessing it inside. Then I told him that that was more than enough. At any rate, it was better than the works of hate. He saw himself accurately in all his hard egotism, and judged himself accordingly.

And now the game has been lost in this newspaper battle against Falk.

It was in the square that I last saw Graber. He claimed that he had allowed himself to be betrayed and that I am the betrayer. He had refrained from punishing evil with the result that evil had grown. He had left it to God to avenge and administer justice, and his wife had become more evil and indifferent. And it all was my fault. He didn't say goodbye as he turned on his heel. He was the one of my children whom I loved best . . . and I lost him.

I knew Mrs. Graber only through her husband's word-etchings and he had never calumniated her; rather, he praised her good qualities. But I gathered—or thought I gathered—what a nightmare from Hell she must be.

She entered the room without dreaming that I knew her husband. I had expected a wanton and saw instead a likeable, somewhat reserved woman. She was thin, tense, but with a most beautiful melancholy expression. She defended her husband, fought for him like a lioness! No sham. Complete sincerity! She declared outright that she knew Falk was behind those scandal-sheet accounts of her husband and Helene Gritz. Falk answered that he had nothing to do with it. I thought that lightning would surely strike his lying head. He viewed the affair "entirely from the interests of the State." God deliver us! She bore his lies without answering. Then she lowered her eyes to the rug and said: "I should like to make clear to you—to you both—that everything that my husband has done in no way changes my view of him. He is a man of integrity. He is an idealist. He thinks little of his own advantage. If he has made this mistake it is because I could not give him the love he needed and which he had a right to demand. I do not blame him."

That was as well said as if I had said it myself. She spoke of her boy—what his friends had said, how he had been crushed by the many rumors and scandal articles. She appealed to Falk's fatherhood and begged him to put an end to the press campaign.

So that was the woman whom I for more than a decade believed a monster. My knowledge of human nature is really penetrating! Obviously I am well suited to deal with human beings and their deep spiritual problems. I was flabbergasted. I believe I closed my eyes. I was ashamed of myself.

The man to whom she was speaking had been her paramour twenty years before. He didn't betray it; they addressed each other formally. I saw that he feared her power to betray him. How would it be if the truth about their relations should come to light? He would have to resign and give up all authority. His whole family would most likely be broken up. She did not use this weapon, but by her silence indicated that she looked upon everything as her own fault. I was overcome with sympathy for this woman whom I had misrepresented in my mind for so many years. In the past I prayed for her with a cold heart. What she did remains and her guilt is terrible. But she is a human being; she has a soul; God never gives up.

And the Prime Minister, the Father-of-the-Country! The poor hypocrite. The interest of the State . . . He has nothing to do with the affair . . . Graber has attacked him . . . He has no desire to become involved in private affairs . . . He will do what he can . . . He will speak with the Minister of Justice . . . He has no power over the press which must remain free in a constitutional state, but he will try . . . He is a Catholic and has not taste for revenge. . . .

And then she was gone, poor woman. He disappeared behind his protective cloud of cigar smoke, grumbling and muttering. I stole a march on the great man. He said, "Yes, that was quite touching. How naive people are. They never understand until it reaches close to home that always, *always,* one must atone for wrongdoing." Strike down, lightning! I thought. Open up, polished parquet floor. Thunder down upon his head, ancestral portraits on the wall! I answered: "Quite to the contrary. Fortunately, one does not have to, my son." He stared at me uneasily. "What do you mean?" he snarled, and disappeared again in the smoke cloud behind the desk. "It would be quite awful," I said, "if we were to be punished after our crimes. If that were the case, wouldn't many of us be in prison? And none of us could avoid disgraces of the sort that Dr. Graber is suffering."

Like a nodding Buddha he popped out of his smoke. "You mean," he said, "that Christ forgives us our sins: of course! From the religious point of view—of course! I'm not trying to make that a point of issue. But in the world as it now exists, crime draws punishment in its wake—with almost automatic certainty." For a whole long moment I believed he was honest enough to consider his own case. "Yes," I answered, "almost always. Especially if the persons connected with the criminal fit themselves into the chain of cause and effect, sin and punishment; if we accept the principle of unmerciful retribution. But we Christians do not so accept it, do we? We are members of the Mystical Body of Christ, Who sacrifices Himself for the sins of the world." His mouth was hanging open—he, the superman, the master manipulator and father of his country.

Now let's take number five, or is it six? And that is Christer Wendt. Where have I seen him before—and why don't I like him?

Well, here is the hospital where we will speak words of

peace to the sick little old ladies. How merrily they lie. They confess their intemperance and their little quarrels. If they could see into the bottom of their souls they'd scream in horror and fall right to the deepest pool in Hell. So it's somewhat of a blessing that they see nothing. I must be particularly nice today to the sentimental old *dame* with the mustache. When she asked what I really thought of her husband, who is continually tippling, cursing and swearing the live-long day; otherwise he appears to be an excellent taxi-driver—"well," I answered, "I think when he comes to the Pearly Gates they won't let him in." "I think so too," said the pious old witch. "Saint Peter won't let him in," I continued. "No, of course he won't," and as she spoke she could see herself being greeted in the Heavenly Anteroom by the approaching cherubs. "Then he will have to whisper a few words to Saint Peter," I said. "What words?" "Watch out, Peter, he'll have to say, Remember the rooster!" Where have I seen Wendt before?

9

GEORG left the Residence early, but did not go to Mass. He had gone regularly only at certain times of unrest and anxiety. During these periods he had usually attended first Mass at the Dominican Church. Often he sat with his pocket missal, a gift from his mother, which he read distractedly. And he dreamed. He didn't always go to Communion and sometimes he even fell asleep.

There had been a time when he always felt secure after beginning the day in this fashion. Before the newspapers arrived, before he spoke with another person, before the noise of the city began in earnest, he was able for half an hour to try to listen quietly with the ear of the spirit. Even when he didn't arrive at clear spiritual focus, he nevertheless could cast off unrest. He had been thankful for the conviction that there existed in the world a point of orientation like the Church, where he could recognize his sins, receive absolution, and go to Communion.

Now he was through with all that.

One day he sat quite far back in the Lady Chapel. It had been some time since his last confession; he had grown weary of hearing the old priest repeat fatherly counsels which had nothing to do with his real problems. When he looked up he noticed that a young woman was kneeling in front of him. Her close-cropped hair and her soft neckline appealed to him. He gazed, fascinated, waiting to see her face. Without so much as a glance toward him she rose and walked noiselessly past with a light, confident step. Her entire appearance suggested a quality strikingly associated with the remarkable slenderness of her body. Georg got up and left through the opposite side aisle. He managed to open the door for her; she acknowledged with a nod. Outside on the street a book slipped from under her arm to the sidewalk. He quickly retrieved it.

At the inn on the corner they took tea together. Physically, she was not very interesting and he was never to become particularly aware of her body. She was not beautiful—her face was too strong-willed, with craggy features and Alpine-black eyebrows. She dressed with appalling carelessness. Yet Georg was fascinated. Gertrud von Felsen had one interest—the Catholic Church. She had an unimportant job in a small, insignificant business and she never discussed her work. But she was filled with the doings of the Universal Church. She knew the "ins" and "outs" of every bishop and cardinal in the land; she could report everything there was to know about

the famous theologians. She spoke a strange jargon that first repelled and later enchanted Georg, with its mixture of English
and German plus frequent quotations from Italian and
Latin. She constantly brought in the mystics—in their original languages. Slowly, with pedagogic clarity, she cited them
as if recognizing that her listener was on a lower level and
had difficulty in following her.

Georg was bewitched by her puritanical severity and
power. Here at last he had found a girl who held her life in
her own two hands and walked her own path untroubled by
the currents of the time and the caprice of fashion. She
steadfastly refused to read novels, poetry or philosophy. The
only literature that appealed to her was the writing of the
Fathers. Once, in passing, he referred to the Middle Ages
and she set him straight immediately: the Middle Ages
was a degenerate, premature modern era with its mystique
of suffering and its ecclesiastical conflicts. The great period of
the Church had been the early Christian era. After the Evan-
gelists, the Church's true authorities were, she said, Augustine,
Origen, and Irenaeus.

Georg met her regularly for several months. He surren-
dered to the force of her personality and docilely followed
her direction, unconcerned at the unusual fact of his being
under the domination of a plain, thirty-five year old woman.
She was completely free of sexuality. She was not a woman
but an angel, and he felt quite relieved in this rarefied
atmosphere. He began to believe that in their friendship—
external as it was—he was experiencing a counterpart of the
selfless friendships of the great Christian personalities. Thus
it was that for him there now existed an area of human existence where the springs of unrest, anxiety and continual
striving became neutralized. In her company he found the
same peace that he had found in the companionship of
Spinoza or Wittgenstein in the university library.

During the period following their meeting Georg went to confession regularly to Father Leo. Gertrud had asked him whether he chose his confessor carefully and he had to admit with embarrassment that he had always left it to chance. It *was* difficult, she admitted, to find a good confessor. In her whole life, she had found only two priests who understood her spiritual life at all. One was the Cardinal, the other a country priest in an Alpine village. She furnished this information in such a nonchalant and matter-of-fact fashion that its arrogance slipped by without any astonishment on Georg's part. Perhaps that was as it should be; perhaps this insignificant woman about whom nobody cared and who, from the external point of view, played no significant role in society—perhaps she had attained the highest peak of the spiritual life. Most likely, Georg mused, he would never have even an inkling of her kind of experiences. He realized that he was still a novice.

When Father Leo discovered the cause of Georg's interest in religion, he warned him that nothing was more common than for young men to believe that they have found the elements of true sanctity in a pious woman. Georg was irritated and argued back. He had at last found a girl who demanded no adulation, who did not desire that she be paid solemn court. Father Leo smiled and when he realized that he could not convince the boy he made a suggestion: "Try for a whole week to attend another church, our horrible old suburban church, for example, and then come back!"

Georg obeyed and suffered complete martyrdom. When he went to Communion he was distracted and indifferent. He was bored during Mass and was not even able to follow in his missal. Was the Dominican right after all? He spoke of this to Gertrud, who merely smiled and said that most priests were unskilled in the direction of souls. Certainly the fat

Dominican's intentions were good but he really didn't know what he was talking about.

When Georg came home after an Easter vacation in the Alps he met Gertrud again. She was being escorted by another young man who followed her slavishly. Georg saw in the other young man a reflected image of himself. He saw in his rival his own envy and infatuation, which burned with a double flame because he thought his emotions were sublimated above the dangerous realm of sexuality. This caricature provoked him to shame and fury. He had it out with Gertrud, who listened quietly, then merely smiled. She didn't deign to reply.

Georg recovered quickly from his disillusionment. He told the Dominican that he had been right in his diagnosis, but that he himself drew another conclusion: not only was Gertrud a fake and a hypocrite, who masked her self-seeking with ascetic and pious veneers,—so also were all dead woman saints and living pious females. He was excited about his discovery and attempted to prove his theory by putting the women saints of Church history to the test. In each he believed that he found the same pattern: early sexual shock, trauma, an Orestes complex; eventually, an extended daydream made up of pious exercises. Under the apparent protection of honest confessions and self-control the feminine soul then hurled itself into the area which she thought was the spiritual life. Within such a frame an unsurpassed cult of the ego could flourish in contrast to the healthy, honest workings of an ordinary, simple and zealous life of humanitarianism.

He saw how Gertrud thanked God that He had endowed her with such incomparable spiritual beauty and serenity. He also saw how she reveled in her power. No one could be more deceitful than she had been—or more corrupt.

Father Leo, of course, refused to agree with him. It was all well and good that the boy no longer believed that he had met a saint, but it was equally foolish for him to believe that the girl was a pharisee. "She is working with only half her heart and is a bit deceitful—like the rest of us. She wants purity of soul—a little bit. She may be a saint with a very small portion of her soul and the rest is deceit and half-heartedness—like the rest of us—like you and me."

Georg listened without objections, but from that day on he gave up the practice of his religion. He was happy to know what actually lay behind this thing called holiness. Obviously the time had come to find another path. In his own home he saw even graver forms of spiritual *malaise*: his father's inability to see his own errors combined with self-righteous, sententious judgments of others; his mother's soft sentimentality. Thanks—he had had enough!

One day, in the university coffee shop, Georg chanced to sit next to a young girl who was leafing through a chemistry tract. She had straight blond hair and an energetic face of almost Mongolian cast. They began to talk and he was immediately won by her confident, peasant way of speaking. She was from the north country, one of those reliable girls raised on a farm. Saturated with the religious observances of their region, they come to the city and diligently pursue their studies without taking any part in the student life.

The girl said that she recognized him from the student discussions, especially from the great debate about Communism:

"But it seemed that you did not quite know which opinion you wanted to adopt."

This angered him. Her tone was almost motherly, though not without a suspicion of mockery.

"I said that Communism in one country is not the same

as that in another. And I spoke of the difference between Communist theory and practice."

She nodded. "I remember."

When he helped her into her coat he noticed her strong, well-knit physique.

"Haven't I seen you at Mass?" she asked.

"That's possible," he answered, blushing. His guess had been correct. A pious peasant student. He added with irritation:

"But that must have been quite awhile ago . . . ?"

"Oh," she replied. "Don't you go to church any more?"

"No."

"It amuses me," she answered quietly. "Religion has always amused me."

"Religion amuses you?"

"Yes, and it interests me, too. By the way, I am a Communist. But I have always believed that Christianity is a matter of historic interest. Indeed more than that. It fascinates me—it is so pathetic in its helplessness and blindness."

"You're a Marxist and at the same time fascinated by Christianity? That's a rare combination."

"Why do you say that?" She paused and looked at him intently. "When I think of obsolete old women and priests, and the universal weakness of the Church it upsets me a little. Once the Church was a great revolutionary movement, just as strong as Communism. It was headed by gifted men and women who were prepared to sacrifice their lives. Now it has become the flabbiest of flabby habits of the flabbiest social class—the bourgeoisie. Oh, pardon me—perhaps I have offended you?"

"No, no!" he answered, stimulated. "As a matter of fact I was brought up a Catholic, but I think exactly as you do. Only I'm not amused or fascinated; I detest the whole swindle."

"Most do," she said softly. "But not I. I love every movement that wants to do something and which is furthered by human beings who place purpose ahead of personal interests. Just imagine, a once young revolution has been transformed into a sentimental affair for old women! The rich young man has become a fat old man who has joined forces with the pharisees. And the whole bunch think of themselves as Christ's children. It's a bit of a joke, don't you think?"

She spoke so quietly, with such lack of antagonism despite her hard words, that Georg was intensely interested. She was not beautiful, but she radiated an impression of confidence, healthy human understanding, and strong, sound instinct. It was with complete loathing that Georg recalled Gertrud von Felsen. He had never met such a woman as this and suddenly his entire circle of earlier acquaintances appeared anemic and sterile.

"How did you happen to become a Communist?"

"It's not too difficult to understand. I come from a rural area where we are all Catholic and I am accustomed to take things seriously. When I realized that the Church doesn't mean what it says, I determined to find out whether there might be in my generation a group which would be willing to sacrifice themselves like the early Christians. Naturally I found the Communists. You know I can't read a line in the Bible without seeing the great Russian pioneers before me. They had to suffer exactly the same persecutions, they had to live in exile, they had to sacrifice everything—they never gave up. In one land after another they were beaten, murdered, tortured in prisons. Finally they won in Russia."

"But with somewhat different methods than those of early Christianity," Georg said, extremely anxious when he realized how very much he had been influenced by her remarks. (Why was it that he was always the one influenced rather than influencing?)

"Are you referring to the struggle for power? It's an insignificant trifle if you compare it with all the blood that the bourgeoisie spilt through the centuries protecting their privileges."

He had no reply. His mother, his father, Gertrud von Felsen—all these experiences fitted her theory. He had often heard Communists before but they had been terribly abstract, with their harangues on class warfare and the materialistic concept of history. But here he was face to face with a confidently alive and warm young woman. Only among the Communists had she found the qualities she had grown to admire in the early Christians back in the times when they really were Christians.

He attempted to object that Communists had long been betraying their ideals and had erected a new state consisting of classes, in short, a system more unjust than capitalism itself.

She smiled patronizingly and reached for his hand:

"Don't tell me that an intelligent person like you is going to come out with such stupidities! Just read Lenin or Stalin. They predicted that before we attain the classless society— throughout the whole world—we have to undergo a transitional period of a hundred years. During this time everything must be sacrificed so that the proletariat can seize power, and it is precisely at this period that we have now arrived. Do you think that the leading Communists are fools and bandits? Don't you think they know what they're doing?"

She waxed eloquent.

"The faceless proletariat. It's the only class that can bring about what Jesus dreamed of. You say that the Communists in Russia are worse off than the workers here. Of course! Any child can see that. The very objection smells of capitalism. Why should we bother about how "good" we have it during the brief century of struggle prior to the creation of a new

103

world? America's easy way of life, hygiene and beautiful clothing don't bother us in the least—all that will come with time. But first we must win!"

Georg listened, deeply affected despite himself; mostly, perhaps, because he always found himself agreeing with an opinion he had previously rejected. The peasant girl won over his intellect in exactly the same way that Gertrud von Felsen had. Could he ever build his own system of values, he wondered.

Agitated, he at first stayed away from the girl. Then he found some Communistic literature—some, oddly enough, in his father's library. He sought out Communist students and was distrustfully accepted by them. For some time he went about in continual anxiety. He compared Regina with the new girl in his life. What a sterile *milieu* he had sprung from! Could he ever learn to live as an individual? Around him was the raucous herd, riled to the heat of passion and ready to explode. Hundreds of thousands in his own city were cases of obvious need, with military and police lined up over against these working masses. This was reality. And he was living outside of it.

Then, with increasing frequency, he sought out Alexandra, who lived at the other end of the city with a Communist worker family. He paid her a visit and was served Russian tea beneath the powerful heads of Marx and Stalin which graced the wall.

To his gratitude, Alexandra never tried to "convert" him. With a kind of mothering friendship, she treated him like a comrade and smiled at his capitalistic background. It was a shame that an otherwise clever young man was so tragically handicapped. It was as if he had been undeservedly stricken by a crippling illness against which unsentimental and realistic methods must be used if he was to be cured. He found himself becoming increasingly bound to her; on her part she was politely tolerant when from time to time he managed to lure her into excursions to town or on boat outings. Yet he never dared take her home; he was afraid she would have felt nothing but pity for his expensive mansion and the degenerate condition of his family.

One afternoon he discussed his new experience with Christer Wendt, who listened with his usual matter-of-fact friendliness. He did not act particularly interested and warned Georg against rushing headlong into anything.

"If you really want to make an active contribution, don't be over hasty. Test the materialistic concept of history until you are convinced that it is correct. And don't let yourself be upset by this girl's poetic visions. She's seen too many Russian propaganda films. By the way, are you in love with her?"

Georg had not given the matter any thought. She had been more his "comrade" and mother, but at this moment it occurred to him that he was more attached to this confident, warm person than to any other human being. There had been a time when he believed that all women were pale in contrast to Regina. Now there was no question of beauty; it was not that blind desire to take possession of a beautiful shape or to enjoy a premeditated pleasure. Here was warmth and an earthy reality; warm soil, safe refuge and above all, intelligence.

Smiling he answered, "Of course I am in love with her. But she isn't with me; you may be sure of that. So far as she is concerned I am nothing but a poor predestined step-son of capitalism infected with bourgeois habits and economic privilege. That's the worst thing that could happen to anyone, she thinks."

"What do you think yourself?"

"I'm beginning to think the same way. I'm beginning to

believe that my entire family *is* a ghastly caricature—that life can't be really lived in the bourgeois form where every idea is a camouflage of selfish interest."

Wendt nodded.

"And don't you think that possibly on the other side things are exactly the same? I do. That's why I hold myself aloof."

Georg was standing at the window; he could see his father approaching with Father Leo. He let the curtain fall back with a gesture of repugnance.

"Just take a look at my father. Now he's going to tie himself up with the Church. How many times a week does that Dominican come here, anyway?"

He recalled the scornful Alexandra's application of the parable of the rich young man who had now grown old and joined the pharisees. It was as if he now could see that same unholy alliance stealthily approaching across the asphalt.

"Christer," he said. "Pretty soon I won't be able to stand this house. I'm going to have to get out."

"Original," Wendt answered. "No son of a bourgeois family has ever said that before. I congratulate you."

Georg hurried from the hall so that he could reach his room before his father arrived. He drew the bolt with closed eyes and took a deep breath. He then went to the window and looked out. The villa section lay in the suburb to the northwest on a high elevation overlooking the river. On the distant side factory smoke rose toward heaven while the sun shone on roofs still sparkling from the gentle morning rain. The air refreshed his face and for the first time he believed that he could see an intelligent pattern in the rushing chaos. A new world in its birth-pangs and a fabulous world-transforming opportunity seemed spread before him. Powerful forces were massing on both fronts while an unknown hand guided affairs ever closer to the inevitable explosion. Behind the world of technology, collective struggles, hate and envy, an intelligence was working with patient method until one day it would reveal itself. History had a meaning and he, for the first time, was becoming aware of it.

As he turned around he noticed the family pictures above his bed and was suddenly wrenched by shame. Barely a year ago he had been a part of such stupidity. He had revered the past and had even been proud of these stingy, diligent burghers, these learned professors. He had even placed his grandfather in the most favored position because he had been a general. He began snatching the pictures down and then hurled them across the room to the sofa. The General fell to the floor with a spatter of shattered glass. As he moved again toward the window he could feel the satisfying crunch of the fragments beneath his feet. Would he finally be rid of his boredom and uncertainty? Would he at last be able to bring some meaning into his life? He thought of Alexandra, tellurically warm, and didn't know whether he loved her or her ideas. All he knew was that he loved. He would break out of this spectre-ridden house, where the very walls spoke of self-seeking. He would break out of the constraining frame and attain living contact with altruistic forces. He smiled, noticing that through force of habit he had folded his hands. The old dead formalism—like almost everything in his life. But that was all in the past. A sensation of gratitude swept over him, but he did not know to whom he should direct his thanks. The transcendent world which had once preoccupied him and with which he had sought in vain to establish contact had been blown away by the breath of spring. Before him lay the earth, naked, waiting for activity and seed.

And somewhere on the other side of the high factory chimneys, sitting in a poor room, was the woman whom he loved.

10

GOD has plopped me squarely in the center of an interlocking series of human destinies. The reason, most likely, is that I am supposed to make a contribution in some form or another, as confessor for example. But my experience tells me that everything goes wrong when I try to influence other people. When I give advice I can be quite sure that it should be exactly the other way around.

The Prime Minister obviously likes me, and I really don't know why. He can't make heads or tails of my brothers in religion, who are interested in social and political problems, but he loves to talk to me—or use me for a sounding board. The only thing he dislikes is my view of the natural sciences. When I told him that mysticism is an exact science and that the natural sciences are poetic fancy with constantly changing myths, he stared at me. He was embarrassed for me. I know I am right, of course. Does anyone believe that a shred of our scientific concept of the universe will be accepted a thousand years from now? Yet the rules of the spiritual life laid down by John of the Cross are as valuable today as they were in his time. But I should be careful, I suppose, about saying such things.

Old dame Elisabeth is the quintessence of zeal. Yet she interests me the least. Her little worries will clear up before long. She is so preoccupied with her own spirituality, she reads such dismally edifying tracts, she prays such a weird amount—all that we will have to drive out of her.

But she is beginning to wake up. Yesterday I was out at the Villa. It was a windless day, almost as warm as summer and the fruit trees in the garden were already white with blossoms. The chestnuts will be along soon. Elisabeth was propped on her cane, walking back and forth between the rows of benches which she has had placed in various sheltered areas. She was supervising the tireless Stephan's work in the flower beds. We sat for one or two hours—I really don't know how long because I suspect I dozed a bit when she spoke most feelingly. She said that she suffered from the religious indifference of her husband and children, but had become aware that this sorrow was her necessary sacrifice. (I always get a jolt when I hear rich, well-born people talking about sacrifice.) She was prepared to humble herself, to recognize that she might perhaps be of service to her dear ones only by living in the Dark Night. (When this mystical night is so casually brought in, I become more than shocked. I get mad. It means, of course, that the person talking, now vastly familiar with the lofty experiences of the mystics, has become one of the suffering elect.)

I thought her voice unconsciously began to resemble someone else's—perhaps that of her previous confessor, Father Bruno. I didn't crack my head trying to find her an answer but simply sat there fingering the white twig of a fruit tree.

After she had gone on for awhile about how she might be able to "win" her children, I was forced to break in.

"Why do you think your children can't make heads or tails out of the truths of the Church?"

"I don't know," she answered unsuspectingly. "Can one know anything at all about such things? Isn't there an element of mystery here?"

"Certainly," I answered. "One can't see to the very bottom, most likely, but one or two things can be isolated. Whenever one shuns reality it is usually because it is encountered in an unconvincing form, or, perhaps, in a distorted or spurious form."

She sat quietly. I could hear her breathe.

"You believe, Father . . . ?" she asked in a trembling voice.

"Yes," I interjected vigorously.

There was a painful silence. Stephan approached on the gravelled surface before the ancient facade. A lark rejoiced unseen and the fruit trees stood like motionless white witnesses. In the distance the far barking of a dog all but vanished in the vast expanses. On the steps in front of the facade the great dane slowly raised his head in the sunlight. I sensed that Elisabeth was undergoing something like anxiety. This is good, I thought.

"I speak from my own experience," I continued. "I am convinced that I have hindered people from seeing the truth, precisely because I wanted to show it to them."

"But you conquer souls everywhere!" said the foolish old lady.

"I can tell you," I answered, "that my parents and my brothers do not imagine for a moment that my point of view could possibly be correct—even so far as they themselves are concerned."

"Christ Himself must have had the same experience," she remarked.

"All the more reason why we should not be consoled so easily."

She sat quietly for awhile and then spoke again. I feared it was going to be another sentimental autobiography—which I would hardly be able to bear. Instead she began to talk of Regina. This girl interests me tremendously, among other reasons because I still don't know in what net she has actually been caught.

When Elisabeth realized that her husband had been unfaithful she did not share her sorrow with another human being. But Regina—she said—had immediately understood. She was in on it from the beginning. She knew that her mother was suffering even before Elisabeth had spoken of it. Despite the fact that she was still a little girl, Regina comforted her mother long before she really understood why comfort was needed. It was a mysterious sort of precocious empathy. She didn't even have to think before choosing the proper words. Her closeness to her mother was so great that Elisabeth's suffering was reflected in the girl.

(This was stolen from Madame de Sévigné, I thought; but so what? I, too, borrow my expressions from wherever it happens to suit me.)

I asked a few questions, probing uncertainly at first, but gradually the matter began to clear up. I sensed that something was false here. But what? It had been a fine story that Elisabeth had related, but in the background, grating and off key, lurked a second theme. Finally I saw how the devil's stitches worked into his fabric. As usual I was astounded at the refinement, at his unerring ability to falsify, corrupt and confuse the most noble motives!

I pointed out to Elisabeth that even though she had made no derogatory remarks against Falk, she had herself awakened Regina's distrust of her father. What a familiar story: avoid speaking about or complaining of something; even display magnanimity; excuse and defend for the sake of form. But underlying and penetrating it all sounds the counterpoint of frivolous self-indulgence. It is particularly insidious when combined with: I suffer—but see how generous I am, how noble!

Elisabeth sat quiet and pale as I talked; I could see how hurt she was. I had touched upon her inmost secret and it had now been given away. I was sorry for her, for I had the example of my own experiences. At the same time I realized that I was beginning to like the old lady.

Then she told me something else. When Regina was fourteen or fifteen years old—that is to say, exactly at the critical moment in this family's history,—she began reading the mystics and saints. She went to confession every week, displayed holy pictures in her room, and refused to wear beautiful clothes or to dance. One night the mother found her lying on the floor beside her bed. Another time she found a thick cord that the girl wore tightly bound around her waist for mortification. Elisabeth mentioned it to Father Bruno, and then had some serious words with the child.

Somehow Regina had finally learned the truth. Elisabeth didn't know how; possibly it was through the gossip of Bertha, the cook. The girl was seized by spiritual panic, not only because she saw her mother's suffering and broken spirit, but the poor child also believed her father a lost soul. She saw that the father, who was sending her to a Catholic school, did not observe the principles that he wished his daughter to cherish. He was a damned soul who could be saved from hell only by the sacrifice of somebody else. This somebody else was herself. The idea assumed gigantic proportions as she continued to read the lives of the martyrs and continued to mortify herself.

Elisabeth learned that Regina was trying to do penance for her father and save him. Father Bruno also intervened and told the young girl that there was no better way to help her father than to be doubly affectionate and attentive toward him. She accepted the advice. At the lunch table she would explore the terrain and then be at hand with ash trays, lighters and similar little needs.

The exaggerated nature of this stage passed, as it usually does in the life of the idealistic young. One day at breakfast, however, Elisabeth—without bad intent but certainly without tact—mentioned to Falk that he had a daughter who "wanted to become a saint."

"Nonsense! Sheer stupidity!" he snorted.

White and trembling, Regina left the table. She turned

against her father at that moment, until now she hates him, abhors him.

I had supposed that something of the sort lay behind Regina's present indifference. I pointed out to Elisabeth—without being able to prove it, but at the same time not in the least doubting I was on sure ground—that to an extent she must share the guilt. On the surface she had regretted her action and struggled to correct her daughter's agonized reaction. Interiorly, however, she had looked on it as a triumph. She herself had learned to pardon her husband. (That is almost true.) But she had passed on to Regina the first image of Falk that she constructed after her discovery of his infidelity. The daughter saw her father with the eyes of a wife suffering deep wounds to her pride. This image was a blueprint of hate. In short, without clearly realizing it, without putting it into so many words, Elisabeth's stratagem had been to convince her family that she had been made sick and broken by her husband's brutality and indifference.

She continued to stare at the ground; I believe she wept. She had no rebuttal.

Finally, startled at my own sharpness, I said:

"I am not at all sure that your physical condition is not also a weapon against your husband. You will yourself sick to show how much you suffer."

She raised her eyes and I was moved by her confused, tired features; she certainly does not lack sincerity and seriousness.

"You mean to say," she asked softly, "that self-indulgence is the cause of my physical pain?"

"No," I answered, "not entirely."

This was enough. I had introduced her to the idea that she had been pious and forgiving on the outside only, despite her prayers for her husband. On another level and at the same time, she had taken pleasure in the fact that her daughter took over her hate and thereby continued the punishment

113

of her husband. In all these pious practices she was taking a most sophisticated revenge. But the deeper I see into the deceitful soul of human nature the more I am convinced of its needs. Elisabeth can't stand it any longer. She wants—at least with a part of her soul—to be selfless and self-denying, and that is more than enough.

I thought to myself: all that is happening inside you, all the tearing and sundering caused by the merciless, piercing light of self-knowledge—all this is God's work.

The convent bell sounded and I looked up, blinded by the white snow of blossoming trees. I thought awhile and then said:

"Yes, it hurts. But be thankful. The fact that it hurts means only that God lives and has not forgotten you!"

It occurred to me again that I, too, have a similar fondness for pious phrases which I had plagiarized from others. At the same moment I heard within me the familiar voice of the devil. I knew that if I had had some money, and if it were not too far to the tavern, and if the sun were not shining so brightly, and I were not so lazy, and were not so likely to be ashamed of myself—I knew that I would go directly to that very tavern and get a bit drunk, just as in days gone by. Why? I don't know. But I recognized the temptation and was shocked.

I broke off the interview. I can imagine that I appeared reverend, dependable and well-fed as I left by the west garden gate. Actually I was closer to a frightened rabbit at full tilt. I came directly home to the monastery and together with my brothers bellowed the devil away at choir.

Afterwards, when I was leafing through the paper, I read that Mrs. Graber had met a sudden death. The notice was so phrased that suicide was strongly implied. Another soul gone whom I was called to help. I had been placed across her path and was, perhaps, the only one who had ever managed to see her basic goodness. Possibly she never dared to confess to her husband that she was sorry and that deep down she wanted to make up for her wrong doings. Possibly she never really knew her own identity. Possibly neither of the two dared confess his love for the other. I can't actually say why, but something tells me that this is the way it was.

I must contact Graber again. If I can only convince him that his wife fought bravely for him before she died—that she defended him and loved him. It's my nature to come too late. *Ecclesia cunctans.* "The Church Always Too Late." It certainly fits me!

PART II

Pastorale

11

Report 24 a.

1. In code B 22 I am handing over three private letters which were written to officials in this country and four communications to the envoys in London, Berlin, Paris and Rome; also, for Moscow, microfilm copies of intelligence matters as well as the present progress of the mobilization plan for military suppression here.

My next communication will use code o 6.

2. X 4 is unreliable. He nodded to me in the presence of a cabinet member. On 22 March when I passed him in the corridor he handed me a communication which was not absolutely essential. I request to be left alone. If my work is to succeed I must work entirely alone both at the Executive Offices and the Prime Minister's Residence.

3. Our press commentaries about Falk's interest in the Catholic Church are clumsy and forced. We must wait in this matter until some authentic material can be produced.

4. Falk is planning a blow against Communism which is supposed to take place simultaneously in this country and in the two neighboring countries. He is investigating the extent to which military control in the three countries can be brought under a common command. Exploratory talks have just begun. We can organize a general strike in all three countries without difficulty, but we must first have the factual evidence in our hands. Our press must not even hint at any of this until I have procured a microfilm. The negotiations are being conducted in secret and I do not have access to either the minutes of the discussion or the draft-plan. But there are certain other means.

5. In order to provide necessary jolts to the Prime Minister's nerves some violence in his personal orbit as well as in the Capital itself would be of the greatest value. I leave the choice up to you and warn against any extremes that might cause fatalities. Above everything else in the world the Prime Minister loves his summer Villa, with its collection of books, sculpture and paintings. It is not under guard and as a rule only his sick wife lives there, an hysterical woman devoted to religious meditation.

I would be grateful if nothing were undertaken before I have an opportunity to approve of any plan which may be decided upon. At the present moment, however, I can under no circumstances consent to any personal interview, and I reserve the right to indicate in what way communications should and can reach me.

6. I worked it so that A. made contact with Georg, the Prime Minister's son. Her work was easy. He has discussed Communism with me and spoken of his wish to join the movement. I considered it the right tactic to warn him against it. Nothing must be mentioned concerning his Communistic leanings until I have given the word. In the event that he should take part in Communist meetings and discussions, our press must continue to remain silent. When the time comes the scandal will be that much more acute.

For the same reason A. must leave it to me to reveal her relations with Georg both to the father and to the public. Falk's authority is primarily that of a dignitary, an incorruptible bourgeois, a great jurist. Consequently any "moral abscess," either in his private life or that of his family, would be of inestimable value for our plans. The Prime Minister's wife can be passed over as completely insignificant.

7. A Dominican priest has recently appeared in the Falk family. I know him and unfortunately he recognizes me, though up to now I have denied this. In Falk's presence he said that he had once seen me on a lecture platform. I am still uncertain when this could have been.

8. No. Of course I do not need any weapons.

Christer Wendt wrote his report on the paper and machine of the Ministry and used one of the engraved official envelopes. He put the completed letter in his brief case and immediately paid a visit to the Ministerial toilet. There he happened to meet a man dressed as a chauffeur to whom he handed the envelope.

"You are not supposed to smoke here," he said sharply.

The chauffeur nodded, snuffed the cigarette on the lime-whited wall and threw it away. Then he left the room without a word.

Wendt returned to his office. He had a quarter of an hour to himself before the Prime Minister was expected. He sat down at his desk, leaned back and folded his hands behind his head. He could not deny that Regina still blinded him. Her obvious downward path attracted him more than ever. Strong, healthy, well-balanced women left him cold. But those with a moral sepsis—beautiful women in the slow process of interior consumption—awakened his lusts.

He closed his eyes. Around him whirred the bourgeoisie, confused and nervous, living on empty ideologies, led by their "interests," their "privileges," their impulses. He himself was an instrument which, from the bourgeois point of view, was useless. But viewed from a higher level, he worked perfectly, never making a false step. None of his superiors suspected the ice-cold precision with which he functioned. He knew that he was under scrutiny and smiled when he considered the party members who thought they understood him. He understood the system and realized that he had to be an object of reports and investigations. Let them write what they chose!

In the midst of the battle, in all the convulsions of society, a law of absolute Necessity was at work. It took no account of the individual; the many who screamed in wounded pride or disillusioned hope would be broken and mangled in its wheels. He knew better. This Necessity could be served only if account was taken of all the possible consequences—and if pleasure was experienced even in the mangling of the dying and the destitute! The reason for his extreme effectiveness rested, he felt, on the fact that he enjoyed watching the process from the inside while in a certain modest way he furthered its progress through his own efforts. Some day, of course, he too would be spewn away, torn down and dissociated from the inner workings of the machine and he knew that he would feel even this "defeat" as a triumph.

This close contact with the absolute absence of pity and mercy filled him with security. Actually, the early Christian thinkers had a profound insight into this Process. What they called the realm of the demons was precisely this awesome law of Necessity. But they also calculated with another world. How touching were their attempts to fasten themselves to these little illusions. Metaphysical reflexes, nothing more.

Wendt heard footsteps outside his door. He opened his eyes, rose, glanced first at the desk and then into the mirror.

He flicked off some cigarette ash that had clung to his sleeve.

12

GEORG was a new person. Even his father noticed it and remarked that his son had "fallen in love." Elisabeth thought he was warmer toward her than previously and when she discreetly inquired how he was getting along with his father he answered, to her joy, that they were getting along better than ever.

He had thrown himself into Communist literature and had even ploughed through the philosophical writings of Lenin and Stalin. These, however, he considered mere theorizing and felt no need to expose himself to a detailed theoretical justification of what he powerfully intuited to be the one correct way.

His discussions with Christer Wendt were frequent and the latter continued to recommend his own cool attitude of watchful noncommitment.

Georg had no success with Regina. She had now abandoned herself completely to a bohemian group which appeared to Georg to be sadly lacking in good taste. He had seen her in café in the company of a crowd of half-mad sidewalk litterateurs. And he had often caught glimpses of her in the expensive car of a young surgeon who had quickly carved out wealth and an unsavory reputation for himself. It saddened him when, on his way to the University, he sometimes met her on the steps after she had stepped from the car, leaving behind a man ashen and tired after a night of dissipation. Georg would nod to her but avoided speaking. She rarely came to breakfast and her father seldom saw her.

From the empty estheticism of his sister, the unreal religious imaginings of his mother and the sterile conservatism of his father Georg now turned with rising enthusiasm to his new comrades. He survived certain tests made on his nerves. Often they were inconsiderate, and showed an astonishing lack of intelligence as they parroted Marxist wisdom in grossly simplified formulas. Many of them spoke with menacing bias about his own social class. He grew accustomed to this, however, and realized that only a short time before it had really applied to him.

Alexandra treated him like a young invalid who was beginning to regain health. She led him out into reality, showed him the Communist quarters of the city and convinced him that determination and idealism were to be found in this socially neglected area. Formerly he had felt rather uncomfortable when he had watched the laboring masses streaming from the factories at five o'clock or when he passed them on their way to work in the morning. Now he spent many an evening in tiny, evil-smelling taverns where bad beer or raw whiskey was the only fare. In such places he found incredible stimulation. He met self-taught individuals unshakable in their belief that their vision encompassed the future. He found a fiery sensation of brotherhood and solidarity and an uncompromising will to struggle and sacrifice. These people were not the scum of society, but fighters, often of high moral integrity.

Like all lovers he wished to explore his beloved's past, and he asked frequent questions about Alexandra's childhood, home and brothers and sisters. At first she was evasive, but one day she suggested that he accompany her to her parents' home. She had to make the trip whether he wanted to come along or not. He accepted immediately.

He got up at five o'clock and was waiting in the dark outside her door exactly half an hour later. She came down on the dot, as always. He was embarrassed when he saw how elegant his bicycle was in comparison to hers. Obviously hers had been borrowed; it was a man's, and she was wearing dungarees. He fastened her luggage to his wheel and they rolled off through the quiet suburbs.

Garbage cans on the edge of the sidewalks waiting for the huge trucks from the disposal department. Dogs ripping and slashing at the evil-smelling contents. Past a blackened church where a few individuals—mostly old women—were filing like shadows to Mass. Then the house rows thinning out and the increasing freshness of the air. Suddenly light. Finally,

124

as they passed the limits of the city, where the bunkers from
the German occupation were still standing, the sun broke
forth over a low-flying mist.

Georg was happy. It seemed to him that he was rolling
toward the land of his future. At his side was a strong healthy
girl who pedalled so briskly that he had to struggle to keep
pace. When he contrasted her appearance with that of his
sister he trembled with joy. At last he was finally in touch
with the fresh wellsprings of life! This was health and real
beauty; the other, to which he had too long been a slave, was
a false refinement that poisoned vital living.

They breakfasted in a small inn, where they ordered white
wine. Georg reddened when he saw the difference in their
packets. Thoughtlessly he had taken the first and best of what
was on hand in the pantry. To go with it he had snatched
two chicken legs and a piece of rare cheese. She had nothing
but bread. He asked her to share his packet with him and
received a negative shrug. He insisted, passed her more than
half, and kissed her quickly on the neck. It was the first time
he had kissed her; she permitted him to, but with a shake
of her head.

"I suppose kissing is bourgeois and capitalistic, too," he
said.

"No. But making an idol out of another person is. Or
pretending that the woman you occasionally desire is better
than everyone else!"

"Well, that's not my trouble," he answered.

"Good. Keep it that way. Love is the perennial theme of
the bourgeois novel and the bourgeois theater. I know of
nothing that so much makes me want to vomit."

Georg sat motionless for awhile, holding his wine glass.
Her words shocked him, but he tried not to be bothered and
concentrated on the pleasure of gazing at her. She had shed
her jacket and sat in her short-sleeved blouse, her elbows

propped on the table, her head a little to the left to avoid the rays of the sun, which was shining directly on her face. Georg observed her throat; he saw how the sun gilded the hair which fell to her shoulders; he felt a tremendous love for her conviction and her peace, and he hated to leave the intimate table at the inn.

When they were still approximately twenty kilometers from her home, she began to talk about her family. She described her brothers' egoism and pride of class: they wanted to protect and defend their possessions—nothing more. All thoughts of common purpose with social groups—even less fortunate farmers—were strange to their way of thinking and deeply disquieting. Her parents as well as her brothers were hard-working, law-abiding and loyal people. But to what were they loyal?

"How will such people eventually be integrated into the Communist state of the future?" he asked.

"They can't be," was the quiet reply.

"Can't be?"

"Farmers and the bourgeoisie can't be convinced to surrender their privileges willingly. They fight for them—as for their lives. We have already had White counter-revolutions in Finland, Austria and Hungary. These classes simply rose up in bitterness. They rose up to defend what they called fatherland, or culture, or even religion. Actually all they wanted was to regain their heap of inherited class privileges." She fell silent and trod her pedals authoritatively. He noticed sweat glistening on her tanned neck.

"Sooner or later they must be forced to surrender," she said.

Again he glanced at her. "You mean liquidated," he ventured. The attempted irony in his inflection was weak.

"You're afraid of that word, aren't you? But it really means nothing more than making people politically impotent. A well-ordered society simply cannot come into being as long as there are certain classes plumping for their own privileges. What's to be done? These people must be forced to give up what they won't hand over freely. In Russia, too, the peasants were backward and uneducated; nothing could convince them to give up their cows and fields and integrate themselves into the collective system. I know what they suffered. They lost what they had been taught to believe in as the real value in life—or what the Church and their priests had told them was sacred—the right of private property. This was the inevitable outcome. One period, one generation alone, had to bear the punishment that hundreds of generations, above all the originators, had earned. It can't be otherwise here."

She's so logical, he thought. But could she calmly look on as her own flesh and blood suffered the same fate as the Russian peasants? Before he could even ask the question she was upon him with the answer.

"I know what lies ahead for my own family. It will be a terrible day when the revolution takes over out here. But if I have to choose between this peace and the future of the entire people I won't hesitate for a moment."

They had reached the highest point of a steep grade. At their feet the river coiled past two villages, each with houses clustering around a church. At this level the apple trees had not yet burst forth but the pear trees were in full bloom. He sprang from his bicycle to stand directly beneath a blossoming tree, majestically proffering its wealth. In the heavens a dark cloud. Rain would come later.

Leaning against her handle bars, Alexandra stood catching her breath while her eyes quietly swept over the countryside. He watched her and realized that he had never heard her speak of her own future. The only thing that interested her was the future of the people. Calmly she anticipated a period of blood and struggle, beyond which lay an empire of permanent peace. Nothing could prevent its inevitable achievement.

Rain drops, gentle and refreshing, splattered on the pavement He raised his face and caught a few—one on his forehead and two on his right eyelid. Smiling, he noticed that she was doing the same. He took pleasure in the contours beneath her blouse and in her calm, tanned features. Her hair had shaken loose and lay half way down her back.

"We still have several kilometers more," she said. "Let's try to get there in time."

They let their bikes coast down the steep grade. But the rain came, first in heavy drops, then in a lashing torrent. He noticed the blouse clinging to her body; soon he was himself thoroughly soaked. He didn't want to be the first to suggest that they look for shelter, and it was she who finally capitulated. A spruce tree proved no help, so they rode further and at the edge of the forest found a barn. The front overhead door was solidly locked, but in the rear they found a loose board which was easily removed. They pushed their wheels ahead of them and found shelter.

Georg had never possessed a girl. When after some effort she had peeled off her wet blouse and underclothing, he reached for her damp body. She responded with a level glance that made him feel like a schoolboy, an apprentice. She understood immediately that he had had no experience and as a result felt a kind of motherly pity for his nervous embarrassment. She murmured that she wanted to spare him humiliation and would be pleased to educate him physically as she had already done intellectually. She gave him a gentle lecture on consideration and tact. He was, she pointed out, bourgeois even as a lover. Above all, he must not be immature. Shocked at first, his mood soon melted into gratitude and happiness. This wasn't ill-intended criticism but tenderness and concern, he thought, as he held his still-wet arm around her. After awhile she got up. It seemed as if the daughter of the mother goddess were standing before him, confident in the fullness of her strength. Here was something different indeed from the skinny bodies and mousy features of the waitresses and students to whom he had previously been attracted. Together, they walked out into the meadow; the rain had stopped and the sun had broken forth. They hung their clothes to dry and then sought privacy on the damp, soothing grass of a sheltered nook. Georg fell promptly asleep and the girl lay quietly at his side.

Two flowering pear trees stood directly in front of her. She lay awake, her head propped on her arm. The boy was delightful. What a shame—sooner or later he would become bourgeois again. Well, she had done as she had been instructed and it had not been unpleasant. She had no wish to enter upon a bourgeois love affair, certainly not now just before spring exams and the propaganda trip that was in the offing. She woke him. He looked up, and at once the tides of passion again surged through him. She said quietly:

"We can go on now. Our clothes are dry."

Like the well-educated boy that he was, he obeyed.

13

AT TEN O'CLOCK every morning the King was accustomed to drive in an open car from his summer residence to the city. He refused to listen to suggestions that he use a closed car. Occasionally he drove the car himself, and when he did it was at a very leisurely pace. He would often stop at a point which took his interest, leave the car with his adjutant and stroll into the villages to converse with the peasants. Or he would roam the woods looking for flowers or collecting butterflies. His herbarium was considered impressive; his occasional speeches before the Academy of Sciences had appeared to the learned audience as unusually well-informed. He was fifty-six years old.

The Prime Minister stepped into the small isolated parlor where the King was accustomed to receive his more intimate visitors. He was now standing at the window gazing out.

"Good day," he said without turning. "Today these people over whom you and I rule are especially nice."

Falk had come to discover whether the King objected to the use of force if a general strike were called. His expression became pained as he noticed the King's mocking inflection.

"What do you mean, Your Majesty?" he asked, placing his briefcase on the round table in the center of the room, itself as round as the table.

"Don't you read the liberal press? It is calling upon its readers to storm my crumbling castles! That is, insofar as I can read between the lines—a skill which people really learned in my time, although today it seems to be out of style. Or perhaps I'm wrong? Perhaps that wasn't in the paper?"

"Yes, that conclusion could certainly be drawn," he ventured. "But no sensible person should worry about anything like that."

"I disagree with you," said the King. "Absolutely. Are there really any sensible people left in the country, any more, with the exception of you and me? Are there? Can you name any?"

Falk pursed his lips; he knew that the King enjoyed embarrassing him.

"Don't go making such ugly faces," said the King, who had not actually seen the grimace but knew his Prime Minister. "God sees you, Falk!"

Falk sighed and considered his next step for a moment.

"Your Majesty, the situation has now become so serious that we have to consider the possibility of a general strike. Under these conditions the Government is considering the possibility of using force from the very beginning. But first we wished to determine whether Your Majesty . . ."

The King had turned around. Continuing to avoid his Prime Minister's eyes, he walked diagonally across the room, examined carefully a little table of the Empire period, picked up a silver vase and studied it closely. He was a very spare man whose hands were in constant motion. He would busy himself with extraneous objects during conversation: his hands would fly about in graceful curves; he would rearrange his suit or flick away a piece of lint or handle this or that object. It was a feigned distraction and absent-mindedness, masking what in reality was a complete command of the affair at hand. He could not resist disconcerting visitors. His enemies called him a shamefully deliberate cynic while his friends spoke of him as a "captivating actor." But nobody had called him a well-balanced, forceful personality—except perhaps the press of the present government.

"Have you seen this vase, Falk? I found it one day in the home of a banker in Venice who had the impudence to invite me to dinner. I went, but decided to teach him a lesson. There stood the vase in a corner and do you know what I did?"

"No, Your Majesty."

"I took it away with me. The banker snapped for air like a fish on dry land, but what could he do? He received a tin medal of some honorary order in payment. There are many orders but vases like this are a very scarce item. I know of only one other that can compare with this and that's in Paris at . . ."

Falk did not answer; he wanted the King to realize that he was not interested in the story.

"All silver is interesting," he said finally. "But at the moment it is things of higher value that are at issue, as your Majesty is aware. I wish that Your Majesty, with your incomparable experience . . ."

The King replaced the vase and seated himself in a chair, where he proceeded to light a cigarette.

"So that is why you come to me today. When the Constitutional Monarch occasionally wants to take a hand in things and feels that in a given instance he has a better understanding than his advisors, he is given to know that he should remain passive and say amen to everything. But when the situation becomes critical, then His Majesty is on hand to take . . . to 'share' the responsibility. Or to have the blame pushed over to his corner. Isn't that right?"

"Your Majesty misunderstands me," Falk said seriously.

"Certainly," answered the King. "Of course. When a person has sat for fifteen years compelled to nod in agreement to the unbelievable stupidities that his advisors in a thousand cabinet meetings have served up to him, he risks a tendency toward becoming prematurely senile."

He was on his feet again. He snatched a nude figurine standing on another small table, narrowed his eyes and held it against the light. Then he settled back into his chair and said, after a moment's pause:

"Do you know what a Constitutional Monarch's job is, Falk?"

Falk took a deep breath. Were there no limits? Was he going to have to spend the afternoon standing here listening to these random thoughts?

"Yes, Your Majesty," he said heavily. "I believe that I do. I have written several volumes on the subject which Your Majesty certainly has not read . . ."

"No. You don't know anything about it. Oh, the Constitution and the Laws of Succession and all that you know. But in spite of this you haven't the slightest idea."

He returned the figurine to the table and turning to the Prime Minister said brusquely: "Listen closely, Falk, because I won't explain it twice. If you don't understand, you will have only yourself to blame."

"I will certainly try to understand," Falk answered. He was still standing, for the King had not yet asked him to be seated.

A few brisk steps and the King was again at the window. "Just imagine that from here you have a view of this entire horrible city. Understand? The funny thing is that I continue to believe that it actually is here. Imagine you can see the Parliament, the Opera, the Parade Ground, and all the ants teeming about, and all the fury against me and against you —God, they're fierce against you, Falk—all of it . . . it's nothing but scenery! It's as if one were sitting in a theatre. It all lies beyond the realm of reality."

Was the King going to assume the role of a religious man? Anything was possible in an interview with him.

"I'll go along with that," he said tentatively. "True reality, spiritual reality . . ."

The King whirled around and answered with sudden vehemence:

"Poppycock! The Archbishop is always making similar remarks which he doesn't believe for a moment. No. I don't care two figs for spirituality. In fact I believe that no person is less genuine than the soulful. I'll even go as far as to say that a soulful person is the worst type of which I have any experience. No, I'm thinking in entirely different terms."

Falk considered it useless even to raise the issue about which he had come, so he thought he might just as well continue the conversation for another fifteen minutes before he would leave.

"Your Majesty is embittered," he said automatically. He no longer cared how his words sounded.

"Embittered?" the King answered quickly. "Not in the least. To be embittered means to have lost one's style."

He looked at Falk and noticed that the latter had sat down and was fussing in his attaché case.

"Well, why aren't you listening to me?" the King demanded with feigned unfriendliness. "Why don't you pay attention when I am trying to explain to you the role of a Constitutional Monarch? Can't you try to concentrate a little?"

For the first time Falk could not help but laugh.

"I'll try, Your Majesty."

The King raised a didactic finger. "The role of a Constitutional Monarch is to get married to a princess whom he does not love, to ally himself with people whom he loathes, to be nurtured on the advice of those incapable of giving it, to proclaim opinions at which he laughs, to rule in conjunction with those whom he disdains, to represent that which he abhors and in which he does not believe, and finally to be beheaded for misdemeanors for which he is not in the slightest to be blamed."

Falk became serious again, for behind the humor there was a profound truth. The King was a cynic, even though he had acted with high courage and absolute loyalty during the German occupation.

"No, Your Majesty. Not too long ago Your Majesty proved that the role of a Monarch is something quite different. That is why the country continues to love you."

"Love?" the King parodied. "Thank you! Because I held on to the Constitution during the occupation and didn't forthwith become a Nazi, that is supposed to be a deed of heroism. I go down in history as "a great King." I was "the living conscience" of the people, and so forth. Even you preach such nonsense when necessary. Don't you realize it's an outright insult?"

"No," Falk said almost in a fury. "It is gratitude and love."

"It's effrontery, I say," the King interrupted. "Is the clerk a hero because he doesn't steal the cash box? Is the general a hero because he doesn't turn tail when the bombs begin to fall? But when a King does his primitive duty and remains tolerably loyal to the Constitution which he swore to uphold when he mounted the throne—then he becomes celebrated as something quite extraordinary. Just imagine. The King didn't betray us. He did his duty like the rest! What a great King! He will go down in history . . ."

He had risen to his feet and was gesticulating in the center of the room in genuine anger.

"Thus, the normal pattern is to expect the King to be a traitor and a hireling. I consider that insulting. But you can't understand it. It's of no importance whatever. My father, who really was a great monarch, was hissed off the stage, even though he won victories over himself in most difficult situations. But I, who have not made the slightest creative contribution—I shall go down in history! It will be a fine gathering if everyone in that category is like me."

"Your Majesty," Falk said, "knows very well that Your Majesty has an exalted task to perform. And precisely in the situation in which we now find ourselves . . ."

The King threw his monocle in the air and caught it again.

"Certainly I know that. One task I truly have. One only. And do you know what it is? Not to complain! My task is to show this excellent but somewhat fickle people how a gentleman handles himself; how a fine old gentleman makes his appearance in a scabby world. And I'll continue to do it. To the end. *The Art of Being Beheaded—Handbook for Older Gentlemen.*"

He walked up close to Falk and took hold of his sleeve. "Do

135

you know what the proper word for my task is? *Style,* Falk!
Nothing more than style! And style is something completely
useless, but by now I am head-over-heels in love with the useless."

He stood quietly, then dug harder into Falk's sleeve and
said in a tone that both commanded the Prime Minister's
attention and reminded him of the war years:

"Falk! Now I'm serious! What do you intend to do?"

Falk looked at him. Slowly he answered:

"Hit hard, Your Majesty, if it comes to that."

The King released his grasp immediately and with rapid
step was off to the window.

"Right," he said. "Apparently there is no other way. If
the affair goes well, yours will be the credit. If it goes awry,
you can shove the blame on me. All the rest will do it anyway.
Goodbye. And regards to your wife."

Falk bowed and went slowly to the door. He felt considerably relieved. His visit had not been in vain after all. The
King realized that these strikes were being conducted by re-
mote control from another country and that all the talk about
a spontaneous people's movement from within was complete
nonsense. Thus, the King was prepared to give the government loyal support at a moment when it faced its most serious
crisis to date. Once he had given his word he was unshakable.
He would never try to escape responsibility. And if there
should be need of his voice he could be expected to throw the
weight of his still considerable popularity onto the scale and
speak to the people.

At the door the Prime Minister turned. The King, his arms
crossed, was gazing out the window. Beyond the royal figure
Falk could see a dark and threatening sky. As he stepped into
the vestibule he heard the distant growl of thunder. Pausing,
he thought he could also hear a roar from the boiling sea of
humanity.

He gripped his cane; portfolio in hand, he walked heavily toward the door that a servant had opened.

14

WHEN REGINA was seven years old, her father returned one day from the hunt. She met him on the croquet lawn.

That morning he had left the house very early. She had heard him and his friends rummaging about preparing provisions in the kitchen. Unable to go back to sleep she had crept to the window and moved the curtain aside.

The autumn fog lay damp on the grass and dawn had not quite arrived. She heard someone trying to stifle the baying of the hounds, then their almost tortured howling. The men cursed. It seemed that hunters were always cursing. Carefully, in order not to waken her mother sleeping in the next room, she opened the window. Steps crunched on the gravel, then faded.

All was quiet. Then the unearthly baying began again and though she was afraid she was mesmerized by the sound until her blood ran cold. How could dogs that lazed around day after day, sleeping, suddenly transform themselves into howling monsters? In her mind's eye she pieced together a picture from fragments remembered from her colored children's books: the gentle little hare with the funny ears of the child's story was being hunted to death by howling beasts. Cursing hunters stood shooting from behind trees. She had often heard the rifle report—it sounded like the crack of a whip.

Shivering, she closed the window and crept sobbing back to bed, but she was unable to fall asleep again. She leafed wearily through some books only to be haunted still more vividly by the pictures. Then she dressed and wandered, a lonesome little figure, through the unearthly house of pre-dawn. Her footsteps reverberated and she hurried to reach the living room, where a large Turkish rug lay like a mottled lawn. Some old cigar stubs in an ashtray caught her eye; to her their odor had always been unbearable. How could men smoke such horrible things? Filled with revulsion she picked up the tray to empty it; it slipped from her grasp to the rug. Horrified she fell upon her knees and tried to remove the still-intact ashes. But they crumbled. When she touched the dun-colored butts she felt she was griming her fingers with filthy oil.

She began to cry. So loud were her wails that she woke her mother, who came in, dazed with sleep, to lead her back to the nursery. The child spoke of dogs who had mangled her bunny and of "ashes that had broken in two," all as if she had been sleep-walking.

She was now able to sleep, but soon the sun wakened her and she jumped in alarm. It had been like a bad dream. Perhaps it was only a dream? She peeked into the living room, which by now had been straightened and aired. Fall flowers and large sprays of yellow foliage burst from the vases; the copper etchings on the wall continued to remind her of "the Palace of the King." She forgot her ordeal and the morning passed uneventfully.

At breakfast she heard her mother speak about preparations for dinner. The hunters usually returned around four or five, and liked to eat almost immediately. Regina listened distractedly to the arrangements.

Not until late afternoon, when her playmate had left and she was lonesomely gathering croquet balls together on the lawn behind the Villa did Regina hear the fearful sounds again. The hounds were returning—no longer lively, swift and wild, but sluggish and tired. Behind them came the hunters, sweat-spattered and muddy. Her father called her to see his prizes: from each hand he dangled a hare. She didn't wish to go, but she obeyed and saw to her horror that the animals had fir twigs stuck on their bellies. On her father's hand she saw spots of blood.

She heard the hunters laughing as they clattered up the steps in their heavy boots. She wandered out into the park and spoke a few words with Stephan, who had unleashed the dogs and "talked" with them in his mysterious fashion. He praised them, examined their paws, which he said were painfully wounded, and then led them to their kennels.

Regina went through the service entrance and slipped upstairs from the kitchen to the hall between her mother's bedroom and the bathroom. Through the open door she heard her mother's voice. It sounded as if she were trying to protect herself. Regina stood stricken: she wanted to flee but could not resist looking in. Falk, who had just taken a shower, had gone with a towel draped around his middle through his wife's bedroom toward his own where he intended to dress for dinner. Regina peeked in and saw her father embrace her mother, Elisabeth warded him off playfully and without fear. Regina saw her father's thick-set body from the rear as he pressed her mother toward the bed. The little girl thought she had never seen anything more horrible. His body was not smooth; it was hairy. On his back the hair extended from shoulder to thigh.

She screamed. The parents turned, although neither released the other. Her mother's face had an expression which she had never seen before.

"Get along with you! And close the door!" her father shouted, loudly but without anger.

Regina obeyed. She stood trembling outside and heard her mother laugh—an unfamiliar laugh.

She crept down to the kitchen, stumbled on the stairs and landed heavily against the lower door. The cook was nervous about the coming meal and so Regina was scolded for her continual carelessness and unceremoniously put out into the garden. There she continued to sob in her loneliness. On his way from the barn Stephan saw her. He called and asked why she was crying, but she turned her back and ran down to the shore. Familiar with her ways, he paid no more attention to her.

Hours later Falk and Stephan found her silent and crumpled in the bath house. Exhausted by tears and almost stiff, she gave no explanations and refused to answer her father's gentle questions. How could he understand? Or anyone else for that matter?

It had been the first time that she had seen a man naked. Gradually the image disappeared, but it cropped up now and then whenever she became agitated.

Later, in the library, she noticed that the men smelled of smoke and something else—she didn't know what it was. When one of her father's friends wanted to lift her in the air she cried out and ran away. She knew what men were like— hard, hairy, and incomprehensible. They shot at fleeing animals and were glad if they killed them. And they mistreated their wives. She had seen it with her own eyes.

Years later Regina looked back with a smile upon this episode, as well as upon the hysterical-religious period when she was trying to "save" her father by offering herself as "victim." She had learned enough psychology to understand the connection between unpleasant early experiences and her present neuroses. Unconsciously she fitted herself into the pattern of popular literature on the subject and painted herself exactly like the average descriptive case-analysis. Then, half-heartedly, she underwent analysis, but soon broke off in boredom and disgust. She was told that she understood herself thoroughly, that all she had to do to become "well" was to face the truth boldly and realize that she was actually jealous of her mother. Her distaste for her father was nothing more than inverted and disguised love. She recognized this theory, but she didn't agree with the doctor in the least. It was true that she longed for a father, but certainly not for the one whom she happened to have on hand.

She made various efforts to fall in love and acquired her share of ardent suitors. Sooner or later, however, the phantasm of her father would rise up in her imagination and repel her. Men were so gauche and helpless. They swore allegiance to her beauty and talents. Indeed, there were some who claimed "to love her soul." She found nothing more irritating and insulting than this. She let them burn. When they went too far she froze them back into their place. If they blurted out in injured pride that she wasn't a woman of flesh and blood, that she was afraid of her body, she had pointed retorts: she knew Stendhal and Proust and had no difficulty improvising scathing analyses of the stratagems and tricks of masculine lewdness.

These victories were really defeats and she knew it. She was ashamed of herself. She felt a basic longing for sincerity and simplicity. Strikingly beautiful herself, she was untouched by masculine grace; rather, it unsettled her to see men who were physically attractive, especially if they were aware of it. Sometimes she experienced a quiet inclination, but always for modest, calm and gifted men. Or at times for old men.

When she finally gave herself to a man it was to a student whose forlorn appearance and reserve had appealed to her. She was attending one of the university dances when she met him. She had not known him previously and when he didn't ask her for a dance she wondered why. He said that he would never dare to be so brash—he was not the man to lead such a beautiful woman on the dance floor. He said this without bitterness, rather defensively, yet with a sort of dumb admiration. Regina brushed off her circle of cavaliers and led the youth out to the University Park. They sat together for two hours while he talked, not about himself, but about his work. Bashfully, yet with a slight pomposity, he developed the subject of his doctoral thesis. Regina seduced him a month later.

The night was a severe disillusionment for them both. Her vehement passion shocked him, and he knew nothing about physical love. She spared him embarrassment but made no effort to continue her sentimental attachment.

Were men either howling hounds, hard and repulsive of body, or clumsy, soft little boys who could evoke only compassion and sympathy? She realized that it was toward the gently tender intellectual type that she was attracted; the others she could never stand. Yet her body dictated its own laws and when she refused to obey she had to pay the unpleasant price of jangled nerves.

After this affair she plunged, ever more unsatiated and unransomed, into her art. She worked until exhausted and burned up her energy dancing. This gave her some peace, yet she hungered constantly. She wanted to whip the tyrannical body that had the impudence to torment her. Who was lord over her life? Her self or her body? She mortified it and forced it into obedience.

Her father was often very considerate. He was proud of Regina and saw that she was upset, though he didn't suspect the reason. At times he blamed himself since he had never been able to treat her with warmth. He made clumsy attempts to enter into closer contact with her and was in the habit of giving her expensive and beautiful presents chosen with remarkably good taste. When he traveled abroad he never failed to bring home a gift which obviously had not been selected at random. He gave her expensive treatises on choreography; he gave her sculptures—copies, of course, but excellent ones. He made sure that she had extra money, but always under a tactful pretext: wouldn't she like to attend that dance conference or festival on the Riviera or take a trip to Montreux? And he had sufficient self-understanding never to suggest that he accompany her.

She was always a little embarrassed when, with what seemed to her the grace of a bear, he tried to be friendly in this way. How helpless he really was, even when he was most thoughtful.

In later years he became increasingly occupied by his political work which, in turn, made inroads on his own nerves. He struggled as before to win her confidence, but realized that he was making no headway. Eventually he began to tire of the effort. He let her go her own way since he was no longer able to follow. She had chosen her art and if this did not make her happy she had only herself to blame. After all, wasn't she a mature woman?

Regina had often toyed with the idea of meeting the woman whom her father had once loved and with whom he had betrayed his wife. What could she be like if she were attracted to that bruin of a legal philosopher? That overconfident pedant with his superior manner of playing self-appointed reigning prince! Was she a pure slave to whom he had condescended? Were there really women who could love men like him?

Actually, she made no efforts at all to meet her, but she knew her name, for Elisabeth had not been able to keep it a secret. Consequently, when at a party she learned that a young Doctor Thomas Graber was present, she deliberately made his acquaintance. He was a slight, self-confident man who already had the reputation of a cool, gifted surgeon. His

143

manner was pleasantly different because he avoided making the usual compliments. He told Regina that he had cut up too many female bodies to allow himself to delight over those not cut up. He never could embrace a beautiful woman without thinking what lay beneath the skin—very unesthetic organs, really.

Regina asked if he had ever thought how women feel about men, whose exterior is just as repulsive as the interior and who thus lacked even the superficial appearance of beauty. He laughed boyishly and told her that she was delightful.

Later, in his sleek imported car, he began to make passionate advances without ever speaking a word of love. He used clinical terms exclusively and jeered at his own physical drives on the assumption that she had a similar disgust for her own. He was out of the ordinary and amused her a bit, so she was pleased when he asked if he might see her again—and again.

For the next six months Regina and Thomas Graber met several times a week. He made no secret of the fact that he preferred her to other women—a young, successful doctor is surrounded by a swarm of sentimental women, he would say, but his waiting room would be as empty as a church if he told his patients how many had died under his treatment and how many mistakes he had made.

Even when he drank too much—as he frequently did—he was in sure command of himself. He never attempted to inquire about her private life and was satisfied to talk about her art and about literature. It seemed to Regina that he knew something of "the affair."

He never mentioned his mother.

15

Georg and Alexandra arrived quite late at the farm.

They were expected, or at least Alexandra was, but his presence caused no surprise, and he supposed that this was probably not the first time that she had brought a young man to her home.

He found himself on a middle-sized farm. Never before had he sat at table with peasants like these and he was amazed at the high standard of living. Nothing offended the eye. The furniture matched, with the exception of high cupboards which had probably been bought at an auction, inscribed with the approximate date and then installed at the farm. Georg was offered "the grandfather's chair," which had been made by the great-grandfather of its present occupant who bore the same name. Similarly the clothing, manners and food had remained unchanged down through the generations. The integrity of these people, rudimentary and self-confident to be sure, amazed him and made the superficial babbling back in the city vulgar and neurotic by contrast. Here no one spoke of himself and refrained as well from speaking ill of others. They spoke rather, in their quiet, steady fashion, of material things such as income, prospects for the harvest and politics. He noticed their strong distrust of the government and of every intrusion of the higher authority.

He ate the ham which the mother, a woman of tall, spare taciturnity, placed before him. He drank the farm's own white wine. It was new and not particularly good but wholesome nonetheless. Though he hardly understood the words, he was touched by the father's saying of grace, and he noticed that Alexandra folded her hands together with the others. She had no objections to paying respect to an external form that once had possessed an essential inner reality. Never would she offend needlessly. He saw, too, how much she resembled her family. The brothers had the same rather heavy, well-knit bodies, the same open, sunburned faces, the same prominent cheek bones.

After the meal, while the men rested, Alexandra led Georg on a tour of the house and fields. She seemed neither proud nor embarrassed as she explained the economics of the establishment. Pointing out how self-sufficiency continued to remain an essential element, she mocked the well-tended fences. Couldn't he see how individual ownership was carefully staked out and fenced off? Let no outsider put a foot in here! If a single calf were to break through these lines of demarcation, squabbles and disputes lasting for months would follow.

The boundary mountains, high and blue, stood to the north, for the farm was located in the last plain before the northern border. It was from that very direction that violence had broken through more than once in past history and penetrated into this ancient seat of civilized existence. Georg learned that the men complained continually of the weak frontier fortifications. They were convinced that in the event of war the entire province would be evacuated without any show of defense, for, from all reports, plans for resistance began at the next ring of mountains and the river. Foreign advisors in the Capital sat in judgment on the plan and agreed. The farmers could only shake their heads.

Georg was wrenched between two impressions. On the one hand, the peace, self-confidence and coziness of this tradition-steeped world attracted him. Nothing new-fangled was permitted and the pealing of the Angelus brought the constant response of the sign of the Cross and the Hail Mary. On the other hand, he was stimulated by the young girl's concise, convincing demonstrations that all this was doomed to death, that this pastoral serenity had been bought at the expense of other people's suffering, that the peasant's security was founded on the poverty of others. He knew that in her mind's eye she could visualize the reorganization of the whole area by division of land and the institution of collectivity. He asked how her father's farm would fare and she answered quietly that it would of course be broken up and collectivized.

They reached the top of a hill where the church stood, white and silent. Alexandra pointed out her relatives' graves. When they entered she genuflected—why not? Georg was astounded at her composure and serenity. Unalterably opposed to the entire order of the region, she knew no hate and constantly showed respect and reverence. What a burning vision of the state and of the future she must have if she could so calmly approve of the disappearance of this society!

Dusk fell at last. After a silent evening meal taken without light in the kitchen he went out with Alexandra to the hill. The men stood at the fence gazing out over the fields or chatting about passing cars. They spoke slowly and methodically without ever raising their voices. Night came, mild and soft as velvet. From the other side of the road at the woods' edge a white horse suddenly appeared, so quietly that no one noticed it at first. For a moment it stood absolutely silent, then just as silently disappeared between the tree trunks. Georg, enraptured, stared after it. In the distance, from the direction of the village inn, an accordion could be softly heard, its tones alternately fading and swelling on the night wind. Soft lights cut the plain's velvet blackness and with languid grace the stars appeared, one by one.

When the coolness of the night began to chill they went inside. Arrangements had been made for them to sleep in the shed, where there were several sparsely furnished rooms over the grain bins. They washed at the farm pump. Georg trembled in the expectation of this night—trembled with impatience, uneasiness and desire.

When he entered she was lying in the dark. Quietly she awaited him, her body cool, her manner gentle and motherly. His eagerness was stimulating and passion suddenly engulfed her. When he awoke before midnight and felt the girl beside him he turned toward her again. She yielded willingly, but later, when he whisperingly asked what her brothers would think, she didn't answer. During the entire night she spoke no more than a few words.

Georg spent the remainder of the night in a delirious state of semi-wakefulness. He did not leave her side until morning. He dressed and went carefully down the creaking steps into the yard. The house lay covered with mist despite the first breaking of dawn. Shivering, he went to the fence and looked out across the glistening plain. Again he saw the white horse at the edge of the forest. It stood quietly and then, with gently bobbing head, slipped slowly along the enclosure until it disappeared.

Georg trembled both with cold and joy. Now he knew. He had become a man. His empty, uneven life had suddenly found a direction, a goal. From this fruitful soil a young girl had sprung forth who had brought benison to his loins and solution to his doubts. Legitimate demands could now be made on him and he rejoiced in the sure knewledge that he would do everything in his power to live up to them. The strength of a sound mind and a healthy body had thrust aside all that had injured him, the narrowness of caste, the opinions which father and friends had forced upon him—everything that was false and artificial. Tears of gratitude welled in his eyes as the white horse once more came into view.

They planned to leave at about ten o'clock, and while waiting for Alexandra, Georg chatted with her oldest brother.

There were no questions about the night or about Alexandra and her life at the University. Her brother offered a spate of moderate and confident views on the harvest, village life, politics and the danger of war. The brother had fought against Nazism and had spent a long time in a concentration camp. He had a pronounced limp from a severe leg injury, but he never complained. Men such as he were unfamiliar with sentimentality. An undertone of hate sharpened their voices when the conversation came around to Communism. They had fought against Nazism; they would know how to fight against Communism.

Georg timidly tried to debate some of these points, but when Alexandra came she realized what was going on and abruptly changed the subject. Her brother gave her a suspicious glance and let the topic drop without commenting on her opinions or revealing whether or not he was fully aware of them.

As they were about to mount their bikes the mother gave Alexandra a package containing a leg of lamb, some butter and country-style bread—less for the journey than for her use back in the city.

"Do you need any money?" the mother asked softly.

"No, thank you. I'll get along fine."

Handshakes all around and they were off. They chose a different route, this time through the woods toward the railway station some twenty kilometers from the village. The bikes rolled slowly along the wooded path, alternately slipping on needles and jarred by roots. At the woods' edge they came upon a broad vista of clustered villages, several church towers and an asphalt ribbon glistening like copper between the fields.

During their rest Georg wanted to make love again but she repulsed him.

"You're incorrigible," she said. "All you want is pleasure.

Can you ever stop being bourgeois? Don't you know it's ludicrous?"

His mood was so full of gratitude and relief that nothing could wound or even unsettle him, not even when she began a sharp lecture.

"I am not capital. I'm not something usable, something to be 'possessed.' Can't you grasp that?"

He grasped it.

During the train journey back he fell asleep. They were passing through the suburbs when the rattling of the train woke him—he was not accustomed to third class travel. The dirty buildings disgusted him. In the open windows of run-down houses drooped pillows and sheets. Wash hanging to dry disappeared in sooty wads of locomotive smoke. The outskirts of the city were as if chewed by a pestilence. Georg looked at Alexandra. She was sitting quietly, reading an economic text, her finger tracing a statistic. How can you sit here so undisturbed? Why don't you fly back to your home country with its healthy breath of purity and peace? Then he had to smile at his own foolishness. She preferred the working masses. A new vision had been enkindled in those benumbed minds and it was now bursting into fire. A time would come when these slums would be made whole, the rich would be liquidated, and justice and peace would be the law of the land.

George was so different when he arrived at home that everyone asked what had happened. Falk was delighted that his boy had sought to explore their country. Wendt asked a few polite questions in his disinterested manner. Regina stared at him; her intuition immediately told her that he had lived with a woman.

When he described the bike trip, his meeting with the peasants, the white horse, the contrast between country and city, she asked in her smoky voice:

"Was she nice?"

He grinned: "Nice is hardly the word."

"Naturally," she said. "You know, there comes a certain stage of bourgeois degeneration when it is proper to fondle stable girls and to whore with meal-spattered peasants. Please —I don't begrudge you your pleasure—just don't become a miller yourself!"

Georg smiled at her sarcasm. How tensely decadent and socially useless was his beautiful iceberg of a sister! Would she ever be able to break out of her shell of sterile artificiality and bohemian second-class existence? He noticed her stylized coiffure and the cigarette in her delicate hand, which trembled constantly, incapable of closing in a firm grip.

"Regina, I have had such a wonderful experience that . . ."

"That . . . ?" she asked.

". . . that I only wish that you could have a similar one," he said childishly.

"A miller?"

"No, but peace, relaxation. And purpose!"

She rose with a shrug and turned her back on him. His eyes followed the contours of her body as if appraising a master work, a Grecian urn, or a youthfully beautiful tree.

"So now you're 'happy'?" she asked in a muffled voice. He caught the irony.

"Yes, for the first time in my life."

When she turned again she seemed too sad—or bored—to mock him any longer. "You poor fool."

He sat motionless for a moment. Then realizing that his father might appear at any moment, he got up and went to his room. At his desk he began to leaf through his books but was unable to concentrate on even a few lines. Heart pounding, he rested his forehead on a book. Well, come what may, there was no price he wouldn't pay to remain the person he had just become.

That evening he came upon a workers' demonstration. It

was a parade with placards protesting, in the name of the starving masses, against police terror. His first instinct was to join the ranks, but Alexandra had forbidden it—he must wait awhile before he showed what side he was on. Not so very long ago he had been uneasy, even repelled, when he came upon such workers' parades. Then the hate-filled faces had seemed ugly and vulgar. Now, every young girl was Alexandra and the procession seemed nothing more than a demonstration of courage, strength and honest purpose.

Because she wanted to work and study in peace Alexandra had told him firmly that he should not disturb her schedule too frequently. He was not to come to her room; they would meet in the city when he had made a date in advance.

But his desire gave him no peace. Late one evening he took a streetcar to the suburbs and climbed her narrow staircase. The anteroom door was open and the landlord's family was absent. He knew that she was not in the habit of locking the doors, for she had nothing that could be stolen.

He knocked slowly. No answer. After a moment's hesitation he softly pushed it open. Before him stood a man clad only in trousers. Alexandra was half asleep on the bed.

He slammed the door and ran. The man's voice rang out as he leaped down the stairs. A window was flung open above but he flew on until he reached unfamiliar streets. Then he ducked into a tavern, ordered a brandy and tossed it down with trembling hand.

16

FOR THE first time in his life Georg came home drunk. From the tavern he had gone to other bistros. The whole evening wasn't too clear, but he had fairly distinct recollections of meddling into conversations with strangers, cursing and swearing, kicking up a row, and declaring that all Communist girl students were trulls.

He got to his room with great difficulty. After shedding his jacket and shoes he fell asleep, only to waken a few hours later with reeling head, nausea and all the other classic symptoms. A strong sleeping pill gave him a few more hours of total blankness but his second awakening found him as sick and confused as before.

Louise looked in and was shocked to see that he had not undressed. Finally, after listening frequently at the door, she took courage to slide in a breakfast tray containing a pot of coffee under a wattled covering. With trembling hand he filled the cup and gulped its contents black. Louise really was a faithful soul.

At first the whole incident seemed a terrible humiliation. Then he tried to marshal his recent convictions and to reject his bourgeois self whom Alexandra scorned. He had no success. Helplessly he realized that he had been snared in exactly the same way as the protagonist of the sentimental, middle-class romantic novel, who accused God and the order of the universe because he had no proprietary rights to the woman he loved. He hated his beloved because she was now loved by another; and he hated his fellow suitor for having reached the same goal that he had formerly achieved. Thus Georg had no trouble cutting through and rendering a supposedly sound judgment. But it didn't help him in the slightest. He had fallen in love with a Communist girl who had magnanimously set about to reconstruct him. She had brought him into contact with the proper people, had given him a cosmic insight and a task to perform. She had further given him the gratuity of that memorable night. He had been profoundly appreciative and had not the slightest doubt that she had led him toward an essential liberation.

Now what would happen? He had seen a half-naked man in her room—the very room which he was forbidden to enter unless he made a date in advance. He had no way of knowing whether she had given herself to him, or whether she loved him. Nevertheless the fleeting glimpse was enough to plunge him into the most bitter despair he had ever known. It was ridiculous, debasing.

He took lunch with his father and failed miserably in his efforts to pay attention to the conversation. Falk realized immediately from his son's condition that something very unpleasant must have happened, but he said nothing. When he left the table and saw Georg sitting with a blank stare he passed close to him, patted him lightly on the head and said softly:

"I know that fathers aren't much help. I was young once, too. But if there's anything I can do, Georg, let me know."

The boy looked up in surprise. Falk went into the library. Was this really his father? A wave of gratitude surged through him and quickly receded. His father had nothing to do with this business. In fact, he was now suffering because his father's prejudices had been engrained in his being. He was a victim of the perverted opinions of an entire cultural caste that looked upon woman as hardware that could and should be possessed.

He rose with determination. He would not back down.

After leaving the house he wandered a long time in the city. One thought obsessed him. Had he become a Communist only to prove himself able to share the intellectual *milieu* of a girl whom he wanted? Or was he a first-line Communist, independent of the girl? He couldn't solve the problem, but suspected that the right answer might be humiliating in the extreme.

There was no one to talk to. Regina would answer with her mocking laugh. Finally he sought out Christer Wendt and told him a good deal of the story.

"I thank you for the trust that you have shown me," he said. "But you must realize that my experience in such matters is considerably limited. So far as I can see there are two possibilities. One, naturally, would be to break off immediately with the girl. If you can't approve of her moral code, she will continue to torment you until you are completely broken, if you do keep on with her. The other possibility would hinge on your effort to win her."

Georg looked up. "What do you mean?" he said.

"Win her by showing her that you are stronger than the other; win her by beating the other on the field of battle. *Make* her love you."

Georg shrugged.

"How? She's superior to me. In her eyes I am the inveterate son of the bourgeoisie."

"She's right, of course," Wendt said quietly. "But that certainly doesn't prevent your winning her. If you whine, you're just going to chase her away. But if you can show her that you are willing to bear a little unhappiness for the sake of your love you will win her, believe me.

Georg stared at Wendt, then stepped up and grasped his hand.

"But Wendt," he said. "How can you . . . ?" Wendt turned and Georg let his hand fall. He moved to the desk, sat down and began arranging the letters and documents as usual.

"Yes," he said. "I am quite different. I stand . . . outside of things. I'm a misfit. But you are young and strong—and quite admirable. It would really be unusual if you couldn't win the girl you love."

Georg breathed heavily. At any rate he had a real friend in Wendt, who in a few words had showed him how his problem might be solved.

For the rest of the day he was unable to read or work. Again he went for a long walk and took lunch in another quarter of the city. He compared his lot with that of the tired workers around him. Everything had fallen into his lap: he was wealthy and independent; he had education and a future; he was handsome and had quickly won every girl to whom he had been attracted. Now, simply because he had come up against his first real difficulty, he had lost his head.

It occurred to him that he was still a victim of the image of the "pure" maiden. Ridiculous. Am I pure myself? Are there really any pure men? Am I not exactly like the bourgeois youth of the nineteenth century who wanted sexual liberty for himself but wouldn't tolerate it in the girl he selected? Should she really have no emotional outlet? He was living in a bygone world. There was bound to be friction and unhappiness when two distinct systems of moral values collided, particularly when this happened within the same person.

He did not risk looking for Alexandra immediately. After a few days he wrote a letter of apology for his irresponsible behavior and asked if they couldn't meet again. Her answer was swift. They met in a small café opposite the University. Georg, who expected a lecture, resolved to accept it calmly. But there was no lecture. Alexandra seemed completely unconcerned and didn't mention the incident. After a half-hour of general conversation—during which the girl directed heavy attacks against his father and his regime—he said:

"Will you forgive me again for my stupidity?"

She laughed her motherly laugh and placed her hand on his.

"Forgive?" she said. "That is another word that I wish you would avoid in your association with me. When I make a stupid mistake—something that happens often—I regret it and try to avoid repeating it. But absolutely never will I ask any other human being for forgiveness! That would be to admit that another has the right to make decisions concerning me. This no one has!"

"You're so strong," he ventured. "I'm not."

"Of course not. How could you be? I know exactly what's hurting you. If it's any comfort to you I might say that I once went through a very similar experience."

He stared at her, astonished.

"And I carried on much more miserably than you have."

He shook his head, smiling in disbelief.

"But there's no need for you to hear this story, you can read it in the first penny romance you pick up. Now, about the man you saw in my room: I am not in love with him, have never loved him, and never will love him. And I am not living with him either. He had taken his shirt off because it was dirty and I washed it for him. He was waiting for it to dry."

Georg stared at her. Was this really true?

Alexandra noticed his joy and added:

"Your delight displeases me. Now you are thinking that I am 'yours,' as the saying goes. I'm not. I don't even know if I ever will be. That depends entirely upon you."

Wendt was right, thought George.

"What can I do?" he asked awkwardly. "You know that . . ."

" '. . . that I will do everything in my power to win you.' That is what you were about to say, isn't it? Well don't try! No man will win me who does 'everything' for me!"

She gazed quietly at him:

"I think that the man who wins me will be the one who sacrifices everything to remain faithful to ideals that he knows to be good and true!"

He snatched her hand and she said, smiling:

"No sentimentality, if possible!"

But she leaned across the table and, despite the crowd, kissed him on the cheek.

"You idiot. You know that I like you a lot. I'm no 'pure maiden' and you should be glad of it. I'm your friend, your comrade, and if you don't scare me off with bourgeois selfishness and rights of possession we two can have a lot of fun together."

She spoke simply, with great warmth and no cynicism. Then she looked out over the crowd of students around them.

"Just take a look at these fellows," she said quietly.

He pulled himself to attention.

"How many of them, do you suppose, want anything more than to pick out a nice girl and a well-paying job? They'll become lawyers, officers, businessmen, and they'll all amount to something. They'll get good jobs and possess property. And not one of them ever thinks that less than a mile from here there are people who don't have enough bread to last through the day. Maybe some here will not have a particularly easy time of it. In that case they'll go on dreaming always of better days to come. They all bump and push and fight in order to come up in the world. I hate them. They're a pack of riff-raff. And these clowns have the nerve to call our comrades rabble. Our youth who gather in clubs after a hard day of unrewarding work, to study and to stay up for the rest of the night planning a new and just social order."

"Alexandra," he said enthusiastically, "thank you for opening my eyes. I was just like them before I met you."

"Oh, no. You were not like them. At least you were uneasy. You saw that something was wrong and knew you hadn't found the right path. I let you come to me that night because you pleased me by at once recognizing what was right—and because you have changed your views."

Oh, how wonderful! After that night of humiliation and ridiculous grief, to be able to breathe again in her clear and rational world! Never would he deceive her and the confidence she showed him, however much it might cost his pride.

With a light kiss, she was gone. He watched through the café window as she boarded the bus. She didn't wave as the bus rolled off, but he could still glimpse her as she took out a newspaper on the crowded rear platform. He forgot to pay when he left the restaurant. A waiter ran after him and he produced his wallet, flushed with embarrassment.

Again he began to wander the streets, and, with no place in mind, finally boarded a streetcar going out of the city. Before long he noticed that he was not too far from the Villa and decided to visit his mother. He took the route through the forest, where so often in the hunting season he had rested at the lodge. At a fork in the path he came upon a madonna before which a lighted candle fluttered. He had never before seen this particular statue, although he had gone this way many times, but he knew there were monks in the vicinity who were in the habit of erecting such images here and there.

As he stood in the half-light and watched the candlelight play over the face of the cheap, plaster-of-Paris madonna, he knew that he was standing before the Virgin to whom love and devotion had been paid for two thousand long years. At the point of passing on with a shrug, he realized that he was by no means through with the problem she presented. Here was purity in a deeper sense. Was it only vestigial middle-class imagination that made him continue to feel reverence for this unknown, insignificant Virgin who had given birth to the greatest Man in history, a point which even Alexandra conceded?

For awhile he stood hesitating. Our Lady would understand us, he thought.

Another moment's reflection: Would she . . . ? Alexandra has a certain purity, too. She is not biased; she is unselfish and ready for sacrifice—even if she does soothe an occasional comrade with her body. But . . . ?

Deep within he felt new unrest. Night fell suddenly and eventually he realized that he would be unable to reach his destination by going through the woods. Perhaps it was just as well. Probably his father was at the Villa; he had been visiting Elisabeth more frequently—apparently a reconciliation was taking place beween them, no doubt through that Dominican who was always around these days.

He stopped. He realized that sooner or later a radical break would have to be made with his father. That didn't mean that personal enmity had to be kindled between them, however. Surely no one demanded that he hate his father. Yet, it was Falk who was responsible for the reactionary policies, who wanted to succeed in his political purposes with the help of the military. The Communist newspapers were clear enough about that. Perhaps Georg himself could be of some service to the cause. Possibly he could show himself worthy of Alexandra by cutting all threads binding him to his father and putting himself shoulder to shoulder with the fighting masses.

He trembled at the thought. What if a great task waited for him right here. What was Alexandra asking of him, though she never explicitly mentioned it.

He realized that he was getting close to the hunting lodge. Provisions would be on hand there and he knew where the key was hidden. Deciding to spend the entire night there, he turned and arrived at the clearing. If he followed the meadow two kilometers to the south he would arrive at the lodge. There he could think in peace. After a good sleep he could probably reach a final decision.

17

THE PRIME MINISTER told his secretary that he planned to take a few hours' rest in the country. Though Wendt showed no surprise he was puzzled. Right in the midst of a crisis? Why?

"What if something should happen during the day?" he asked. "I mean political developments."

Falk shook his head.

"Nothing will happen and I will be back tomorrow."

Wendt felt he had to gain time.

"At any rate I would appreciate instructions on what to do if you do not return."

"Impossible," said Falk.

Wendt nodded. Apparently the Prime Minister had determined not to inform anyone of the purpose of this excursion.

"There is just one more thing . . . ," he began.

But Falk shook his head. "Don't overdo your efficiency, Wendt! I have taken care of everything that was to be taken care of. Don't worry!"

Wendt nodded again and closed the door of the limousine with precisely the required force to make it snap shut without the unpleasant noise that the Prime Minister found annoying.

He thought Falk drew a sigh of relief. The chauffeur, who had been idling the motor, now slipped slowly off in low gear. As Wendt turned back to the Residence no other cars were in sight. When Falk's limousine was barely a hundred and fifty feet away, a black sports car careened into view, braked and was on the point of stopping. Wendt made a barely perceptible gesture in the direction of the now disappearing limousine. The sports car continued on. Wendt cast an uneasy glance toward the armed house across the street. That one had been extremely dangerous, more risky than anything he had done in recent days. The police over there may have noticed his gesture. Would they suspect anything? Well, it had been a risk impossible to avoid.

Falk had his chauffeur drive directly to the Villa. Spring had come and in the park the chestnut blossoms had burst forth in glory. Lawns were fresh and green; the small fountain was pleasantly murmuring, and as always Stephan was busying himself with the garden. Falk called a greeting and mounted the classic stairway, flanked by the pillars which were his pride and joy. One had come from Rome and was obviously of Grecian inspiration. The others had been copied from it.

The Prime Minister was overworked, uneasy and nervous. The political situation was intolerable. After the riots and attacks two weeks before an unhealthy foreboding quiet had settled in. Falk could sense the charged atmosphere but could not foresee what would burst from it. In his Cabinet several of his colleagues were beginning to think his policies too severe, and there was a growing sentiment for lifting the irritating state of mobilization. It was felt, too, that at least some age groups should be sent back from the army, for there was work in the spring for which these men were badly needed.

The police had acted quite sharply in quelling the riots and Falk had acknowledged that they had done so on his instructions.

It was a commercial treaty with Russia, however, that was creating the greatest problem. Falk had blocked it, even though it would bring great advantages to the country. But he felt it would also signify a rapprochment with a deadly enemy, who, he knew, would break all agreements whenever it was to their advantage to do so. Above all, such a rapprochment could be construed by the Russians as the beginning of capitulation. The Communist press at home harrassed him and accused him of having sold the country to "the capitalistic powers." Indeed, in the depressed economic state in which the country was now floundering, it seemed unnatural to do without the goods that Russia wanted to export. But it had to be so. Falk was convinced of it. He would never enter upon compromises of this sort. He was convinced that the country would be lost once a new regime came to power which believed in the possibility of winning Russia's help by giving in to her.

The great drawing room, Falk's favorite retreat, was located in an area framed by the classic pillars. The room was not high, but the sun was able to play over carefully selected antique furniture. In one corner were two familiar views of the Cathedral of Chartres; in the arrangement of the flowers he could recognize Elisabeth's touch. Where could she be? In recent days—without any particular cause—he had begun to long for her again. He felt terribly alone and wanted to confide in her. Without actually noticing how it came about a new feeling of warmth had expanded within him. Always she had caused him pain; how he felt that he needed her.

She was not at home. He went through the entire house until he came to the kitchen and heard that Mrs. Falk had gone to the monastery. The Prime Minister reflected a moment and thought he would drive out there, but changed his mind.

"I'm going for a walk in the woods. Please tell Mrs. Falk that I will be home for lunch. Alone. I don't want any guests."

He went through the library. Here in the country he housed his classics; his official books were in the Residence with his scientific books, periodical series and reference works. He paused and let his eye run over the rows of leather bindings which owed their carefully selected colors to Elisabeth's taste. You silent, true friends, he thought. You never betray. I am the one who has deserted you. Why do I ply my present trade when I could be out here in your company, listening to your voices and slowly pressing a little closer to my own inner identity?

He told the chauffeur to drive on. A path turned into the woods bordering on the King's hunting park. They drove along the high fence protecting the royal deer and finally turned into the depths of the woods. After about ten minutes Falk told the chauffeur to stop.

"I'll get out here. Come for me in three hours at my hunting lodge on the other side."

The chauffeur got out and went quickly around to the other side to open the door. He nodded, his face stolid as usual.

"Does Your Excellency wish to take the briefcase?"

Falk paused a moment.

"No. But give me my cane. And a pack of matches if you happen to have any!"

For a moment the Prime Minister stood quietly and listened to the even purring of the motor until it faded. Then he walked slowly into the woods.

His senses were flooded with the beauty of the forest and he deliberately allowed the quiet coolness and the high, rustling majesty of the evergreens to work on him. But his nerves had been so badly stretched that it was difficult for him to relax completely. He felt as if a motor were running inside him and he was unable to shut it off.

He lighted a cigar, and when the branches under his feet ceased to crackle he could hear all the intimate noises of the forest: the wind's sigh as it rose and fell, the birds, and here and there a knocking or a dull thud as something fell to earth. He went slowly toward the north—there was no hurry. If he walked fast he could reach the lodge in three quarters of an hour, but he intended to arrive considerably later.

Culture grows as slowly as a forest, adding ring upon ring, year after year. The old dies off imperceptibly and the new takes its place. The shoots become stronger, shrubs push in here and there. But in the great over-all view the forest is today exactly as it was a hundred or two hundred years ago. Behind this apparently peaceful growth—I am well aware—

164

lie tremendous tensions and struggles for life and death. Beneath the moss muffling my footsteps hundreds of roots fight implacably for the nourishment of the soil. I can see the does in flight and hear their hooves beat with the sound of graceful poetry. But I never see them sick, or wounded, or even dead. They are hunted, too; they struggle and perish. How many animals are frightened unto death in this quiet forest-temple? They can neither seek comfort nor give voice to their fear.

He loved this forest. But he loved infinitely more the Western civilization into which he had been born. Today the entire cultural form that he loved was tottering. In the opinion of many it was already condemned to death. Was there a possibility of saving it?

He had always maintained that every culture, every epoch of a cultural development, had to reckon with some crisis of this nature. A balance, an absolutely foolproof balance, between the vital forces and the form of a culture had never existed. To hope for it was a myth, a dream-wish. Possibly, he thought, our time is not in exceptionally greater danger than the classical epochs. The structure of culture is always the prey of dangers. The Persians invaded Greece; the Germans destroyed Rome; the Arabs pressed as far as Poitiers; the Turks stood before the walls of Vienna. Were these less dangerous experiences than Russian Communism? Wasn't a grinning Caliban always standing before the wall of the city ready to lay waste, to desecrate and humiliate?

The thought, frightening as it was, was not without its elements of hope. What had been the factor that in all these critical moments had signified salvation? Always it had been the same—the emergence of the strong, independent, creative personalities of men of genius. It would be a fatal mistake to deal on the one hand only with the dying form, or, on the other, only with the destructive forces breaking in. From

165

nature's abundant womb exceptional individual creative spirits also sprang forth. They stood in no need of the means of might—history proved that. St. Francis threw off his clothes to stand naked. But his spirituality spread like a prairie fire enkindling thousands with purity and holiness. The great poets often lived in lowly circumstances, misunderstood, their work reaching no further than a highly select group. But after death their words found echo and their visions flamed up in unnumbered hearts. Truly original creative contributions did not always spring from the well-defined cultural institutions, but from free lancers and solitary geniuses. Society, in fact, does not create—at best it administers. And the commonwealth unable to embrace the new accretions of genius was doomed to death. The proud edifice of the law, painfully and deliberately erected stone upon stone, was crowned by the most significant experiences of mankind, experiences inviolably and inexorably necessary for the human community.

He paused a moment on the mossy forest floor. His feet had left deep traces on the soft carpet. Suddenly he saw a fox slink by and followed it with his eyes until it disappeared. He was now breathing quietly as if in church and it seemed to him that the trees were forming a quiet cathedral around him, their tops arching over and the sunlight breaking in as if through lofty rose lunettes.

His thoughts turned to Father Leo. And to the Church. In the center of history stood one single power which never had been brought low. It had suffered defeats, it had been humiliated, but its defeats had been turned into victories and its standards flew best in an opposing wind. The blood of martyrs is the best seed of the Church. The degradation of her individual members works for her triumph. This axiom he knew by heart and saw it borne out in Church history. A well-reasoned course of action, of itself, enkindled no spirits, evoked no new creative energies. But wherever man injected his entire being into an enterprise and unhesitatingly fell in love with what he considered to be sacred, then only would a thousand youths spring up fired by the same vision. Nothing was easier to affirm or prove. It was a law.

But if this were true—and he did not doubt for a moment that it was—how then could he stabilize the present order? Could he claim that the State which he served would really conform to these past experiences? Was he not precisely on the point of employing the tools of force to shore up a building in whose interior there no longer was room for sacrifice? Where could men be found who would offer the selfless sacrifice? Was there not after all a terrible truth—not expressed in the choicest language to be sure—in the Communistic critique of the bourgeois? Would not Christ Himself be able to subscribe on all essential points to the Communistic condemnation of the "burgher"?

And was not he himself a burgher? Even when he spoke of sacrifice?

But—he banged his cane against a fir tree—*if* he were to follow literally the demands of the Gospel, *if* he were to abandon the thought of force and merely pray and sacrifice, the entire edifice would dissolve in chaos. It took centuries to build a culture; it could be torn down in a decade. Hitler proved that. Did anyone seriously believe that a hundred thousand Hindus, following Gandhi's example, could actually save their land by passive resistance or by hurling themselves beneath the treads of Chinese tanks?

Could martyrs save a culture?

This thought gave birth to a fresh one that horrified him: perhaps the most important thing after all was not the saving of a culture? Perhaps he was putting in first place values that should be in second place? The Church had achieved permanence only because the Christians had assented to martyrdom. The Church was born at the very moment when all the Apostles fled and the Master Himself was put to death. It would be difficult to imagine a lower water mark, but Christianity's true strength had sprung from this source. He knew that. And yet for more than four years he had put forth all his efforts to create the tools of might and to bend opinion to do battle with men of violence!

He longed to throw off all his senseless burdens, and to retreat to his research and study, to let others shape the conclusions, all of which would be compromises in one way or another. Politics has been and will remain compromise. The end is sought through the use of means opposed to the end. Purposeless. Ridiculous.

Falk got up and proceeded slowly on his way.

When he reached his hunting lodge the limousine was waiting for him, the chauffeur lying asleep at the edge of the woods.

Falk's steps were soft on the grassy sod and the chauffeur did not wake until the Prime Minister gently laid his hand on his shoulder.

"I beg pardon," he said and struggled, half drunk with sleep, to his feet.

Falk climbed in. He looked forward to lunch with Elisabeth. Perhaps he might even phone the monastery and ask for Father Leo. He suspected that the monk had at least partially stimulated his meditations and might be of assistance in working toward greater clarity than Falk had achieved.

Not until he alighted from the limousine in front of the Villa did Falk realize that his case had disappeared.

The chauffeur was numb with fear. He had put it on the back seat. He had not left the limousine for a single moment. It had to be there.

But it wasn't.

A few moments later Falk was standing at the telephone, his face flaming, his brow bathed in sweat. He was calling the Chief of Police.

"Get out here! Quickly! My briefcase has been stolen! Absolutely! My most important papers!"

18

I PUT a call through to Dr. Graber. For a long time he said nothing and when he finally spoke his voice betrayed the effects of alcohol, or sorrow, or both. He would not tell me where the burial was to take place.

"The Church has no interest in a woman who has committed suicide," he said.

I answered that the Church took greater interest in no one more than an unfortunate human being. I added that I knew one or two things that I thought I should tell him. Among other things, I knew that Mrs. Graber had defended him vigorously in a highly revealing conversation. He fell silent again. Then I heard some strange sound that at first I mistook for sobs, but which soon proved to be spasms of laughter.

Then all at once he became obviously ashamed of himself, stopped laughing and curtly informed me that his wife would be buried without the ministrations of a priest at her country residence which she had always loved. With that he hung up.

I decided to attend the funeral. The trip takes half a day—streetcar, local train, bus, and then a quarter hour's walk. Why not? I had a lot of things to think over.

And in mulling them all over, I think I gained a new insight. The thing that is causing harm to each of my little flock is not so much their actual deeds, but the image that each constructs in his own mind of the deeds and characters of his antagonists. Georg's and Regina's view of their father is absurd. They don't see that he is closer to being a timid, slightly retarded child than a brutal superman. And I certainly have to try to correct Elisabeth's picture of her husband, too. Then again, the idea they have all had of Elisabeth —myself included—is completely false. She is pietistic and has come close to lying self-idolization. But in the midst of all her giddy sentimentality there is an astonishing will and an unbelievable toughness. She may seem wrecked, but she has the strongest will in the family. She doesn't complain the way Falk does when she sees herself in all her hatefulness; she merely nods and continues on her way. I'm very happy that she doesn't often weep—a most unusual phenomenon.

This confusion about Graber is extremely important. The children and Elisabeth are sure that Falk had one of those ordinary extra-marital affairs with a certain lady X. From it Graber suffered a deep psychological wound that ruined his life. But there is the other face of the coin: in Falk's presence and in mine she conducted herself calmly and defended her husband. It was not play-acting either; she was in dead earnest. And Falk? He certainly is blind in many respects, but here he seemed to show not the slightest remorse of conscience. This fact suggests that all the interlocking relationships are different from what appears on the surface. Something deep inside me tells me that all of us have constructed a completely false image of Mrs. Graber. If her husband's wound was not so tremendous—almost pathological— I would almost be inclined to believe that Falk and she have never had relations. How in the devil does it all hang together?

The facts lie open before me, yet I refuse to accept the common answer to a situation. Something tells me there is another solution. Perhaps that's because I am rather slow-witted and unable to hold together all parts of a syllogism. They thought so in Rome.

Why did Mrs. Graber take her own life? It couldn't be the newspaper campaign, it couldn't be all those disclosures about her husband's life with Helene Gritz. I take Mrs. Graber absolutely on her word when she said that her idea of her husband had not been altered.

Something else must have happened. But what? Could that son of hers have something to do with it? Of all the actors in this poorly written drama he seems to be the one furthest removed from everything human. Perhaps I think this because I know him the least.

My little flock! I could weep for it: the human raw material is not so bad; the human conflicts are not really so terrible; the catastrophe was not necessary. A demon blinded the actors, magnified their sins into unpardonable crimes, increased their pride and rancor into something pathological. And out of this miserable confusion arose a dilemma that threatens the entire country. Dr. Graber's fight with the Prime Minister cuts off the possibility of a union of his party with the Catholic National party. And that is probably a triumph for the Devil, who takes, I suspect, a keen interest in politics.

Characteristic of the *ecclesia cunctans,* I lost my way and arrived too late for the internment. Presumably I got the proper information at the bus stop, but I was too deeply wrapped up in my own thoughts. I always arrive too late.

When I did finally get there the grave had already been closed. To my surprise, it was some distance down from the house, in a little thicket, the site selected with the clear intent of not caring for it or visiting it. A farmer was shoveling back the soil when I came on the scene. I prayed a few moments for the poor soul. When I turned around I saw Dr.

171

Graber moving off slowly while his son stepped into his car. It was obvious that the father preferred to walk back. I ran a little race with him—with great effort, of course. I think I could hear young Graber's scornful laughter as he drove away. The elder Graber and I walked on together in silence for awhile. He didn't answer my questions.

Finally he paused and I shrank back from the expression on the face turned to me. I had seen him distraught many times but never so violently. The faces of the damned must look like this, I thought. But I felt again that I loved this man. With great deliberation I told him the story of his wife's bravery in the presence of Falk and myself. I repeated her statements of confidence in her husband, her belief in his idealism, and her self-accusation.

He looked at me with dead eyes.

"Yes." His voice was so hoarse that it kept failing him. "She gave me the same story."

"Don't you believe she was sincere?"

"I told her that all my life I had heard nothing but lies from her. I told her that I valued her hate far more than her love. I told her that she had corroded and destroyed every fibre of my being. She wept. Then I told her that even if she made herself into a saint and recognized her guilt it would mean nothing to me. Her crime stands. Neither repentance nor self-accusation can wipe it out. The simple fact is that I have lived for decades chained to a woman of deceit, while I myself, for the most stupid religious motives, have bound the chains still tighter."

He walked on. His manner was dreamlike, his gait was unsteady. We walked in the gray drizzle to the last stop on the bus line. Without saying goodbye he mounted the first step; then, oblivious of the other passengers, he grasped the handrail and leaned down to me.

"There is only one thing that bothers me: which are the most to blame, my wife's lies or the lies of the Church?"

"What lies of the Church are you thinking of?"

"The lies about a God of Love, the lies that claim God cares about mankind," he said evenly. "If there is a God—something I consider highly improbable—he is a devil."

I resisted the temptation to accompany him. My presence tormented him too much. I decided to wait for the next bus and stood in the incessant drizzle looking out across the plain. Far down the street a woman was slowly approaching the bus stop. When she arrived she sat down, hood thrown back, on the bench. I finished reading my Office a short time later and she looked up. It was a pretty, somewhat flaccid face. Where had I seen her before?

Before I could reach any conclusion she edged closer to me and spoke in a remarkably clear and pleasant voice:

"Apparently you recognize me."

"Yes, but I was just trying to think where . . ."

"Helene Gritz," she said softly. "Forgive me. It was stupid of me to come out here. I got out very early, as soon as I found that she was to be buried here. I stayed out of sight and no one saw me. I didn't intrude."

"Why did you come?"

She blushed. "Because I wanted to put some flowers on her grave."

This was the woman whose name was on every tongue, the woman scorned throughout an entire nation. This was "the woman of the web" to whom Dr. Graber has been so long attached. This was the one whom I knew Graber avoided when he was still going to Confession and Communion and into whose arms he threw himself when everything collapsed. I knew her not only from her pictures but also from his confessions and conferences with me. I knew that she was liberal in granting her favors, but I knew there were other things to be said, that in her own way she had loved, that she had tried to comfort another human being, that in the midst of her dissolute world there was gentleness and goodness. I knew that she had never made demands on Dr. Graber, that she had always been the one who gave. It suddenly occurred to me that she might possibly be the most human of all the hardened, narrow players in this drama.

"Was it wrong of me?" she asked softly.

"Was what wrong?"

"That I came out here?"

I took her hand without answering. No, it was not wrong. I don't condemn her. Furthermore, I have no aversion for such women. They have kindness and affection and they want to love and give themselves. The only trouble is they don't do it the right way. Helene Gritz is not at all proud and only slightly selfish. But right now she is publicly considered a most contemptible sinner, and no one is willing to forgive her. What was her crime? Simply that with her confused sense of values she tried to comfort a mentally distraught man with her body?

So ran my thoughts. When I was young, I too was stupid enough to say the things that are being said today. Now I know better. The very moment that the words of condemnation are spoken the Devil spits on his hands and takes over. I'm more careful now.

"Of course it was not wrong for you to come here. You came for the same reason I did—to pray for an unfortunate woman. And perhaps, like me, to regret that there had been no better way for you to help her."

"Oh, yes," she said. "But what could I have done? He despised her. He spoke terribly about her. I knew that she couldn't be as bad as he painted her. But what could I do?"

It was raining harder, even though the skies flamed in sunset around us. We sat on a small elevated area in the midst of flat land which stretched off in all directions. A wind was blowing and we trembled with cold. She wanted to go to confession right then and there, but I explained to her that the normal procedure was for her to come to my confessional.

God had granted me insight into the soul of a sinner. I was overjoyed. He *has* borne our iniquities, and He rejects no one. He continues to work in the stony hearts of Drs. Graber, junior and senior, and He bends down to a prostitute who prayed behind a bush for a poor woman who had killed herself. God's grace is with us.

I won't abandon Helene Gritz. I have seen people who were morally perfect and spiritually corrupt, yes, even dead. When I looked into that poor face, damp with rain and tears, I couldn't help thinking that there are morally imperfect—even corrupt—people whose souls are still childlike. Their real trouble is that no one has ever bothered about them.

She promised to come to Confession. Perhaps she'll regret the promise and not come. She is going to have a difficult time of it, but if she doesn't come I'll seek her out. She's honest and humble.

19

THE POLICE came in half an hour. Chauffeur Kolbe was put under questioning and could only say that he had fallen asleep for about an hour and that the attaché case had most probably been stolen during this time. His testimony was not particularly convincing; Kolbe was arrested and brought back to the city.

Falk tried to think back systematically on the flow of events since he had taken the attaché case from his study. He had

had a conversation with Wendt during which they spoke about the preparation for preventive mobilization. Falk had found certain faults with the plans and said he intended to make some revisions before sending them in their entirety to the Field Marshal. Then he had taken the dossier and put it in the smaller of the two cases which he habitually used when carrying valuable documents. No one but Wendt had been in the room.

Could he have left it in the library? No. Then, had he possibly left it in the great hall where Louise helped him into his coat? No, he remembered having it in the limousine. Of course, he had spoken about it with the chauffeur. But perhaps that was a mistake. Perhaps his case was not actually in the limousine even though he discussed it with the chauffeur. Perhaps, after all, he really did leave it at the Residence. Together with the Chief of Police he went carefully through the entire sequence of events, but his memory tallied so exactly with Kolbe's that all doubt vanished. He now clearly remembered seeing the case near the chauffeur as he stepped out of the car.

Had Kolbe had a rendezvous with anyone while he was in the woods? Had he really stayed with the car the whole time? Had he locked the rear doors or hadn't he? Would it be possible for anyone to open the doors without making any noise?

Kolbe gave unequivocal answers. He hadn't seen a soul, he had stretched out beside the car and had fallen asleep. Furthermore, he had had no idea of the importance of the case's contents. The Chief of Police's view, however, seemed to prevail: the chauffeur was lying and would continue to lie. He had been bought by the Communists. Falk accepted this theory, despite the fact that Kolbe had been his chauffeur for eight years. The Chief of Police would now undertake a complete investigation of the man's past.

Lunch was a nightmare. Falk had looked forward so much to a little peace here and perhaps a serious conversation with his wife. Now his nerves were so badly shaken that he couldn't converse at all. The suspicion of his old friend and servant horrified him, and the thought that he was surrounded by spies, that he could trust no one sickened him. Even his summer Villa was caught in the web.

After lunch Wendt arrived. He thought that in all probability the case had been stolen by the Communists; most likely the police would soon have the matter cleared up. But he had another plan to suggest. Why not let the Communists keep the case? What could be more advantageous than to have them send to Russia the very plans with which Falk was dissatisfied and which he intended to alter? A new plan would have to be drawn up anyway. Perhaps bad luck could be turned into good fortune. Now Falk would have no difficulty in trying to convince the generals that a new plan must be worked out. The enemy would be duped and the generals forced to yield to the views of the Prime Minister!

Falk listened in admiration: What a clear, quick mind Wendt had. The secretary was indispensable!

Wendt was completely right. Of course. This was the only solution. The misfortune was changed into a blessing. Falk's mood turned to one of great good humor. He called for a bottle of sherry and drank more than was his custom. He had survived both the attack of pessimism and the incipient conviction that his task was hopeless. His fighting spirit was enkindled once more. They'd see with whom they were dealing. So politics is the art of the impossible? He'd show them that the impossible is possible!

Elisabeth had been a passive witness to all this activity. Nobody had said anything to her but she noticed the uneasy glances of the Chief of Police. He had wanted the details kept from her, but since this was now obviously impossible she was given specific instructions never to so much as mention the incident.

Falk padded nervously about the house, relieved about a

solution which was both promising and frightening. Though Wendt had driven back into town the Prime Minister had decided to stay at the Villa and try to calm his nerves, if at all possible. Perhaps for once he would take a sleeping pill and go to bed early. Tomorrow would be a strenuous day. The generals were always difficult, especially Sturzebecker. But this time they would have to give in.

Elisabeth brought him afternoon tea at his favorite spot under the balcony between the pillars, where a vista extended across the park toward trees which he himself had planted.

Elisabeth's new understanding of her husband pressed in upon her. He was not the strong, inconsiderate man that for years she had supposed him to be. On the contrary, he was weak, vulnerable and upset. The furrows which political life had left on his features brought forcibly to her mind the burdens he had long carried without the least support from any member of his family. She had imagined all these years that her interior silence and patient suffering of his indifference had helped and supported him. This comfort had given meaning to her life. The past months, however, had showed up this illusion for what it was. Almost without her realizing it, Father Leo had taken apart the house of cards one by one and showed her that it was flight from reality, even self-deception. Not only had she been of no help to her husband, but her martyr's pose before Regina had actually been an attempt to do him harm. She had laid the foundation for her children's deep mistrust of their father. Now her entire life seemed nothing but an edifice of self-pity built behind a facade of piety, sacrifice and humility. How could such deceit be forgiven?

And yet she felt that her new outlook, in some mysterious way, gave her security. To have herself unmasked bit by bit had been fearfully and eternally humiliating, but the whole process showed clearly that God was constantly showing her

178

the way to truth and concrete reality. Wasn't Christian life after all the ultimate realism, an acceptance of facts as they are, a readiness to deal with everything as it is rather than the way one wishes it to be? "I am the Way, the Truth, and the Life." She had done her best to bend this severely clear teaching into sentimentality and syrupy self-pity.

Naturally, Elisabeth did not speak about this, for her husband most likely would not have understood her. But she suffered quietly when she reflected upon her life. She had been unable to bear such insignificant pain as wounded pride. She had contributed to the disintegration of her own home, to the suspicion that was spreading among the members of her family. Now she watched Georg stumbling far from the truth; Regina nervous, distraught and malignantly hostile; her husband alone, beset and afraid, with no member of the family to help or comfort him.

His care-worn face and heavy breathing as he stared blankly over the flowering garden appalled her. At last I love him. I have finally learned to see him exactly as he is. Had I been different his life would have been easier. Instead of barricading his way to Christ and the Church, I might have helped him find them.

Once in the confessional she had discussed with Father Leo the possibility of helping her husband in the light of her new insights.

He answered in his dry fashion: "By no means! Of yourself, my child, you can do nothing. Not the slightest . . ."

Again, he was right. She would only open herself to further defeat if she thought that she could help her husband in religious matters. God, however, could do everything, if she would only let His will be done.

This stripping of pretense from her new insight had been a fresh humiliation. But how good, after all the fog, to feel her feet at last upon some solid ground! She was not to be

179

granted understanding of problems closest to her. Not an inch could she penetrate into God's purposes; she had no idea what His plan was, what was going to happen to her husband, her children, or herself. But He was there. His strong hand was guiding everything. Nothing escaped Him. *Felix culpa. Etiam peccata.*

That afternoon Regina took the train out to the Villa. She called from the station to ask for the limousine, heard the news that Kolbe was not available, and took a taxi. This irritated her. She became increasingly ill-tempered and sarcastic when on arriving she could get no information as to Kolbe's whereabouts or why he had gone. Elisabeth could see that Falk was being tortured. But he said little, merely held up his hand, powerless against his daughter.

"Dear Regina, I simply can't tell you why Kolbe is not here. I can only say that most likely he will never come back."

She stood before him in the sunlight between the pillars, elastic, lank, poised like a feather.

"Shouldn't he have been given notice? Why wasn't he?" Her father shrugged.

"Probably because he's been as faithful to you as a watchdog," she said sharply. "Because he loves you, Father; because he has put his entire life at your service. That should be reason enough!"

Shocked, Elisabeth looked at her husband. He raised his eyebrows and she was moved when she saw the terrible efforts he made to control himself.

"Regina," he said, "don't talk like that. Someday you'll know the whole story."

"That's not necessary," she answered. "The explanation is very simple. All real devotion, real warmth, real human decency dies in this house! In our family it's been dead for a long time. It looks like a home here, like ordinary human life, but it's something quite different."

Falk rose heavily. A word would have put an end to it, but he felt the duty to remain silent even though her accusations were pressing in upon him. What kind of a life was his daughter leading? When had she ever been grateful for what he had given her? Hadn't he given her an expensive education? Hadn't she been allowed to lead her own life—with the exception of that godforsaken stupidity with Christer Wendt? How many young girls had been as pampered as she had been?

He was tired. Too tired to refute accusations and defend himself. Heavy and obtuse he stood before her:

"Perhaps you're right," he said softly. He went down the steps to the garden and turned again to the two women: "In spite of everything I have only wanted to do good," he said heavily.

"I have the feeling that those who have experienced your good intentions decline them with thanks," Regina said hotly. "Your indifference is hard to bear, but your paternal solicitude is a monstrosity, Father!"

Again his tired eyes were upon her. The veins of his forehead were swollen, as always when he was angry, but he was too beaten, or too sad to answer her.

His passivity irritated her; it hurt her to know that he had more self-control than she. Deep down inside she knew that she admired his discipline and this made her furious.

"Recently I have made an acquaintance that I think will interest you," she announced.

Falk didn't move. She looked at his broad back and seethed with rage.

"His name is Thomas Graber."

Her mother's groan was audible from the chair. Falk turned slowly. He looked at her with a face that she had never seen before and she was shocked at the turmoil that she could see in his soul.

"Who is he? Why should he interest me?"

"Because he's his mother's son. Because he has to pay the price for what others have committed. Because he can't live a day of his life untouched by the tragedy that marked his mother!"

Elisabeth closed her eyes. Now, after so many years, the reckoning was coming.

Falk plodded back up the steps. He stood in front of his daughter, clenched fists shaking, ready to strike. Regina watched him, not so much in fear as in horror at her own words. She felt as if she were being driven by a demoniacal power.

But the fists relaxed, his hand moved toward her, and she noticed that it trembled. She dared not strike off the paternal caress that was laid on her shoulder for the first time in many years.

"You are cruel, Regina. Are you really so unhappy that you have to flog your parents, have to cut into old wounds?"

With heavy step he passed her, bent down and kissed Elisabeth on the brow. Then he went to his bedroom and closed the door. The key could be heard turning in the lock.

Regina flew to her mother's side, fell on her knees and buried her face in Elisabeth's lap.

"Mother, Mother," she wailed. "Don't hate me. I don't know what I'm saying . . . I don't know who I am any more."

20

WHEN Regina learned who Thomas Graber's mother was she was swept by a feeling of excitement, a tangled mood which vacillated between discomfort and joy, unrest and expectation, ordinary curiosity and a dose of sadism. Now she would learn the full truth about her father.

It was not easy. It was fairly evident that Thomas had not the slightest idea who his mother's lover had been and Regina did not give this secret away. Whenever the subject was mentioned, he withdrew completely within himself, and refused to discuss it—almost as if this self-assured, urbane doctor were afraid of the entire affair. Apparently it tormented him and whenever he managed to speak about it a look of youthful anxiety would cloud his eyes.

Regina's curiosity so gripped her that she had to find out all she could, and she eventually came to realize that she sought Thomas Graber's company only because through him she hoped to learn the truth both about her father and about herself.

She had already reached certain conclusions. She knew that the past binds. She herself was bound fast by it, although she could not always judge exactly how. But she felt that her personal unhappiness was caused by the circumstances around her—tensions which she had to take on against her will, conflicts into which she had been born. If these conflicts were to be attributed to a particular individual— her father, for instance—then he alone would be responsible for her unhappiness; and she would have the carrion comfort of knowing that she was being forced to pay the price for his lust and indifference.

She took many long trips with Thomas. When he had finished his work for the day they would meet somewhere, eat at a wayside inn or in some small town, and drive for hours. Occasionally they spent the night together. This time, however, she had inspired the admiration of a man who did not wish to conquer. He didn't want to possess her; he wanted to see her.

He never talked about his father, whom he seemed to despise.

One day she didn't keep their appointment. He waited for some time and finally went off uneasily. On her way to the appointment Regina had met Isabelle.

She had sent no advance notice, and Regina had no suspicion that Isabelle intended to visit either the capital or the country itself. They had written each other long letters for a time, but the correspondence ultimately caused each so much pain that they abandoned it. Regina had never told the girl how much she longed for her, since she felt it wiser to have Isabelle believe that she had become weary of the attachment.

Suddenly Isabelle was here, standing in the sunlight in front of the Prime Minister's Residence. She had not risked calling or entering, but simply waited until Regina came out, as it happened on her way to the date with Graber.

Habitually preoccupied, Regina didn't see Isabelle.

Isabelle, on the opposite side of the street, was at once swept with joy yet extremely worried. Would Regina be angry, would she want to have nothing more to do with her? She called her name. A quick look at Regina's face showed that her fears were hollow. Regina had stopped short, a pillar of stone. Then, her entire face suffused with light, she bounded across the street to enclose the girl within her arms.

"My dear. What are you doing here?"

Isabelle began to weep within the tight embrace. Realizing that her father would have a full view from the library window, Regina hustled her friend around a corner. A policeman on guard at the gate had saluted and then looked on in amazement as the two disappeared.

They went to a bench under the trees lining the boulevard. Alternately laughing and crying, Isabelle gave a nervous report, fearful yet happy, her great black eyes flickering.

184

She could stand the situation at home no longer. Her mother had wanted her to become engaged to a distant relative, a young industrialist from Basel. She liked him, they had met often, he was very nice. But to marry him? Finally she had refused and this led to a scene. The following day she had left without saying goodbye. Fortunately her passport was in order.

"And now no one knows where you are?"

"No. If I had said anything, they wouldn't have let me leave!"

Regina, touched, smiled at this naïveté. For a full year she had longed for this girl. She had told herself that a complete break had to be made and that every further contact would only lead to further pain. Yet what an indescribable benison to have Isabelle with her again, to be able to comfort her, put an arm around her, sit beside her, and finally call forth that sparkling smile. Aware of its implications, she had waited for this moment and was thrilled when the smile broke out at last. Isabelle pressed closer, her dark head on Regina's shoulder, and closed her eyes in confident happiness.

The first thing to do was to bring some order into the situation. A telegram would have to be sent. Isabelle refused. Her parents would certainly come after her. But Regina insisted. Some way must be found to set the parents' minds at ease. They then discussed the contents of a telegram and settled on a terse message: Isabelle was visiting with Regina —the parents knew and esteemed her—and she would be home soon. In this way the girls would at least gain a few days and could discuss the next move later.

But there was nothing to discuss. Isabelle had but one thought. She knew that she had to meet Regina and could not live without her. Couldn't she stay here permanently? Couldn't she study dancing with her and then possibly become her assistant? She looked at Regina with pleading doe-eyes.

Regina forgot her appointment. First she must find a place for Isabelle to stay. Why not out at the Villa with her mother? Certainly Mrs. Falk would be delighted to have her. But perhaps it would be too lonesome out there. She didn't want Isabelle to look upon it as a kind of exile, but proposed it nonetheless. Isabelle was overjoyed, assuming that Regina would live there with her.

Isabelle's sorrows were blown away. She followed Regina through the city. They took a streetcar to the country district and walked the remaining kilometer, pausing to refresh old memories. All problems were forgotten and they tried to live carefree in the moment as they had before.

Despite her great happiness, Regina continued to be quite unsettled. Could it really be true? It seemed to her as if everything were happening in a dream or were vicariously experienced in a book. Their relationship was set apart, so far as she was concerned. It didn't belong to the realm of ordinary reality; it couldn't grow, find normal extension or sink its roots. It was like an ellipsis mark, indicating that the sentence could not be completed. What would follow? She refused to think about it, because all thoughts became one thought: How could she risk bringing down on this young girl's head all the pain she had won for herself during these sad years.

Isabelle was jubilant. Regina had neither forgotten her nor been angry with her. She had found—without a word—that Regina was exactly the same. Her eyes confessed that she still loved.

As they walked Regina felt, with a shudder compounded of both joy and fear, that her feelings for Isabelle had altered. Possibly her whole being had changed substantially. In the earlier days of their friendship her chief emotion had been a kind of motherly warmth. The attraction now was quite different.

186

It was at the edge of the woods just before they emerged in front of the summer Villa. Isabelle's kiss was upon her cheek. Then her head was taken in two hands and she was kissed on the mouth. She realized suddenly that she had never really kissed before.

Elisabeth was happy about the visit, although she was somewhat concerned when she saw how young the girl seemed to be, and thought it a bit strange that she had come almost without any baggage, for the girl said that she had left only one small bag at the station. She gave instructions for a guest room to be prepared and suggested that they enjoy a springtime lunch together. Company pleased her and she was happy to feel that she could be of some help to those she loved. The girl's attentiveness and charm enchanted Elisabeth, and she readily agreed to write an explanatory letter to Isabelle's parents telling them that their daughter was staying at the Villa.

Thomas telephoned after lunch. He accepted Regina's explanation calmly, and was relieved there had been no mishap. Might he call for Regina at the Villa?

Receiver in hand, Regina stood undecided for a moment. In the parlor, Isabelle, framed by the conservatory window, was relaxed and happy as she chatted with Elisabeth. She really didn't want to leave her friend alone; on the other hand it would be difficult to say no to Thomas, whom she had already disappointed. He could come.

She told her mother and Isabelle that she was expecting a visit from "her doctor." Isabelle appeared not to have heard. She was moving excitedly about, examining flowers and period pieces. Her rapport with the poetry and good taste of the Villa was immediate and she inhaled deeply the atmosphere of quiet peace. When she caught sight of the King's deer on the other side of the fence beyond the park she was so touched by their delicate beauty that tears shone in her eyes.

She is like the does, Regina thought. Delicate, graceful—and helpless. She stared so intently at Isabelle's lips that the girl finally exclaimed:

"Regina! Why are you looking at me like that? Is my lipstick too dark?"

When Regina tried to answer, her voice was hoarse and blurred by her inner excitement.

The open convertible glided slowly along a forest road that they both loved as Regina talked and Thomas listened. When she had finished sketching the details of Isabelle's flight from home and her anxieties about the future, he said without turning his head:

"It's obvious that you're in love with her."

"Yes," said Regina with no trace of doubt.

"Do you also realize that you . . . desire her?"

She didn't move a muscle although she inhaled deeply. This time he turned toward her with a friendly smile.

"Yes," she answered hoarsely.

"I knew it without having seen her and despite the fact that you only spoke of her once before."

"But how—how is it possible?" she asked, almost in pain.

He gazed intently ahead and laughed again.

"Nothing is more natural—considering the life you have had. Just don't be afraid! If a person has enough courage to follow nature, there is no need for fear. Pain is the result of going against nature."

She saw that he was not trying to be cynical. He was simply making a dispassionate, medical-psychological judgment, and she knew that he had her interest at heart.

To combat her uneasiness she brought up his own problems. She must reach a closer rapport with him, and if he was going to speak so openly she could risk being equally frank.

With quiet sadness he told the story of his childhood, how he had learned to hate the man whom his mother had illicitly loved. Regina thought of her father. How could that stoutish, insensitive feral man have won the love of this unknown woman and held it all through the years. Within her she felt her old hate asserting itself. That was just like him; pushing his way into another person's life, then remaining smugly respectable while the other went down to defeat.

"And this 'other man,' " she said "You must hate him!"

"Not any more," Thomas answered quietly. "Why should I hate him? I feel sorry for him. He was a coward, and that just about sums it up."

"A coward?" Regina repeated. Had she heard correctly? It certainly was not an act of cowardice to force one's way into the life of a friend, seduce his wife, fling her aside, and then become a patriot and statesman.

"Yes, a coward," he answered. "Don't make the same mistake he did!"

She gazed at him without understanding. What parallel could there possibly be between her feelings for Isabelle and her father's love for another man's wife? Her father had done precisely what she had not done.

"I don't understand you," she said. "You may not hate him, but for my part I can feel nothing but scorn for a man who takes and conquers without thinking in the least . . ."

He brought the car to a gentle stop, shut off the motor, turned toward her and leaned back. A melancholy smile played across his pale lips.

" 'Take' did you say? And 'conquer'? My only complaint is that he did *not* take my mother and did *not* conquer her!"

She looked at him speechless. Her entire childhood had been under the shadow of her father's betrayal of her mother, and his conquest of another woman. She recalled her girlish dreams when she had wanted to atone for his sins, her ridiculous mortifications. She felt driven to confide to Thomas that she knew who the unknown man was, but at the last moment she controlled herself.

"Do you mean to say that he was not your mother's lover?" Her voice was so strained that he looked at her bewildered, unable to understand her excitement.

"Of course he wasn't," he said. "If he had been, there would have been no tragedy. My father would have flown into a rage, my mother would have got her freedom, and that would have been the end of it. But he was too cowardly. Or, if you wish, too 'idealistic,' too 'noble'! He loved her but he couldn't give up his honor, his family, and his what-have-you. Actually, he was simply too much afraid of what people would say. He was afraid of bourgeois public opinion."

Finally she said: "How do you know all this? Are you sure you are right?"

"Of course I'm right," he said. "After her death I found the diary that my mother kept. The story is clear—and pathetic."

She grasped his arm. "Tom, could I read that diary?"

He looked at her in astonishment. "Of course, Regina, but it makes dull reading. It doesn't reveal his name, and Mama destroyed all traces of him. There is no letter, no photographs. And Papa never said who he was; I doubt if he ever knew. You can read the whole miserable story, and three more wretched people would be difficult to find."

He threw in the clutch, pressed the starter button with his left hand and slipped into low gear. They drove slowly beneath the cool arches of the beech woods.

Regina leaned back and closed her eyes.

21

GEORG woke up early and was hungry. He went to the cache at the rear of the lodge, found the key hidden behind a loose stone in the wall, climbed down and got a few cans of food from which he prepared breakfast. After eating, he took the boat and rowed out on the small lake to refresh himself and think things over. It was still too early for a swim, even though the water in the small calm lake warmed up remarkably fast. He was not happy, for he was still eaten with jealousy, but he felt free. He would make progress. He felt that one day he would conquer himself enough to become Alexandra's unselfish comrade and nothing more. He knew that he had to break completely with the entire tradition which "home, school and country" had given him.

The most important thing was to take the first step. Only if he proved himself an instrument of the great cause would he be able to win her. On the spot, he grandly resolved to leave home, renounce his father's support and get a job. But what sort of job? His Communist companions naturally looked upon him with a dose of skepticism. Would he ever be able to win their confidence? If only there were something he could do, something that with one blow would clarify his relationship both to Alexandra and to his father.

As he approached the pier he let the boat glide up softly, as his father had taught him when he was a little boy. He secured it and climbed up on the knotty, dry boards. As he turned he saw a car—his father's. Had it been sent out for him? Or had his father come out here? Perhaps at this very moment he was inside the lodge, angry at the disorder. Angry because there was an unemptied ashtray on the table and because the bed was not made, or because of the tin cans that he loathed. He always said that tins should never be put on a bare table; if there were no cloth, a piece of paper, at least, should be put underneath.

Georg went slowly back to the lodge and looked inside. No one there. He went to the auto. Everything was quiet. Not a soul. Not until a few moments later did he discover the chauffeur, collar open, sleeping at the edge of the forest.

He was about to wake him but changed his mind. Where was his father? He looked inside the car and the only thing worth noting was Falk's small leather attaché case, a cross between a briefcase and a traveling case, with two compartments. Almost automatically he reached in, grabbed the case and went back under the trees. He retreated quickly to the lodge, cleaned up everything, locked up, pushed the key back into place, checked to be sure that the chauffeur was still sleeping and ran off. He didn't head toward the forest for fear of meeting his father and a hunting companion. Towards the other side was an opening into a clearing.

It proved to be a long detour. First he ran, but couldn't keep it up very long. He slowed to a fast walk and finally to a normal pace. Had he done something stupid and irresponsible? Or had he really bumped unexpectedly into the big chance of a lifetime? Supposing the case contained only unimportant papers?

He ducked into the bushes where he opened it with the attached key. An envelope was marked "Top secret" and one glance was enough to prove that it was a defense plan, or part of one. Trembling he thought of the moral that spoke of "ready-made destiny" which required nothing but that it be seized.

Now to reach Alexandra! Quickly, before his father came back and sounded the alarm! The time for the break had come; doubting was past. Blindly he had thrown himself into an entirely new world, a world of action. His resolute hand had moved to change the world for himself and his fellow men. The deed would have its consequences; his entire life would be different. But changed, too, would be the general situation in the country if what he had done would only prove to be of value to the poor, oppressed revolutionaries. Alexandra had opened his eyes to their plight. His soul was a turmoil of joy and childlike fear.

Arriving at a village he boarded a rickety bus which brought him to the suburbs where he could get a streetcar. Then he remembered that he no longer had a home. Where would he sleep tonight? And money? And clothes, overcoat, books . . . ? He tried to stifle his growing fears. Alexandra was the only one he could trust. He would have to find her.

The long trolley ride to her street was a nightmare. Would he ever get there? Would she be furious at him for intruding again? But what else could he do? He got off and stood on the sidewalk. Passers-by stared at the distraught young man with the expensive briefcase, and he realized that he was acting carelessly. If the case had been reported missing, the police would be on the watch. He entered a shop, bought a newspaper, and wrapped it around the case, securing it with a string supplied by the clerk. From there he proceeded to the home of the worker family where Alexandra boarded and asked that the case be given her. Was there any message he wanted delivered? No, none at all.

As he came back down to the street and walked toward the bus stop, he saw Alexandra in animated conversation with two men. One was young, approximately his own age; the other was in his fifties. Georg watched them from the concealment of a doorway. After a few minutes the young man went off alone; Alexandra and the older man, dark and vigorous, came towards him. Georg withdrew further into the doorway and turned his back as they passed. He could hear their voices faintly and then he heard Alexandra's bright, uninhibited laughter—the laugh he loved. He was poised to run after them to tell her what had happened. Then he thought this might be unwise. On the other hand, was it any wiser to let her go to her room with a man who might not be a Communist and who would be on hand when she opened the case? But weren't all her friends Communists?

His desire to report to her, however, won out. He caught up to them as they stepped into the doorway of Alexandra's house.

"Alexandra," he cried.

She wheeled and he saw that she blanched in fury.

"What are you doing here?"

He could hear the man mutter, "Who the hell is this?"

Confusedly Georg pressed closer.

"Alexandra, I have something very important to tell you. I must speak to you—alone."

She stepped closer to him. Despite the hall's half light, he could see her eyes flash.

"Get out of here," she said in a tone he had never heard before.

The man took her arm in an intimate grip and eased her back a bit. He stepped close, menacingly.

"Get the hell out of here, college boy," he said softly.

Georg raised his hands as though to ward off a blow.

"Listen. I have a reason for coming. I left something important in your room . . . I have to . . ."

"In your room!" The dark man turned, seized Alexandra by the arms and shook her. "What business does this kid have in your room?"

Georg grabbed the man and pushed him aside. The next moment he stumbled back from a heavy blow to the face, hit his head against the wall and sank to the floor. He could hear the rustle of people gathering, other voices, Alexandra's voice. As he struggled to his feet he could see the man holding her in a brutal grip that stretched her blouse over her breasts. He staggered, tried to hit back, but the next blow flattened him. He heard Alexandra's quiet voice: "Throw him out! He's drunk!"

The words paralyzed him. When he finally reached his feet he didn't even try to parry the next blow, which sent him down the steps to the sidewalk. He got up to the sound of laughter, dimly saw people ringing him around, felt blood rill over his face, and then he stumbled from the scene.

He stopped when he had reached a narrow street where there were not so many passers-by. He stepped into a little shop, told the terrified proprietress that he had met with an accident, and asked if he could wash his face.

He was led to a sink in a dirty kitchen. A sour stench arose from it.

Georg remained hidden for the next twelve hours. He bought an adhesive bandage in a drugstore, ate at a run-down restaurant. When dawn broke he went home. The pain in his head was excruciating and his self-confidence had oozed away with his blood. The entire incident now seemed vulgar, ridiculous and senseless, even though his imagination was still dominated by the unknown fifty-year-old. His manner of handling Alexandra left no doubt that he was her "friend." Men do not speak to women that way unless they have power over them—physical power. Were these the relationships he had to accept if he were to be her co-worker?

He arrived home brimming with fear, spied Louise and almost ran to his room, where he locked the door. His pulse was pounding and the wound smarted painfully under the adhesive. He threw himself on the bed and wept. At any moment his father might come. What could he say? Mercifully, he blacked out for an hour.

A rap at the door woke him. He leaped up in confused

anxiety. His father would be implacable, would disown him, perhaps even beat him—a thing he had never done before. But when the door opened he found someone whom he had never dreamed of seeing in his room. It was Father Leo.

"Excuse me," said the Dominican and walked in.

He spoke softly and moved quietly.

"Don't be frightened," he said. "No one knows I'm here. I come as your friend."

Georg looked at him distrustfully. The priest's face was serious and open, yet with a twinkle in his eye that made the boy incapable of disliking him. The Dominican whistled soundlessly when he saw the wound and adhesive plaster.

"Wait a moment," he said.

He found a bottle of alcohol, made Georg sit down on the bed, removed the plaster, bathed the wound, then bathed his face.

Georg felt like a schoolboy. At the same time he felt an odd gratitude toward the monk who neither criticized nor asked questions but simply helped.

All the while the Dominican muttered to himself about the wound. His manner was relaxed and quiet. "Now then," he said when he had finished. "That's a little better."

He stood smiling before the boy. "Tell me, where did you put the briefcase?"

Georg shook his head.

The Dominican's smile was neither sympathetic nor sarcastic, but friendly.

"Can't you see," he said, "that sooner or later everyone will realize that you were the one who took it? The police have been to the Villa and I rode to the lodge on my motorcycle and found that you were the one who borrowed the briefcase."

Georg looked up.

"How did you know that?"

"Oh, it wasn't too difficult. Who else could have taken it? Who cleans up after himself—carelessly to be sure? Who smokes Lucky Strikes? Who throws wooden matches on the floor? Who has the key and locks up behind him? Who wears a size 12 shoe with rubber soles and is likely to forget about such things at moments of crisis?"

He pulled a comb from his pocket, carefully detached three hairs which he held against the light and then let fall to the rug. He laughed, a jolly loud laugh.

"I have no intention of turning you in. It's completely natural that you should find yourself on an opposing side. When I was your age, I left home intending to join the Foreign Legion. But I got no farther than the next city, where they caught me. I don't want you to think that I want to change your ideas on politics."

Suddenly his expression became serious.

"If you are convinced that Christer Wendt really is a political authority, you must naturally stick with him."

Georg propped himself on his elbows.

"Christer Wendt?" he said questioningly. "He has nothing to do with this affair."

For a moment the Dominican gazed searchingly at Georg. It seemed most unlikely that the boy at a time like this would dissemble.

"I only know that he is your friend," the priest said.

"Wendt," Georg said, "is a man who wants nothing. He's even indifferent to the way people treat him. He'll never take a stand. Never."

"Well," Father Leo said, "however things may be with him, you're going to be hauled in for questioning. They're bound to find out that you spent the night in the lodge—and that you took the case from the automobile. They'll follow your trail, easy enough since the sand was quite wet in the direction you took. It's going to be unpleasant, and you should make up your mind to follow what you consider to be the most reasonable course of action. I think you would be wise to tell me the whole truth. Where is the briefcase? Why did you take it? Who has it now?"

Georg closed his eyes; he looked up.

"What briefcase?" he asked. "I got drunk and got into a fight, as you can see. Did I really steal a briefcase? Where? You're getting me worried, Father."

The Dominican looked piercingly at him. Such fine qualities to put to the service of stupidity, he thought. Now you want to be loyal toward your comrades and you feel you shouldn't betray Wendt's confidences. If only the right causes were followed with the same heroic courage as the wrong ones.

"As you wish," he said. "Choose for yourself. Either the police, questioning, humiliation and misery, or a simple little confidence with me. Do what you yourself think right and understand one thing: you can have people who share your political views—who are in no way your friends."

He went to the door.

"Now try to sleep! And afterwards give these things a little thought."

He opened the door as noiselessly as when he had come, nodded and disappeared.

For a moment he stood in the corridor. Poor boy. He went slowly down the stairs. As he was reaching for his hat the library door opened and Wendt appeared.

"The Prime Minister would like to speak with you," he said coolly.

The Dominican entered.

Falk came towards him with flushed face and quick steps.

"It's eerie," he said. "The police chief just called and said that the briefcase was turned in at the lost-and-found."

"Was anything in it?" asked Father Leo.

"Yes. And that's what makes it even stranger. The police said it was full of papers. Apparently the dossier is still there."

He paced the room.

"The whole affair is getting more enigmatic. My chauffeur continues to lie. How did it happen in the first place? If someone took it, it was for a reason. *Cui bono?* No action can be conceived without some sort of a selfish motive."

The Dominican smiled and looked at the secretary.

"Perhaps. What do you think, Wendt?"

The secretary merely glanced at him, but said nothing.

"In any case I am happy about one thing," continued Falk, "and that is that there's no foundation for the suspicion about my boy."

The Dominican looked at him. "I am happy, too," he said.

Falk laughed.

"So there. You're not a Father Brown after all—despite all your other merits."

"I don't know everything that was in the briefcase," Wendt said slowly, "but it is not hard to imagine that the interested parties had time to copy the contents, or at least a part of them."

Falk looked at him.

"Yes, of course that's possible. Not everything, but a large part of it, if they worked at it. But why did they give it up? If I could only understand that. It's a beautiful case—superb leather. I bought it in London. No one makes leather goods like the English."

"Perhaps the thief wanted to cover his tracks," said the Dominican. "He wants us to think that he's not interested in the papers. It's an old trick that always misfires. No one betrays himself as quickly as the one who tries to seem disinterested."

He looked smilingly toward Christer Wendt.

"Right," said the secretary.

PART III

Evensong

22

THE CEILING of the downstairs living room was half gone and
the walls were seared with fire. The blackened pillars remained standing—with the exception of the genuine one that
had served as Falk's model. This had been toppled, perhaps
intentionally. The lawn was completely ruined, trampled by
heavy boots and criss-crossed by fire engine tires. Outside stood
a pile of furniture, much of it partially destroyed. They had
been able to save about half of the objects in the house.
Stephan and some young helpers were now slowly trudging
back and forth carrying undamaged pieces to the shed concealed behind a huge lilac bush.

Georg was in the library busying himself with the books.
The first sets carried out had later been damaged by water,
and most of them were ruined. The fire did not reach the
library, but water from the burning bedrooms had flowed
down through the double ceiling, damaging most of the
volumes. The library would have to be considered a total loss.

Georg heard steps in the parlor and looking through the
door saw his father, in overalls. Falk surveyed the scene, his
expression dark and embittered.

Georg raised his hand in a helpless gesture.

"In this section almost everything is ruined. Over here,
too."

He stepped to the window overlooking the rubble on the
front lawn.

"They certainly didn't take much care of things when they

threw them out on the lawn," he continued. "But I suppose there wasn't any time to be careful . . ."

"No. There certainly wasn't," came his father's sarcastic reply.

Suddenly Georg thought: When your wife collapsed you didn't feel so terribly sorry. You've been able to hold up in spite of Regina's disintegration. But when you lose your books and furniture—that breaks you!

He held up a painting and showed it to his father.

"Take this, for example. All they had to do was to keep it under cover until they got it outside and then put it down under a tree, and fifteen thousand marks would have been saved. But what does Stephan know about a Courbet?"

Falk stepped over and took the painting in both hands. The linen had been thoroughly torn and damaged by the water beyond any hope of repair. In one corner, woods still showed forth dark splendor. After awhile, his voice hoarse with bitterness, Falk said:

"And he certainly could not have known that this was the first painting of any real value that I ever bought. I got it shortly after your mother and I were married."

He hurled the picture away from him. Two piles of books that Georg had arranged toppled to the floor. Georg looked anxiously at his father. He had seldom seen him like this.

"I've looked through the books," he said. "Many of them have been scorched, some hopelessly. But the majority were destroyed by water—rusty water. It was ridiculous for them to use so much water. Or maybe they had to? What do you think, Father?"

"Yes," Falk answered as he measured the room in long strides. "Yes, it was necessary. From *their* point of view. It was absolutely and completely necessary from *their* point of view. It was absolutely and completely necessary that in the interests of their class and cause they destroy everything they could get their hands on, everything that the fire spared."

He approached Georg and stood before him, hands propped on hips.

"You are aware," he said, "that these stupid fools are supposed to be 'idealists.' They go about rescuing the worthwhile things of humanity from us, the capitalists. I'd like to know if these bandits have thought of one aspect of the question—namely that I have been able to collect all these objects here and construct my home, not because I have inherited money, not because I have carried on a profitable business with a continual eye for profit, but because I have worked ten times harder than other men, because I have driven myself, slaved, sacrificed, if you must hear the word. But that's a criminal offense, of course."

He wheeled and continued his pacing, snatching a book here and there, then hurling it away. All through the years Georg had seen these expensive volumes handled lovingly. In the entire collection there was not an item that had not been tracked down personally—in auctions along the quays on the Seine, in the second hand shops on *la rue Bonaparte* or *la rue de Seine*, in Venice, in Rome.

"Yes," Georg said weakly giving ground outwardly, yet feeling a mounting inner anguish. "They are pretty stupid."

Falk's fury mounted slowly once more.

"Most of my life has been work. You know that. Life has never given me anything for nothing. Whatever I have gained has been gained in struggle. All my life I have felt myself like a commandant of a beleaguered fortress. At night I have had to go out to inspect the walls lest new enemies appear. It hasn't been very pleasant."

He's right, Georg thought. But what has he accomplished by all this?

"I have gained a few things in the process," Falk continued. "A few true friends who never have betrayed me."

His son looked at him in consternation. Had he intended to be sarcastic? What friends was he thinking of? The cynical

General Sturzebecker? Or his friends in his political party?

Falk had snatched another book, a parchment volume blackened by smoke. He let it fall to the floor.

"My books," he said, "who have given me my riches, and have never hurt me. My pictures that gave me beauty and relaxation, and have never attacked me or criticized me. My furniture that has silently taught me the beauty of form and the values of the past—and which I had hoped to leave to you, my children."

Fists clenched he walked to the window.

"The trees that I planted myself. Year after year they have rustled above my head."

He turned around again, mottled with bitterness.

"Did you see my tall ash?" he shouted. "My favorite tree? Of course the rabble couldn't ruin it completely. It survived. But my Greek pillar that cost me so much trouble to bring home twenty years ago from Rome—knocked over and smashed by the damned barbarians. Oh, those people have a good aim. They must have had a clever leader, who knew how to hit me in the right place. They didn't miss!"

Georg felt helpless. His feelings were split in two. He heard the misery in his father's words. These externals were the center of his life and he openly and naively confessed the fact without realizing how much it unmasked of his entire philosophy of life. If he had put value on things other than books and furniture all this might not have happened. From another point of view, Georg felt genuinely sorry for his father. He seemed now like a tragic figure, a dumb sacrifice to the cult of possession. He was somewhat amazed at himself when he stepped toward his father and laid a hand on his shoulder:

"Father," he said, "I can understand."

Falk was rigid. Slowly he raised his head. His arms hung limp against his heavy body.

"You understand me?" he said dully. "Really? For a long time I thought that no one understood me any more. But it doesn't matter. I don't need understanding."

He drew a deep breath and said menacingly:

"Now I have made up my mind!"

His voice was so violent and strong that Georg stepped back a pace.

"About what, Father?" His voice trembled.

Falk, standing in the middle of the ruins, snatched a broken statuette and fingered it as he spoke.

"Never was I so completely convinced as I am now that our adversary is pure barbarism, complete stupidity, a grinning, weak-witted Caliban. For a very long time I was willing to toy with the idea that perhaps even the Communists had ideals along with a colossally stupid good will. I tried to believe that, in the last analysis, Communism was charged with a kind of touching faith, a sort of religious readiness to sacrifice."

He strode over to a chair and gave it a kick. One of the legs snapped off. It was an Italian chair from the sixteenth century upon which the children, when they were little, had never been allowed to sit.

"These heroes of the future, these propertyless, unselfish, idealistic, pious proletarians," he screamed. "They're the ones who stormed my house which was built in beauty. They're the ones who trampled and sullied everything, befouled the grounds with their urine, drank my wine and then set my villa on fire, probably as they sang one of their hymns on the brotherhood of man."

He fell silent. Then the fists balled again and he said with tautly controlled violence:

"Now I'll strike!"

Georg scarcely breathed.

"What do you intend to do, Father?"

207

Falk didn't look at him.

"I've tried to be humane too long. I had hoped for at least a minimum of responsibility and understanding."

"What do you intend to do, Father?" Georg asked again.

"The General of the Armies will have the answer to that this afternoon," came the reply.

Georg sprang to his side and tried once more to lay a hand on his shoulder. He was pushed aside.

"You mean bloodshed?"

Falk was not looking at his son. He continued as if talking to himself.

"I mean exactly that. Machine guns and automatics, if police clubs and fire hoses don't do the job. Now is the time to show them that a civilized state like ours cannot tolerate their barbarity."

"Father!" Georg shouted. "You wouldn't dare!"

Falk turned slowly.

"Who is to prevent me?"

Father and son both turned as Elisabeth, propped on her cane, came through the parlor. Georg walked quickly toward her and offered his arm. He was about to lead her to an armchair, but she declined.

"You shouldn't have to see any more of this misery, Mother!" he said. "It would be better for you to stay at Stephan's."

Her soft voice brittle, Elisabeth said:

"Just imagine, Georg. My birds are still alive. Achilles has come back and Proserpina stayed in the gallery. I found her there, the poor thing. She was sitting very still and her heart was pounding, but at least she's alive."

Falk stepped close to his wife and gently caressed her cheek.

"If they had any idea that you love your birds, a couple of idealists would have been sure to twist their necks."

Elisabeth acted as if she had not seen the destruction around her. Georg thought: one worries about birds, the other about books.

After a pause she said: "I can't imagine how Stephan was able to come up . . . I don't understand how he . . ."

Falk's expression became alert and vulpine.

"What time was it when he woke you?" he asked sharply.

"Possibly seven o'clock," Elisabeth answered. "I don't know for sure."

"There you have it! Two hours before they got here! Doesn't that prove he was in on the job? He could stand being around while destruction was wrought on something that he has worked on for twenty years. But he wouldn't want to have a murder on his conscience. The noble gardener!"

Georg shook his head.

"No, no. You're wrong, Father."

Elisabeth heard neither of them. She indicated that she would appreciate help to the entrance, where both doors had been removed from their hinges.

"It's so strange," she said. "I don't believe I have ever seen the lake as beautiful as it is today. Just look. Isn't it miraculous—the clarity, the stillness."

Both men followed her glance. Georg noticed Isabelle carrying a chair toward the shed. What luck that she happened to have been out with Regina and her doctor friend that evening. He wouldn't want to think of what could have happened if she had fallen into the hands of the rioters!

"No matter what people may try to do," Elisabeth said calmly, "nature remains undisturbed and full of the blessings of peace."

Georg led her to the terrace and she asked with a gesture to be helped down the stairs. Once at the bottom she disengaged her arm from his and nodded her thanks.

"It's a strange thing to say," she remarked, "but I feel at

ease despite everything that has happened. It seems, some-how, as if they did not damage the essential, the things that are really important."

Isabelle came out of the shed, waved to Elizabeth and ran toward her. For a few seconds Georg let his eyes linger on the swift, lithe figure. Then he turned and went back to his father who was still rooted to the same spot.

"Mother is wonderful," he said.

"Meaning what?" Falk answered.

"She is not possessive of things, of objects. She treasures what is more important."

With a quick movement of the head his father looked at him.

"Like canaries and the splashing of waves? Yes, if you think such things of more value than man and the state."

Georg looked doubtfully at his father. The time had come to talk frankly with him.

"I was thinking of something else, Father."

"What was it?" Falk asked drily.

Georg bit his lip. It wouldn't come out very easily.

"I was thinking . . . about peace of heart," he said, to his own astonishment.

Falk glanced up quickly and nodded scornfully.

"Thanks," he said. "I know what you're implying. Your mother is inspired, full of deep feeling, while I am brutal and hard. But won't you see that I am fighting for the com-munity, respect for the other man, cohesion, a stable order—the real values? The others are feasting off the capital, per-mitting themselves every sort of license. I am constructing new values. I am laying the firm foundation."

"Father, don't talk like that," Georg exploded. "I can't stand it!"

His father darted him a quick look: "Why not?" He bore down. "Why can't you stand it?"

"Because it's nothing but talk!"

The veins bulged on Falk's forehead. He took a deep breath to gain self-control.

"So—you too," he said passionately. "So it comes down to the fact that you're reading Marx secretly and going to Communist student meetings. Don't deny it. I know everything you've been up to!"

He grabbed the briefcase and produced a small notebook.

"You attend Professor Strowski's lectures—he's a Jew and a Communist. You appear at the 'Concordia' with young radical writers of the Communist line. You parade around with a young Communist girl, whose name is . . ."

"Father!" Georg was on the rack now. "If you defend freedom, perhaps I have the right to choose my own friends and read what I wish."

"Go right on slumming with your idealists who have defiled the Villa. Go right ahead! Make brothers of my enemies and the country's enemies. Go right ahead!"

"Father," Georg said, not daring to meet his eyes. "I must speak with you before you . . ."

"Before I what?"

"Before you send the soldiers against the workers."

Falk threw his head back with a scornful laugh:

"I have no intention of discussing that with you, you young puppy!"

Georg added rapidly, "There was something else I wanted to mention."

Mastering fear, he looked his father in the face, his hand grasping a book which, unknowingly, he had picked up from the floor.

"Father," he said, "don't you see how life around you is becoming suffocating?"

Falk stared at him.

"I've been feeling this way for years. I have respected you,

211

admired you—I still do—in many ways. But just look at Regina! Look at Mother! Think of our whole life!"

Falk stood motionless without letting his son out of his line of vision.

"What are you trying to say?" he demanded hotly.

Georg's gesture was one of despair.

"You're certainly able to see that we pass each other like strangers, that we're afraid of each other—at least, *we* are afraid of *you*. We're living an inhuman life. You don't see us, you don't listen to us. Not that we're so important, but at least . . . Forgive me, Father!"

He stood trembling and breathless.

"I should forgive that?" Falk asked as softly as before. "No. That's too much. That's what comes of your hob-nobbing with the rabble."

"No, Father," Georg added quickly. "If I have gone around with people you call rabble it's because I can't stand living here any longer. I'd rather go my own way. I have found people who don't have your talents, but who have hearts and a real readiness to sacrifice."

"You mean the Communists?"

"Yes, the Communists!"

Falk laughed his mirthless laugh.

"Then you were probably in on the plans for the violence here—you and your new friends?"

"No," Georg answered. "You know I wasn't. I detest brutality and barbarism."

("But I steal!" he heard an inner voice whisper.)

Falk continued standing quietly a moment. Then he turned his back.

"Get out of here!" he hissed barely audibly.

Georg's answer was quiet.

"Yes, I'll go. I'll leave the props and appearances where human life has disappeared. I don't want to break with you.

For years I have hoped that you'd see what you're doing. Behind your high-sounding words . . . Just look at Mother; you've beaten her to the ground. Yes, you. And Regina. She's going downhill fast."

Falk turned slowly, his hand clenching the back of a chair. "Go," he said quietly.

"All right," Georg cried in complete despair. (If only I hadn't taken his attaché case!) "I'll go. And I won't come back!"

At the doorway he hesitated, as if in thought. Ruefully he came halfway back across the room.

"Father . . ." he implored.

Falk's arms were crossed. His son had only to look at him for a second before he turned and flung himself from the house.

For a split second the father remained motionless. Then he took a few steps, kicked a book across the room and sat down, arms dangling like a cripple.

Minutes later he got up with a sigh and went to the telephone.

"Line A. Thanks. General Sturzebecker. Hello, General! Yes, we've a terrible mess out here. Yes, naturally, I'd very much like to speak with you, General. In an hour? In my office. Immediately before the cabinet meeting. Thanks."

He replaced the receiver quietly.

"Where is Georg?" he heard from behind him.

Elisabeth had returned. She was leaning on Isabelle. When Falk turned, the girl bowed without releasing Elisabeth's arm.

"He has gone," said Falk.

"Without saying goodbye?" asked Elisabeth. "It must seem odd to hear me say it, but the birds seem to be singing especially beautifully today. Almost as if they wanted to comfort us. And the birches are still standing as white and

213

pure as before, waving and murmuring. What a morning! Don't you feel as though God has something in store for us?"

He shrugged.

"Yes," he said. "I'm convinced He does."

Elisabeth's face brightened. She patted Isabelle's hand.

"You feel that way too. Almost always when misfortune strikes, when something is lost, something else of much greater value comes about. Something unexpected. You will see that's the case this time, too."

Falk nodded.

"Yes," he said dully. "This time it's going to be something else that will come about. Of that I'm sure."

Elisabeth glanced at Isabelle and smiled.

"I was very frightened last night in there with Stephan. I could hear the crackling and roaring. And the shouting. Then the soldiers came and chased the poor unfortunates away. But now I feel happy. But you probably can't understand why."

"No," her husband answered.

His mind on other things, he crossed over to her and kissed her on the forehead.

"No," he repeated. "I fear that I don't quite understand. But I too have learned something important from it all."

"You have? What, dear?"

Both women were looking at him.

"I have learned not to rely on a single human being. I have learned to rely on nothing else than upon . . ."

". . . than upon God? You're right!"

Isabelle led her again toward the door.

She pause for a moment once more.

"What a morning. It's as if He were saying to us: 'All your possessions are pure plunder, without value. But just see what I can give you!' "

23

Locked in her room at the Prime Minister's Residence, Regina flipped through the packet of Mrs. Graber's private papers which Thomas had given her. Voices drifted in from the dining room. Her father's dinner guest was a political subordinate and the conversation was animated. If her father could only see the homework she was doing here!

The diary was quite fragmentary. From all appearances Mrs. Graber had made her entries furtively and often the edges of the papers were crumpled as if they had more than once been hastily shoved into a drawer or under a blotting pad.

The first entries were indifferent notations of friends, invitations, appointments, illnesses. Incisive and attractive, the script became, with the passage of years, more and more strained and nervous. Included were pictures of Thomas's mother. She could not have been called beautiful, but her expression was both clever and serious. It was the ordinary face of a woman who could bear responsibility, but also the face of a woman who had known passion.

Obviously there must have been a time when Falk and Graber had been good friends, if not on intimate terms. Falk was often in the guest-lists included after every party. Three years passed before Regina came upon any pertinent passages. After a matter-of-fact note concerning some extended entertaining, the following entry stood out:

"I like H. better than any other man."

H. was her father. Regina read on hungrily.

The dry factual notations continued. But under the date-line of a Saturday morning they produced a richer yield.

"Today I am twenty-seven years old. Why have I been sitting here writing down things that are not worth mentioning? Why do I pass over the one thing for which I live, that one thing which I fear, the one thing that makes me happy!"

Somewhat further along: "Elisabeth and I chatted together. She is much more intelligent than I, has a broad knowledge of literature and religion. But her modesty is almost sickening. She speaks with such perpetual restraint and humility that she actually seems proud. When she talks it is as if a second voice were saying, 'see how humble I am, how I am trying to bring myself down to your level, you poor thing!' I wonder whether or not I really can't hurt her."

So this was a description of my mother in her youth, Regina thought. This was the way she appeared in the eyes of another woman.

Two days later: "It is best to write this down: I never loved my husband. I respect him and admire him a bit. He's so down-to-earth, ordinary, and proper that I always feel secure in his presence. He's such a contrast to my Papa, who was never ordinary in any situation. But now I am beginning to understand something important. It was a crime to marry for the reasons I did. He loves me; he has never really loved another, either before or after our marriage. But I cannot bring myself to love him. He's so opinionated, so immobile —I don't know. But H. . . . Is it my imagination when I think I'm beginning to love him. He has never taken any particular interest in me. But when he speaks there's always a certain tone . . . he looks at me frequently in a sort of distracted fashion, but it's such a lovely look. He likes to look at me and when he speaks there are always little niceties meant just for me, for he never says them within earshot of others. I understand Elisabeth less than ever. She thinks she's psychic and that she's carrying around a secret that no one else knows anything about. I don't for a moment believe in this sort of spirituality. And H.? Has she ever had even an inkling of who he is? I doubt it."

After this there was a silence of two years; a large part of the diary had been ripped out. Something must have come about at this time which was roughly the time when Regina was from six to eight years old.

Well did the girl remember this time.

When the diary resumed, the handwriting had become almost that of a different person, and the previously well-ordered and well-thought-out entries had been transformed into speedily jotted comments, as though the author of the diary was now making her observations for the purpose of exploring her own heart.

"I don't understand myself any more. I have not grown equal to H.'s intelligence and his expositions bore me. He is erotic rather than attractive. But what concentrated power of personality! It's as if he had been smelted in one solid piece. He listens so quietly, his speech is never hurried. But when he's angry a thunderstorm bursts forth. He is really wonderful when he thunders. My husband is a private person. He is himself and works at his profession. But H. stands for an ideal. He embodies something. He has undertaken a great work and has dedicated himself to it with tremendous strength and determination. He never mentions himself, because he considers himself insignificant, and avoids referring to his private life. When he does occasionally speak of it he seems distracted and disinterested. But when he describes gifted students who have done well in his examinations! Or when he speaks of some stimulating article, or when he gives his ideas on how the University should be improved. Then he's pure fire!

"How narrow and purposeless my own life is in comparison to his! Most men grow from childhood to boyhood to manhood. But a few grow further. He belongs in that class. He has a fourth dimension.

"I love him."

Regina could hardly trust her eyes. What a weird way to fall in love! A not particularly gifted woman knocked off her feet by a thundering legal philosopher. She herself had heard it all before, particularly during those years, and she had always looked upon it as self-exaltation. He always was trying to convey the impression of being exceptional, engaging, or best of all, majestic. And he had always appeared to her as somewhat ridiculous.

And yet . . . and yet this is what had set another woman on fire, hopelessly in love.

The continuation of the diary provided factual details. The two had begun to have private meetings. It had started at a watering place, where Elisabeth Falk obviously had been the one most in need of a cure. This was probably when her paralysis first had begun to set in. H. and Mrs. Graber met each other daily at Elisabeth's sick bed. Then in the evening they would walk together on the beach; the author of the diary became lyrical, almost eccentrically extravagant. Her reactions to H. were as if to a superman, a granite block of perfection. In comparison other men were as schoolboys.

Her father!

It was still difficult to imagine how this idyll could be carried over into passion. How could her father awaken any woman's physical love? Yet it was impossible to deny the fact. He slowly forced his way into this woman's emotional life, filled her subconscious and took command of her. Finally, there was but one thing she wanted: to have done with her past life and to become entirely his.

Mrs. Graber was now writing down everything with reckless abandon. She could no longer stand her husband's touch. If she couldn't live with H., she wanted to live alone. And one day H. told her frankly that he returned her love.

"He recognizes it," she wrote. "He has long recognized it. He says that he has loved me for two years. Though he never speaks of his marriage I can gather how miserable his life with Elisabeth must be. How she must torture him with her pretense, her fake religious humility, her pride. He lets her do what she likes but no longer lives with her. He never speaks of himself. But once he, the great legal scholar, sketched for me the love of the Brownings. In all my life I have never heard a human being speak with such power. True love is as rare as the gifts of genius, in his opinion. It breaks all barriers, it is austere, it seeks neither happiness nor satisfaction. In fact, a great love is a manifestation of the similar drive toward the Absolute, the Unattainable, as is reverence for the philosophical concepts of law, of honor, of the law itself. He loves European legal philosophy the way a man should love his wife. Does that sound absurd? At any rate I know that when I hear him speak I would give my life to be able to share his love, even though it should ruin my entire life and that of my family."

The next hundred pages dealt exclusively with H. External events were either not mentioned or casually passed over. It was not easy to judge when and where they met, though apparently it was with considerable regularity. She referred to his letters, which had obviously been burned. Step by step the two could be seen coming closer to each other until her tone took on the vibrations of a woman beloved. Now she also began to describe him as a man. She attempted to retain impressions of his individual traits and spoke of his clothing, which was always severely prosaic and conservative.

Then it came:

"He says that he desires me, has desired me for two long years! Never have I felt prouder or happier! Yet he doesn't want to love me, doesn't want to want me. It would be contrary to his principles. I understand him. He says that we would gain nothing if we lived with each other. Love has a tragic dimension; it is a gift of destiny that can never be brought to full realization. The human body is incapable of expressing love, for love is hunger for completion, for the Absolute. The hunger of human bodies is but a weak reflection of this great longing. Once man has satisfied the physical longing, an even greater dissatisfaction remains. The lover really wants to possess the soul of the other, but souls cannot be possessed.

"He never moralizes, never raises social or moral objections. He is not afraid. He's no burgher. He simply looks upon love as a great act of fate that must be suffered as tragic destiny. One has a duty not to satisfy one's love, for to satisfy it would be to betray it, to kill it.

"I cannot understand all, but I would always be willing, no matter what, to share his life—or just be near him always. He is like a mighty river, like a great wave always struggling forward. I would give my life if I could let myself be swept away by that wave!"

Regina sat thinking awhile. All this was romantic hysteria. Here were two middle-class people who didn't dare give in to their impulses because they had no knowledge of psychoanalysis and consequently had sublimated, "mystified," their basic drives. The situation was as clear as day: both were frustrated and wanted to possess each other—but didn't dare. To cover up their cowardice he had invented this arrogant philosophy. It was pitiful.

The only pages that she fully understood were those in which Mrs. Graber repeated his views on poetry. Here Regina was able to recognize herself, her own hunger for the Absolute in her pursuit of the dance. But her father was no artist. He was a legal philosopher and a burgher. A judge!

The relationship continued on in the diary. Page after page Regina read, sketches of their meetings, happy etchings of his nobility and strength, sad lines describing unsatisfied longing. H. appeared to wish to educate her in sacrifice. He would continue to be interested in her only as long as she was willing to sacrifice love for the sake of love. Purest sophistry! No divorce had been contemplated, nor even discussed. H. had not the slightest intention of leaving Elisabeth, or, for that matter, of having the Grabers separate. And during the entire mendacious and unreal love, Elisabeth was at home tormented, almost out of her mind. And Dr. Graber was fumbling with one means after another to win back his wife.

Finally H. reaped the whirlwind. For years he had drawn this woman steadily away from her husband, filling her with notions of her own importance. Now he wanted her to "travel the road back." Her love demanded it! At this point there were some confused, incoherent, despairing entries and Thomas Graber had furnished the margins with ironical exclamation marks.

It was precisely during the years described that Regina herself had been so deeply upset by her mother's sorrow that she had begun to fear for her father and to desire to offer herself as a "sacrificial victim." How grotesque! What a miserable game! By his sophistry her father had disrupted every human relation surrounding him. He was indifferent to his wife and let her welter in her pain and unhappiness. He forced his daughter into the blind alley of religious hysteria. He subjected his friend, Dr. Graber, to horrible torture. He transformed the Graber home into something cold and dead—Thomas was the one who had to pay that bill. Despite all this the mystical H. was a proud man. Still! The poor creature he loved now followed him obediently, almost enthusiastically. She who was now going along "the road back" was trying to love her husband and thus to become worthy of H.! He was pushing her into a hopeless corner and demanding from her an absurdity, namely that she love someone whom she was incapable of loving! The result was that she tormented her husband with fresh years of anguish by offering him a dutiful love upon the command of another man.

It was with great excitement that Regina read these lines. Her father was not the primitive person she had believed him to be. He was vastly more complicated. But her basic intuition had been correct: he was inhuman and he succeeded in destroying everything around him. All in the name of the "Absolute"!

Finally Mrs. Graber's obedience and submission reached the point where she even ceased to write his name. In her imagination Regina could picture her father exacting from the woman a solemn promise never to mention his name, never more to think of him. So she suffered. At his command she plunged the dagger into her heart and was proud thus to bleed. He left her, majestically and admired, but his shadow was always to hover over the blighted home. She could not forget him. Finally came the tragicomic finale when one night she burned his pictures and letters. Everything had to be wiped out and the new course of action put in motion. Following H.'s command she tried ever more to penetrate into her husband's heart, to understand him, to win him, to awaken his love once again . . .

What a refined way to torture him! What a way to debase oneself. The diary was a tawdry history of complete self-deceit. A little confidence, a little courage to defy false conventions and inhibitions and the problem might have been solved.

There were some final entries that showed that she was aware of how her own opportunities for happiness disappeared while on the other hand she was bringing problems upon her family.

And yet she never despaired.

"I am wounded, sick, an invalid," she wrote once toward the end of her diary. "My husband is making pathetic attempts to cure me. He doesn't suspect that I would prefer to remain an invalid in the shade of H., the one real human being in my life, than to be cured with himself. What do I care about my sickness? I have only one thing in my heart, to remain true to what he has taught me."

This was the last personal entry. After that the book had been hidden.

Regina studied the series of photographs which Thomas had lent her of his mother. It was amazing, but her expression seemed to have grown more refined and purified with the passage of years. There was no evidence of her pain; rather, a sort of mystical confidence seemed to shine from her dark countenance—as if she knew that she had done the right thing.

"Well, what do you think?" Thomas asked when Regina returned the diary. "Have you ever read anything more gruesome?"

"No," she said. "Are you sure you really don't know who this H. is?"

"I haven't the slightest idea," he answered. "And I haven't the slightest intention of trying to find out."

"Why not?"

"Oh," he said, with a knowing grin, "because then I'd feel I ought to murder him, and that could be a bit of a bore."

24

THE CRISIS had come to a head quickly. Falk had abandoned all plans for conciliatory action, and he now veered completely to the opinion of the generals, which formerly he had considered too radical. A state of martial law had been proclaimed in the Capital and the Prime Minister himself was living under military protection in his Executive Offices. A number of arrests had taken place. General Sturzebecker had been named Commander-in-Chief, a fact which foreshadowed a hard administration, for he was a career officer who had been through many wars.

Georg had disappeared completely and Falk had made scant inquiries. But Elisabeth often phoned looking for news —she was worried. Ordinarily Falk had his secretary answer. In reality, however, he was worried himself about the boy and gave the police instructions to hunt him down. He considered it unthinkable that Georg had seriously made common cause with the Communists. Nevertheless, there was a certain risk involved at a time like this for the Prime Minister's son to be gadding about in the less safe quarters of the city.

The theft of his attaché case now appeared to be solved. Of course it had been Georg, the young fool! There were times when Falk was tempted to strike his son from his memory. He had betrayed both father and country. At the same time, quite illogically, he longed to find him and one day to win his friendship. There was no question but that Georg had reached some unusual conclusions concerning him. If he had only known! Why had he not spoken long ago with his children about the chief problem of his life? Now he was being punished for having vowed never to investigate false accusations.

In recent days he had grown thin. He had dark circles under his eyes and was smoking too much. As was his custom, he was sitting with his secretary in one of the offices, speaking with nervous excitement on the telephone:

"I'll expect you here as soon as possible, General. Do you think that estimate is correct? Fifteen thousand people? Every worker and his wife in the entire city must be taking part!

Yes, I read it. It's the unmistakable signal for the uprising. Keep your telephone lines open and have reports to me every fifteen minutes. Oftener if necessary. Thanks."

He hung up.

"Unbelievable," he said. "Completely unbelievable."

In the southern suburbs, the great factory district, the workers had broken up telephone connections here and there, had torn up the streets and had clashed with both militia and police. Their press had just made the announcement that fifteen thousand persons—unarmed—were going to hold a great mass demonstration. If the armed forces tried to prevent them, they would have only themselves to answer for the probable consequences. In such an event an appeal would be made to friends and protectors of the worker class—outside the country.

"Unbelievable?" Wendt repeated. "Oh, no—it's quite logical after the propaganda of the last weeks. Also, they know that we're considering the possibility of firing on unarmed demonstrators. It's a provocation they can't resist."

Falk had risen and was measuring the room with nervous steps.

"One can't help wondering," he said, "if we're dealing with human beings. Can't they see that the country cannot tolerate such a crisis, that the whole thing is instigated by the Communists for their own purposes? And yet they march! Don't they ever take time out to think?"

"No," Wendt said. "Why should they think? There is nothing that people like to do less."

Falk stood at the window while his eyes swept the open square in front of the Ministry. It had been barricaded and armed soldiers were everywhere. Three tanks stood in front of the Palace and he knew that machine guns were in location both at the Palace and at the Ministry. So it had finally come to this!

"This people calls itself a civilized society," he said slowly. "We pride ourselves on our democracy, don't we? But it only takes the slightest breath of suggestion to put the masses on the march. Against all common sense, even against their own interests!"

Wendt was standing, arms crossed. He was living a moment of quiet peace and icy joy. Step by step he was coming nearer his goal; now there was nothing in his way and the net was being slowly drawn in.

"It is a deep-rooted superstition," he said, "to believe that men are driven by their own interests."

Falk turned to him questioningly.

Wendt continued: "They are influenced by their drives. And by the insinuated suggestions of other people. The strange fact is that this, as a rule, is in a direction contrary to their own interests. I find it all quite amusing."

Falk's nervousness was mounting. For the first time in his life he felt that he didn't have himself completely under control and this further confused and unnerved him.

"Well," he said. "We'll see. Under no circumstances will we let them get as far as the factory district. We have to keep the munitions factories in operation. And we have to be ready for any eventuality on the border. Furthermore, it is the country's duty to protect those who are willing to work. What sort of mail was there today?"

Wendt walked over to his attaché case which he had placed on the little table by the wall. The regular daily program had been suspended and there was an accumulation of things which they still had not been able to discuss.

He opened the case.

"Only some crank letters," he said. "Fourteen of them, I believe. They're not particularly interesting."

"All the same," said Falk with irritation, "I want to hear some of them. Some samples!"

226

"But, Your Excellency . . ." Wendt said imploringly.

"Read some of them, I said!"

Wendt leafed through the sheaf, selected a letter, and murmured:

"Here's a really vulgar one, in an unusually affected hand-writing. I could swear it's from a woman. No name, of course. 'You should resign!' 'You haven't the maturity to serve as Prime Minister!' 'Make way for a younger man capable of crushing the enemies of the country!' Then it becomes less interesting: 'Don't drink so much champagne,' for example. 'What's more, you're too well fed. You're a suety sensualist. The Prime Minister should look like an ascetic.' "

"Into the wastebasket," Falk said quietly.

He was receiving such letters every day. At first they challenged him and he had even taken the pains to answer some of the signed ones. In most cases he found that he was dealing with psychopaths.

"Well. Is there anything else?" he said dryly.

Again Wendt leafed through the papers.

"Yes, here's a letter. I opened it accidentally. It's of a private nature."

"From whom?"

Wendt looked up almost triumphantly.

"From young Mr. Falk, Your Excellency."

"From my son? Let me see it."

Wendt passed over the letter which Falk snatched and was about to open. Instead he crumpled it into a ball.

"No!" he said. "No! This letter I'll not read! First let him come back and ask for forgiveness."

"It does not contain such a request," Wendt said cautiously. "I was able to make out that much."

Falk continued standing, the crumpled letter in his fist.

"Think of it. My own son."

He threw the balled paper into the open fireplace, where

logs had been arranged decoratively, though no fire had been lighted.

"Is there anything else we need to discuss? What about the press?"

Wendt returned the sheaf of letters to the case and reached for the newspapers which he had prepared with blue pencil.

"So far as foreign politics is concerned . . ."

"I'm not the least bit interested in that today," Falk answered from the window."

Wendt smiled.

"With the exception of the strike and mobilization, the papers are discussing Dr. Graber's resignation. Even his own party is treating him severely. Nevertheless . . ."

A heavy wave of uneasiness passed over Falk. This matter had been completely unnecessary. Well, it had been his only blunder.

"Nevertheless?" he repeated. "Nevertheless what?"

"Nevertheless the most damaging part had not yet been made public," Wendt said quietly.

"What are you talking about?"

"That secretly a child . . ."

Falk wheeled, scarlet.

"No," he shouted. "No. Enough's enough."

Wendt nodded, but added:

"I don't know why mercy should be shown to such vermin. The information can be leaked out, very carefully, without anyone . . ."

"No," Falk shouted again in full fury. "I'll have nothing more to do with the matter. In all honesty I don't believe that the 'Gloria affair' is so completely clear. Juridically, formally, perhaps. But hardly from the moral point of view. Basically it was not his error; he appeared not to have known too much about the affair when he became involved in it."

Wendt remained impassive. The Catholic Party had been severely compromised and that was the most important aspect of it for him. Now it was too late for anything to be done. Public opinion had already been formed, for it was now common knowledge that the leading journalist of the Catholics had made money in some illegal munitions transactions.

"And his scandalous attacks on the regime, Your Excellency?"

"Yes. They're scandalous all right. Or at any rate, very stupid. Nevertheless his account has been settled."

"Hardly, Wendt replied, "if he's able to get a clean slate in the 'Gloria affair.' It would be considerably more difficult for him to clear his name if we can hammer in to the public conscience that morally he is open to reproach."

"No," Falk said and struck the window frame with his fist. "I've said it for the last time. Is there anything else to be discussed?"

Wendt referred once more to his newspapers.

"There are a few scandal articles here. They're not particularly interesting."

"You always say that," Falk said irritably, "especially when there is actually something important. You need have no fear of my nerves. If they stood up under my son's becoming a Communist, they'll be able to take anything else."

"This time," Wendt said softly, "it doesn't concern your son, Your Excellency. Rather, Miss Falk."

Falk turned. His face was a pale grey.

"Regina," he said softly. "What does it say?"

Wendt looked directly at his chief.

"Your Excellency," he said vigorously, "take my advice! Don't read it!"

"I certainly will not take your advice. I want to hear it all. What is it this time?"

"For one who knows Miss Falk," Wendt said, "it sounds ridiculous, cut out of whole cloth."

"Read!"

Falk could feel the floor buckle beneath him. He had faced all blows—when they came straight at him. But this unrest behind his back. This eternal lack of security, this choking enmity in his own family. Thanks be to God that he and Elisabeth had recently begun to be close again. And suddenly he longed for Father Leo. The priest knew that he could visit unannounced whenever he wanted to or should have the time. He would always be welcome and Falk had given him a pass which would get him through all the sentries.

"It appears that Miss Falk has been a little . . . careless," Wendt said.

"Read it."

"It's about a sort of artists' cabaret. A private one—or at least semi-private. Apparently someone did some snooping. 'Among some of the better-known young ladies, who seem to take particular pleasure in dancing with negroes and sailors, the vivacious daughter of the Prime Minister was noticed. She was costumed—if that is the word—as a bacchante.' "

Falk ripped the paper from Wendt's hand, yet hesitated to read it.

"Regina," he said. "She, too. That's all I needed."

He forced himself to scan the article. The paper was not a scandal sheet, but rather one of the esteemed, conservative newspapers. Could it be the work of Graber's friends?

"Yes, it's all too clear. Libertinism, colossal indifference . . ."

He let the paper drop and inserted his finger under his collar.

"This suffocates me . . . I feel surrounded. Just when I need complete peace and as much support as possible, I'm left in the lurch by my own family, my own son and daughter."

"That is the fate of all leaders," Wendt said. "All great men."

"I'm no great man!" the Prime Minister screamed. "I'm

230

no genius. But I am a man of good will. I fight for my country and not for myself. But the pack jumps me! Burns down my house! Poisons my son! My wife lives in a dream world. My daughter dances half naked at some third-rate carnival."

The phone rang.

Falk strode to the desk and grabbed the receiver, hand trembling. Wendt quickly shoved the newspaper back into the case. He felt as if he were in a laboratory. An injection now, another in a little while, small preparatory jolts. Little doses—no need to hurry. And the result was as if read off a precision instrument. Politics is a natural science.

"Yes," Falk said, trying to control his voice. "Oh, the General has arrived? Please have him come up. You are sure you are keeping our outside line open? Good. Continue to do so."

He hung up.

"The General has finally arrived," he said. "It will be nice to have two decent, loyal people near me."

He fumbled once more for the newspaper, then hurled it away in fury.

"Wendt! I give you unconditional authority to use any means. Strike down that Graber. Put your foot on his neck and step hard! If no consideration is taken of my feelings, why should I be considerate?"

Wendt nodded. He had understood.

Falk mopped his forehead and stepped again to the window. He felt more than nervous. Formerly he never would have given in to such rage. And it was not many years ago that he lived apart from this seething world, occupied with scholarly research! The only sensational events those days were the academic appointments and the minor University scandals, but they were enough to give him excitement for weeks or even months. Those were the days when he had not worried much about the fortunes of the country. He had never thought that he was living outside reality. Well, he certainly wasn't living outside reality now! Almost every moment he had to make decisions—improvised decisions. One thing he had learned: whenever he found a person in complete agreement with his own convictions, that person usually proved incapable of acting, was a victim of a sort of paralysis.

It was precisely this passivity that his enemies were exploiting. The idealists held back since they could find no policies which were morally unobjectionable in every detail, so they condemned themselves to taking no part at all. Thanks to this sensitivity, this acute scrupulosity, evil continued to gain the upper hand. It was the same way in international politics. The democracies believed they could never start a war themselves, they'll always wait until they have been attacked—and thus start out at a disadvantage. This beautiful idealism had to be paid for by the deaths of a hundred thousand soldiers, the bombing of countless cities. Thus, he thought, he must continually seek compromises if he was to act constructively at all. Politics is the art of the possible, and the possible is never more than a compromise. One had to be content with the knowledge that, at most, one had aimed in the right direction.

At the same time he thought about his specific problem of the moment. He had the feeling in this instance that the events were leading him, rather than vice versa. The situation was self-created. Nor do I think that those on the opposing side are dominating the circumstances any more than we are, he pondered.

The door was thrown open and the Supreme Commander, General Sturzebecker, entered. He was sixty years of age or a little more. Known for his brutality, he nevertheless gave the impression of being a philosopher rather than a soldier; judging by his appearance, no one would have guessed that he had taken part in four wars.

He saluted.

25

ISABELLE had been brought up in Switzerland where she had lived almost completely apart from any contacts with Catholicism. She had grown accustomed to bare, severe churches without altars or decorations. Christian belief in her mind was summed up as a moral imperative, an unqualified righteousness, against which there was no appeal. She had never heard Swiss Catholics mentioned with anything other than distrust.

Regina was nominally a Catholic, but her religion had never seemed to mean anything to her. It was in Elisabeth that Isabelle met a Catholic woman for the first time.

She had felt immediately attracted to the sick woman, who lived so much alone out here in the country. She longed for Regina when the latter was in the city at the Institute for the Dance, but she was nonetheless happy to stroll with Elisabeth in the park, and the older woman seemed stimulated by the company of the reserved young girl.

One day Elisabeth took her to the conventual Mass at the Dominican Monastery. Isabelle assisted, perplexed and not at all edified. At times she was close to irritation. What was the sense of all the movements and bowings? Why all the ceremonial with incense and crucifix? She liked the Gregorian Chant, but it went no further than her ear. When she left, she was more firmly convinced that Calvinism was the only true form of Christianity.

However, one evening after the meal that the two shared alone, Elisabeth mentioned that she would like very much to go to Compline at the Monastery. Isabelle, from motives of affection, offered to accompany her.

The church was dark except for the dim light in the choir

section where the priests were sitting. They chanted the psalms in recollected, chaste tones. Isabelle slowly lost interest. Moreover, unable to understand the Latin or to make any sense out of Elisabeth's instructions on how to follow the passages, she was growing quiet sleepy. Then a monk busying himself at the altar caught her eye. Something odd was taking place. A lamp, quite near her own bench, was lighted, which bathed the area before the picture of the Virgin. Then the altar gate was opened; from both sides the Dominicans filed out, their cowls thrown back. As Isabelle watched the strong, intelligent profiles, they seemed to her like white warriors. Slowly they formed ranks like a small army and turned toward the image of the Madonna high on the wall. She heard them sing:

Salve Regina, mater misericordiae, vita, dulcedo et spes nostra, salve.

Ad te clamamus, exsules filii Hevae.

Ad te suspiramus, gementes et flentes in hac lacrimarum valle. . . . The deep voices rolled under the arched ceiling, their eyes were fixed far in the distance—near to the young Mother.

Suddenly Isabelle wanted to kneel but unable to overcome her reserve she remained standing, her heart pounding. These men, well-formed in secular learning and religious discipline, willingly sacrificing their lives in a monastery, were bowing down before a young maiden, an unknown little Jewess who, once visited by an angel, had answered, "Let it be done unto me according to Thy Will!"

The Madonna. The word had always reminded her of plump female forms, garishly painted, with a helpless child on lap. Images, in short, like the ones found on the roadsides in Switzerland. This time, however, both the picture on the wall and the respectful homage of the monks radiated an atmosphere of purity of which she had never been aware.

What was it? Was there also a gracious, all-pardoning, gentle element in holiness? To her Godliness had always been masculine, the fatherly element, That Which administers justice and punishment. Here was something else, a young woman who knew everything of the longing and desires of her kind.

Moved almost to tears the girl could hardly speak to Elisabeth on the way home. She had loved Regina, and still did love her. Despite her tenderness, however, Regina was cold in comparison to the young Mother of God. She was bewitching—she was beauty and oversensitivity. But had it really been Regina whom she sought?

That night sleep did not come easily, so she tried for the first time in her life to pray to the Mother of God. When she was unable to find the right words she tried to force the image from her mind. But it kept returning and in her state of semi-wakefulness she felt that someone was watching over her. At home she had never felt this security, despite all the order and cleanliness. Noisy vacuum cleaners have a tendency to squelch mystic perception.

Regina had gone to a party and stayed overnight in the city; she would not be home until the afternoon. Isabelle realized for the first time that she did not miss her friend. Usually when she was left alone she became lonesome and restless, and would try to console herself by going to Regina's room to study old photographs of her friend or to leaf through her books. Today she lived in a new conviction. The memory of her previous evening's experience kept sweeping over her like a mysterious wave.

Several times she was on the point of consulting Elisabeth, but never quite mustered the courage. Then she tried to find her way through the Catholic literature in the house, but quickly bogged down in the theology.

After breakfast, barefooted and bareheaded, she went alone into the gently blowing woods. She wanted to go off, away

235

from everybody, into the half darkness. Her steps hesitant she left the path and walked into the depths of the forest. For the first time, too, she entered into herself, anxious yet very happy with the joy of discovery. The music of the beech leaves was a soft murmur. When she paused she felt at once that she was in the presence of a gentle being, vibrant with the essence of life. She turned slowly. The wood stood before her, cool in the half light. High above, the sun played freely among the tree tops; below everything was a muffled, quiet expectancy. To be able to escape from over-loud voices, from the whole world of men, with their technocracy and their ideas! Had she finally found an unknown world of which she had never been aware? How could she have lived so many years without realizing that man has an inner as well as an exterior life? Now she was forging ever deeper into her own soul as she moved slowly across the soft moss, still somewhat anxious, but full of expectancy and peace. For years her life had been shattered by the alarms of the world of men. At this moment something completely different was moving toward her. Carefully, on her guard, she moved farther, her lips parted in a happy smile. *"O clemens, o pia, o dulcis virgo Maria!"*

At last she fell on her knees and felt it both natural and right. Covering her face she remained motionless a long time until her knees, unaccustomed to the position, began to smart. She felt that she was giving herself over to a strange power that wanted neither to possess her nor force her. She remained motionless. But her soul extended its arms, as it were, and whispered to the element of motherliness and gentleness:

"Yes!"

After reading Mrs. Graber's diary, Regina was confused and upset. She was also ashamed, for she realized that she had been spying, prying into a well-kept secret, laughing at the

236

serious confessions of a dead woman. And the reason she had given for wanting to read it was a lie. Rather than being interested in Thomas' past, she really was looking for evidence to convict her father. Even now she was unable to understand his role as revealed by those secret pages, nor could she deny that he emerged a more-or-less imposing figure. She was still convinced that he was inhuman, but if she wanted to be honest she could no longer look upon him as insincere and petty. There was a certain "style" in the whole affair, a certain tinge of greatness.

But most of all she was disturbed by the recurring idea that she was face to face with certain experiences which she was simply unable to grasp. How could such massive will power be delivered up to something as vague and incomprehensible as this abstract "Absolute"? Why, in her own life, was there no such overriding imperative to which she could quietly subordinate her life? Why was her own world broken and splintered? She had tried to erect the white temple of beauty over the neurotic fragmentation of her own existence. But she froze in this temple; beauty made her shudder.

During the following days she spent a great deal of time with Thomas. She came home late, often after having drunk too much. Her desire to be with Isabelle out in the country continued; at the same time she was frightened of the passionate direction her emotions had taken. She knew, however, that things could not drift on as at present; she must come to a decision, and to a course of action. Was she really abnormal? If so, she supposed she had no choice but to be true to this nature. More than once during the recent tumultuous days her desire for Isabelle had certainly been a hot longing. In the girl, unspoiled, innocent, there was something that had not yet been awakened. Regina felt she wanted to be the one to lead her to the shattering revelation, to the realm of ambiguous values out of which true beauty springs.

Not for a moment did she believe that either of them would find happiness in it, for she knew that she was facing a garden of sensuality full of alluring but traditionally forbidden joys. They would be sharing the unveiling of a beauty which the self-righteous scorned as sinful. She knew Isabelle would be willing; the girl would not hesitate to follow the one she loved.

But Regina also knew that the tension between Isabelle's mountain-stream freshness and her own splintered, ambivalent values would ultimately express itself as a sort of demoniacal beauty, of its very nature fibered with pain. But what beauty was not composed of pain and anxiety? To deliver the smashing blow of revelation to this girl who had opened to her full of trust; to reveal to her virginal eyes the world of beauty, lust and pain . . . and then to construct with her a world far removed from the coarse, awkward hands of ordinary people—a feminine fortress of gentle beauty!

She could not reveal all this to Thomas, but she listened to his advice and was spurred on by his own ambivalence. As a doctor, he claimed to be objective and neutral, yet even as he spoke he all but trembled with curiosity and expectation, as if in the darkness of a forbidden and secret theatre.

Regina could see through him, but that made no difference to her. Perhaps he could see equally well through her. He was human refuse as was she. Both were sacrifices to her father's brutality. Very well, let her now turn the wheel of consequence.

She went out to the Villa for lunch. At table she found it difficult to speak. Her mother watched uneasily the tired eyes and restless gestures. Isabelle was more charming than ever, a newly created being, but a bit withdrawn into her own sphere so that her conversation was a little distracted. The talk revolved around banalities, but behind the trifles was a tension, a silent struggle among three worlds that were massing their forces.

Elisabeth prayed, unquiet in the presence of something she didn't recognize.

Regina trembled from the excitement of the rare and the forbidden that was awaiting her. She was trying to find courage to take the young, innocent girl by the hand and lead her into the heart of her own jungle.

Isabelle wandered along her own inner path, which was vibrant with timeless bells, restless with a subdued activity quietly drawing her on like a landscape full of flickering lights and restful shade.

During coffee in the garden Regina's nerves trembled so that she got up and padded back and forth, her mother's eyes following her every movement. The girl seemed tormented and feverish, but Elisabeth knew that it would be useless to question her. Finally Regina announced that she was going to the lake, possibly to have a swim. Would Isabelle like to go along? Despite the rigid control she forced on her voice, both Elisabeth and Isabelle thought she sounded strange. Nonetheless, Isabelle answered that she would love to go. Elisabeth timidly suggested that it might be better for Regina to go upstairs and try to rest for awhile. Without answering, Regina linked her arm around Isabelle's and they walked off toward the shore.

Isabelle's arm was soft and cool. The moment Regina felt its touch she knew that her resolution was now firm. She didn't anticipate physical pleasure—all she knew was that she had to force her way into this young virginal soul, seduce it, take possession of it.

After they had walked along for a while Isabelle slowly disengaged her arm. Regina looked at her uneasily. The girl raised her hand to point at something. Before them hung a garish, crudely painted crucifix. At its foot was a Madonna.

Regina stared incredulously as she saw her friend's countenance brighten. Isabelle turned to her and said softly, with an overtone of secret happiness and peace:

"Regina, you'd never imagine. I've made a most wonderful discovery."

Regina looked at her in horror.

"You have? What?"

Isabelle laughed softly, her glance distant.

"Myself, I think," she answered slowly.

She turned to Regina, who could hardly bear to look at her.

"Can you imagine it? I didn't come here to find you."

"You . . . didn't?" Regina asked.

"No," the girl answered looking quietly ahead. "It was something else that I never even dreamed or could have dreamed . . ."

Regina was trembling.

"What?"

Isabelle did not answer, but looked again toward the garish crucifix and the crudely carved Madonna beneath it.

Regina closed her eyes in an effort to control herself. The Mother of God! So this was how it ended—her grand plan to shelter Isabelle out here in the country with her mother. Christ and Mary are greater seducers of young minds than the very demons of Hell.

She opened her eyes and saw Isabelle smiling, happy, filled with the light of interior peace. She lowered them a little and saw the noble head, the flower-like face, the straight back with tanned round shoulders sculped into curves that invited caresses. She wanted to take her arm again. But she couldn't. From between her tightly pressed lips a moan escaped. Isabelle looked up in alarm:

"What's the matter, Regina?"

"Nothing."

26

FALK WALKED across the room to greet General Sturzebecker.
"Welcome, General! Sit down! Smoke? If you want anything at all, just say the word. We could have a cup of strong
tea sent up immediately. Right, Wendt? Or some whiskey."

The general seated himself, stiff as the ceremonial sword at
his side.

"Thanks, no." It was his furrowed intellectual face that
gave him the look of a professor. He had a glass eye and Falk
could never decide which one it was.

"I have had the telephone line held open," said Falk.

"That was hardly necessary," answered the general. He
took a small box from his pocket and removed two little
black lozenges.

"I have to take my little dose of poison," he said.

This act was more than familiar. Undoubtedly they were
licorice laxatives.

"Do you need them today?" Falk asked laughing. Sturzebecker ignored the remark.

"As I see it," he said as he let his glance sweep the room,
settle on Falk and hold him there, "there are always two
possibilities. A good one and a bad one. However, the first
exists only in the world of dreams. If people would only
realize that the worst is always going to happen, there would
be nothing to worry about."

"Things will always go wrong?" Falk repeated, sensing that
his nervousness was beginning to subside. "Isn't that defeat-
ism?"

"By no means," answered the General. "Naturally, we will

be successful to the extent that we have taken precautions. In the present instance, we will hold the factory district and protect the weak-kneed who don't want to strike. But the point is that the victor also loses—in all war. That's the only thing a soldier can swear to—and it makes our profession very interesting."

Falk had begun to pace once more. His nervousness had returned. The phone rang and he snatched the receiver. After a few exchanges he repeated what was being said for the General's benefit.

"They're marching toward the factories. They still have three kilometers to go . . . The police blockade has been broken . . . Thanks, call me again if anything else happens."

Both parties had hung up and the general went back to his chair. He was still chewing his licorice sticks.

"In a quarter of an hour they should arrive at the Army's barbed-wire barricade. And they'll never get through, because behind it we have a few new weapons that may suddenly start to cough. Such things happen in spring time, as Your Excellency knows."

Falk shook his head.

"You're carrying the joke too far, General," he answered. "I definitely intend to permit shooting, if it's necessary. I have no intention of yielding to threats. But I'm not going to give that order without the deepest reflection."

The general registered no reaction; he polished his glasses ceremoniously.

"Why do you feel that way, Your Excellency? We're the ones that have to bear the brunt of the hate. And we are already hated. A democratic army officer is really a remarkable institution, Your Excellency. It has been said that you've recently taken an interest in religion. Now don't act so embarrassed. It's a very interesting subject and also a nice idea to be on good terms with one's Creator, if possible. The life of a democratic officer is a sort of . . . vicarious suffering. Do you see what I mean?"

"No. Explain."

"If there is a war," said the general, "then we have to die for the very countrymen who have tormented us all our lives. They've made fun of us, they've cut our salaries and our standing in the community. They lash out at us in the press, they take the weapons out of our hands and use the money to build palatial old folks' homes, into which they push all the old ladies in the country, who would much prefer to stay in their dirty hovels. But, of course, when the pinch comes, we have to be ready to stand up and die."

Again the telephone rang. Falk lifted the receiver. This time he would see to it that his hand didn't shake.

"Yes," he said. "It's Falk talking.—They're shooting? The demonstrators? But they were supposed to be unarmed!"

Wendt stood motionless. Falk turned to him:

"Wendt, go upstairs and compose that memorandum that we mentioned a few moments ago—the one for the Cabinet meeting."

Wendt bowed and left the room. At the same moment the general stood up and took the receiver.

"Pardon," he said. "General Sturzebecker talking. Get as many eye-witnesses as possible. Tell Major Planck to get hold of some of the weapons that were fired—it's very important."

He gave the receiver back to the Prime Minister.

"Pardon me, Your Excellency."

Falk gripped the instrument.

"Have any of the soldiers been injured?—Two? Hello—now I've been cut off . . . hello, hello . . ."

He hung up.

"Two of your soldiers were wounded, General."

"Splendid," the general answered as he sat down.

"But this is civil war!" exclaimed Falk.

Sturzebecker shook his head. "Not at all. As long as only one side is shooting, it isn't. Too bad they didn't kill some of my people—then we'd really have something to point with pride to. But we'll make as much out of these little wounds as we can. If it's only a scratch on someone's seat caused by a ricochetting pebble, the evening press will thunder about slaughter, violence and blood. Now we can return the fire with a good conscience."

Falk sighed. He walked to the window and looked out. Two tanks were rolling away. He crossed his arms and closed his eyes, his chin pressed down against his breast.

"With a good conscience?" he repeated slowly. "Can one ever have a good conscience when there are decisions to be made? No matter what you do there is always some group against you. That's the way it is even when dealing with criminals and hoodlums. But when both sides act with the best of intentions and there is still blood spilling and suffering, I feel somewhat uneasy."

The general laughed. "I don't," he answered. "On the contrary. At such moments one is closest to the very heart of existence."

Father Leo stepped softly through the doorway.

"That was cleverly said, General," said the priest. "But it's not the least bit true."

Falk brightened and went toward the Dominican.

"Welcome," he said. "I have been hoping you'd come."

"Well, well. The Church is marching too," muttered the general. "That's very nice."

He bowed to the Dominican.

"Pardon the interruption," said Father Leo, "but I felt that I should come when I saw the extras and read the headlines. The whole city's in an uproar."

"You are always more than welcome," said Falk.

The general continued his train of thought.

244

"My young people who got their share of the bullets are 'workers' just like the others. But now they'll go down in history as 'murderers of the working class.' Why? Because they caught the workers' bullets in their white arses. But if they'd been sent out in the field and had shot the workers in the army of some other country they'd be hailed as heroes. It's grotesque. And quite amusing."

Smiling, the Dominican followed the general's lecture, which was delivered in dry, professorial tone.

"It's quite clear," he said, "that the world has got to seem mad to us as long as we refuse to reckon with God's plans for His whole creation."

The general heaved his shoulders in an ironic gesture.

Falk, again excited, strode over to the priest.

"Father Leo," he said, "you know that I believe in God's love. But in a situation like the present one it's very hard to find it."

"It's never easy to find it," answered the Dominican. "If it were, it wouldn't be God's love." He grasped his rosary. "Don't let the troops shoot," he said.

Falk's tension swelled. Was this the only advice that the priest could give?

"I am the Prime Minister of this country," he declared. "That means that I have been charged by the majority of the people with the country's survival. I am also a Christian. But I know that whoever tries to follow the Gospel in practical politics will be trampled underfoot."

The general nodded. "Right," he said softly.

"You don't know any such thing," replied the Dominican.

"I don't?" Falk answered.

"No," said the priest. "Because you have never tried it."

The general, who had followed this exchange with some amusement, rose and advanced upon the Dominican.

"All this is very nice," he said. "I suppose my soldiers must sit quietly with folded hands. Or try to catch the rioters' bullets with their hands and legs, which are well suited to that purpose, presumably to show the clever Creator a gesture of esteem. That's the kind of mutual love He demands, with His mild, fatherly heart."

Falk twisted his hands.

"I admit I'm very confused," he said. "Politics and religion cannot be made to mix in a situation like this."

The Dominican, who had been looking at the general, now turned to Falk.

"Don't shoot! You'll regret it!"

Again the telephone jangled. Falk's hasty grab betrayed his rising agitation.

"Hello . . . Yes . . ."

He listened, then turned, receiver in hand, to the general and the Dominican.

"The barricade is broken," he exclaimed. "The soldiers have drawn back. There have been a few shots from the demonstrators, none so far from the troops."

"Don't shoot back!" said the Dominican.

General Sturzebecker had gone to the desk, where he snatched the receiver.

"Pardon, Your Excellency.—Sturzebecker talking here. The same order as before is in effect, Lieutenant! Understand?"

He laid the instrument down quietly.

"And that order is . . . ?" asked Falk.

The general lit a cigarette before answering. His hand was firm.

"The fire will be returned at the second line. That is, from the fence at the factory district. Any other way they'll burn the factories to the ground, endanger the ammunition dump, and the non-strikers will be massacred."

Eyes closed, the Dominican stood motionless for a moment before he turned to Falk and said softly:

"Don't shoot!"

Falk looked at him doubtfully, then took the receiver.

"The Prime Minister here. I confirm the general's order!"

He turned to the priest.

"I am sorry. But . . ."

The Dominican sucked in his breath and nodded. He measured the room diagonally and crossed his arms, the others' eyes following him.

"Tell me," he said, loudly and distinctly, "do you think you're going to gain grace before God for this—ever?"

"I don't," said Sturzebecker softly. "I have no intention to go hunting for divine grace."

Falk did not hear the general's answer. He stood staring ponderously ahead.

"Recently so many things have happened to me. I'm being assailed by evil on all sides. I'm meeting it in my own family. I have to resist."

Falk turned to the priest.

"I don't overrate myself. But if I were hailed before Divine Justice at this moment . . ."

A despairing ring crept into his voice.

"Be careful," said the Dominican.

". . . I would say," Falk continued with reddening face: " 'Investigate my life! Test my motives! Consider the circumstances under which I work and live! Judge me! I demand justice! Not mercy!' "

"Bravo!" said the general and applauded lightly from his chair. "That was almost as well put as if I had said it myself!"

"God help you, Falk," the Dominican whispered.

Again the telephone rang. After a long glance toward the priest Falk picked up the receiver.

"Yes . . . Yes . . . Yes . . . Yes."

247

He dropped the receiver apathetically. The general read his features and stepped up.

"How many innocent workers have that bloody Sturzebecker's soldiers laid low?"

Falk stood still, his eyes closed.

"They think close to twenty fell in the first salvo. Four soldiers fell first. The fools stormed them!"

"But we're holding the line?" asked the general.

"Yes. The mob retreated. The mounted police made a lateral attack."

He slumped into his chair under the general's pitying glance.

"I simply cannot understand," said Sturzebecker, "why a politician should be shocked at the thought that he has caused pain, particularly when he has done the right thing. Pain is always the result of right action! No matter what is undertaken there's always a spilling of blood and tears. This double fountain is the history of the world."

"May I speak with them a moment?" said the Dominican, who stood before Falk as if afflicted.

At the permissive nod he took the receiver.

"I am speaking from the Prime Minister's office. It's Father Leo. Are the wounded being taken to the hospital? Good. Are there many dead? Oh. Would you be so kind as to telephone the names here as soon as they are known? Thank you."

He hung up. Then the general crossed the room and clapped Falk cheerfully on the shoulder.

"Just rest now," he said. "There won't be any more. If they had forced their way in, they would have slaughtered the strikebreakers. Even if soldiers aren't counted as people at least a strikebreaker can count as half a person. Right? That makes a hundred men because there were two hundred of them. A hundred complete human beings. So there! If the rabble had gotten any further they would have burned down the factories, the munition dump would have blown sky high—a sort of bonus fireworks display. With a little luck a good part of the city could have gone up in smoke. So I would say you should be quite satisfied with the day's work."

Slowly he brought his heels together. "Your Excellency. Tomorrow I will hand in my letter of resignation."

Falk looked uncomprehending.

"Your letter of resignation?" he said dully.

"Of course," said the general cheerfully. "Butcher Sturzebecker has this act of violence on his conscience. He has murdered innocent civilians and won't be permitted to stay. The unwritten code of the country demands that I go. I know what will be in the morning papers. I shall go abroad. There's always a war somewhere, where one can pretend he is taking part in a just cause. Will you permit me to leave? I guarantee you've seen the last of this affair!"

Falk made a resigned gesture; then the general turned to the Dominican.

"Goodbye, Father. It will be my pleasure tomorrow to hear you preach at the Palace chapel. That is, if I can knife my way in past the self-righteous mob. Good day!"

He bowed and left.

At that moment, Christer Wendt came into the room. He paused a moment when he saw the Dominican and a smile flickered across his face. Falk turned toward him. "Ah, Wendt. What is it?"

"Pardon me, Your Excellency," said Wendt, "but I would like to suggest that the guard here be reinforced. Some uneasiness in this area can be expected."

Falk answered flatly, "Do what you think best. Ask Colonel Robach to come up. I have to call on His Majesty. First, however . . ."

The telephone clamored shrilly.

"Wendt," Falk said in a tired voice, "please take that call!"

Wendt obeyed.

"Hello. Yes, it's the Prime Minister's secretary speaking. Yes. What did you say? Oh. Yes, I'll take care of it. You're absolutely sure? Yes. Yes."

He replaced the receiver.

"Your Excellency," he said softly. "I don't know what to say."

"No more of that," Falk replied with a weary gesture. "Just say what you have to say."

"Nine workers," Wendt said. "A foreman, an engineer . . . and then a student."

"A student, too?" said Falk. "The poor boy. What's his name?"

"Your Excellency," answered Wendt, "it's . . . it's . . ."

The Dominican crossed swiftly to Falk's side. Falk raised himself slowly from his chair.

"Just keep talking. I've told you often enough I can take anything."

Wendt swallowed.

"The lieutenant said this: 'When we looked through his papers we found that his name was Georg Falk!' "

Falk was motionless. "Georg Falk?" he said. "What's happened to my boy?"

Then the truth broke in on him.

"Georg dead?" said Falk. "They shot him? The fools . . . Quick, the letter, Wendt. Give me the letter!"

Staggering, he went to the fireplace, found the letter, smoothed it out, but was unable to read it and handed it to the Dominican with a helpless gesture.

"Ask God for His mercy," the priest said softly and quickly.

Falk slowly raised his hands.

"Mercy?" he said hoarsely. "No!"

He shook his fists at the ceiling.

"Justice!" he hissed. "Justice!"

27

THE PRIME MINISTER'S villa had been swiftly restored, but
a barbed-wire fence ran around the grounds. Falk had not yet
had time to hunt for new furniture and had made use of
what was on hand in the guest wings. The cases had more
empty spaces than books, but there were new curtains at the
windows and a new carpet already covered the floor. Stephan,
who had been able to absolve himself from all suspicion,
worked day and night to provide his employers with a house
fit to live in. During repairs Elisabeth had occupied the guest
wing, but she was now ready to move back to her regular
quarters.

The park had been restored, though the lawn still showed
tell-tale signs which could not be removed until fall. The
antique pillar had had to be sacrificed; in its place stood
another copy.

With the crisis over, Falk was coming home to the country
more frequently. He stayed overnight as often as four or five
times a week. After Georg's death he felt the need to be with
his family. Regina kept out of his way—especially after Isabelle had left for Switzerland. She was more withdrawn than
ever and both Elisabeth and her husband doubted that they
would ever again be able to gain her confidence.

It was a morning in early June. Elisabeth, no longer using
her wheelchair, came slowly through the salon. She seemed
younger now than she had in years. Propped on her cane she
looked into the library.

Falk was sitting in his dressing gown in an armchair. The
floor was littered with newspapers which had been read and

let fall. The sun was bursting through drawn shades and two lights were burning. He sat with arms hanging limp over the sides of the chair. Through the night he had slept little, and now gazed fixedly at a crucifix on the desk.

Elisabeth entered softly, went to the windows, pulled the shades back, and then put out the two lights. She came to her husband.

"My dear, won't you try to sleep? It's six o'clock and you've been up all night."

"No," he said indifferently. "I can't."

She smoothed his hair back.

"I understand," she said softly. "I couldn't sleep either. I lay awake and thought of Georg."

He recoiled defensively.

"Don't mention him!"

"I know very little about Communism," Elisabeth said with her brittle voice—it resembled a fine bell that had cracked. "I know that it is Godless and false. But one thing seems clear to me. If Georg became a Communist, he did so because he found there something that he could believe in and love. What could it have been?"

Falk shrugged.

"He was misled, under bad influence. That's all there is to it."

"Yes, of course," Elisabeth answered quickly. "But somehow he must have found a sort of kinship with them that he didn't find with us."

Falk sat rigid.

"At any rate, he must have been happy when he fell, or don't you think so?"

She went to Falk's chair, took the overflowing ashtray and emptied it in the open fireplace.

"Happy?" said Falk. "A rioter? A boy who defied his father and the whole social order?"

252

Elisabeth went to the window and opened it halfway. A soft rain had fallen during the night and the garden glistened.

"Yes," she said. "But on the other hand he had to fight for something he considered to be right. I am not trying to talk myself into not seeing obvious evil. But I do believe that I am right. He was happy when he fell!"

Falk, who was barely listening, said dully:

"Where do you think we should give him permanent burial?"

She smiled and smoothed his hair again.

"Don't bother yourself now with that. You're tired. Try to rest for at least a little while. You have a heavy day ahead of you."

Falk, only half hearing her, sat like a broken man.

"It's amazing," he said, "that you . . . can be so strong. You, who in other respects are so weak. You don't even weep."

"No," Elisabeth said. "I believe he is in good hands."

Falk rose with a sigh. He stood before his wife but his eyes were riveted on the carpet. His voice was thick.

"Elisabeth, I have always thought that I had faith. I have always had the feeling that I have been sustained by my beliefs, even during my political career. But now I'm beginning to feel that I no longer believe. Everything seems so absurd."

She looked at him as his vigor began to return. His voice became stronger and his eyes regained their accustomed brightness.

"I certainly don't think I'm infallible," he said as he reached for her hand. "I know my weakness, or at least, I recognize my mistakes. But I have done my utmost to bring about what I held to be right. And what has been the result? Nothing but catastrophe! Now they're all howling against me—every single party. And Georg . . . *What does God intend for us?*"

253

Elisabeth shook her head.

"Don't ask me," she said. "I haven't the answer. I don't understand His ways. One thing I do know, however: He does have a purpose. There's no such thing as purposelessness or chance. Everything has a meaning, or else hides a meaning."

Falk took her shoulders in his hands. The gesture seemed new to him and he realized that years had passed since he had last done this.

"I've been hard on you," he said.

"No, no," Elisabeth answered and looked down.

He relaxed the mild embrace and walked to the window, threw it open and inhaled deeply of the morning air.

"I realize that I've slipped a good deal. Yet you come to me now to stand by my side. You. The only one. If you only knew how I need you. And if I only had your faith."

Elisabeth looked at him.

"You should try to believe only one thing. Believe that God is love!"

He turned and said slowly, bitterly:

"You mean that He is now acting with love? Toward me?"

"Of course He is," she answered.

With a wry smile he walked towards her.

"Do you call it love? Would you wish an earthly father to treat his children the way God is now treating me?"

She fell silent a moment. She hoped that now she wouldn't start to be pedantic and zealous and realized that she herself was only on the outermost edges of belief.

"You forget that we don't know His purposes. I'm thinking of myself now. How many long years I was embittered and rebellious, even though I seemed quite calm on the surface! Why did I have to suffer a paralysis? Why did I have to live apart from your life? I certainly wanted to give you my love, I thought, but then I discovered that I had no room inside me for anything but myself. The only way to improve myself was to get sick, to give myself leisure to examine my conscience. Oh, no one could have resisted God's love more than I did! That's why I understand you so well."

Elisabeth went slowly to the sofa and sat down. He followed her and took her hand. It had been an eternity since they had last sat this way together.

"Can you tell me," he said, after a long pause, "if you are always able to feel God's presence? I certainly can't."

"Feelings," Elisabeth said hesitantly, "are not very important. The most important thing . . ."

Falk continued in his own train of thought.

"During all these years, when you were alone out here—paralyzed—and I was in love with another woman . . ."

She put her hand over his.

"Don't torment yourself," she said. "That has all been forgiven and forgotten. Since I really got to know myself I no longer wondered that you couldn't love me."

Anguish gripped him and he reached for her hand and pressed it firmly.

"During those years did you have the feeling that God was with you, that you possessed Him?"

Elisabeth reflected for a moment. She dared not say too much and her story was not terribly heroic.

"I can tell you that twelve years passed without my feeling anything at all. When we were married I lived in what I thought was familiarity with God. There was nothing fictitious then; it was real, and had been since I was a little girl. But then it all disappeared."

"Disappeared?" He looked at her intently. "But you never told me!"

She smiled. "There is a lot I have never told you. It disappeared. I continued to pray, I went to confession, I tried to examine my conscience and learn what sins were keeping

255

me from getting closer to God. And I found them, too. I found that my entire life had merely been—a postulancy."

"And then this contact returned?"

"No. Nothing was more difficult for me than just this," she said. "When I believed myself ready for everything, when I had become resigned to my poor health and paralysis and my separation from you, I thought at any rate that I had God or would get Him back. But it didn't happen. I just simply became empty and still am."

He looked at her, shocked, and dropped her hand.

"That's frightening."

She reflected a moment.

"Yes," she answered. "It's frightening."

"And despite it all you acted as before?" he said. "You continued with your charitableness, your works of mercy. All the people that you helped. You even helped in some way in one conversion after another."

"God was able to use me in my lowliness. Whenever someone I knew, someone through me, became a Christian I remained static. I was doing nothing. I didn't even know that God was there!"

The sunbeams streamed in while outside the birds' songs rose toward heaven. Otherwise it was completely quiet. Who would guess what had taken place here a short while ago? The old had been burned down amid terror and torment —suddenly the new stood glistening in the sunlight of innocence.

"When did it all change?" he asked.

She leaned back on the sofa, thankful that she could at last discuss these things with him, without argument and in peace.

"I waited twelve years. During all that time I didn't have the slightest sign of God's existence. I experienced nothing, I felt nothing, I prayed as in an empty room. And I never received an answer. I was plagued by bitterness and aversion. I blamed God! Can you imagine it—a woman like me complaining against God?"

He stared gloomily ahead.

"That part I can understand only too well," he said.

"Then one day something happened," she continued. "It was nothing extraordinary. It was during the summer eight years ago—after our big banquet out here with all our friends."

"When I was made President of the Bank?"

"Yes. You were so proud and happy, and all the guests were in very good humor."

"You seemed quite happy that day yourself," he said.

She smiled. "I was in despair. Even worse than that. When, toward morning, you and the others went out to watch the sunrise from the hill. I stayed behind."

"I remember very well," he said, smiling. "When we came back I thought you had gone to bed, but instead you had set out our breakfast in the dining nook. And what a breakfast!"

She sat quietly a moment.

"At that very time I could have taken my life," she said. "I was in complete rebellion against God. Then I went into the kitchen, on my cane, and put the maids to work."

Now she was speaking with a certain embarrassment, like a schoolgirl.

"I was in the pantry. I stood there and sliced ham, if you please. It was cold there and I stood shivering amid all the dishes and glassware. Everything seemed strange, I wanted to have nothing to do with all this lifeless matter. And suddenly, as I stood there slicing—I remember it so well— suddenly a ray of light came through the blinds. At once I realized . . ."

Falk, who was listening intently, leaned forward so that no nuance would escape him.

"What did you see? What?"

She smiled. "Oh, nothing—nothing 'out there.' But somehow, interiorly, I realized that in this silence, in this night, this emptiness, God was present. That He Himself was this very silence!"

Slowly Falk got up, deeply disappointed.

"I don't understand a single word. Do you mean to say that God was silence? That's the same as saying that lovelessness is love!"

She looked at him. "Yes!" she said. "Exactly!"

He became irritated.

"Explain what you mean," he said. "Either love or the absence of love. Presence or absence. Either fulfillment or the vacuum!"

Once more she nodded.

"I said exactly the same thing all through those years. But I came to realize that God can show his love by not manifesting it. It was as if He wanted to say to me, 'Your task is to believe—without answer, without echo. Persevere!' "

She thought to herself: And I failed even in this. In spite of everything I managed to transform even this into deception and hypocrisy. Sometime he'll have to learn that, too.

"You shock me," Falk said dully. "Do you think that what you describe is love?"

"There's none greater," Elisabeth answered. "If you could only see that God is working with you and with all of us! If you could only see that every terrible thing that has happened is His work and will."

Falk stood stiffly before her. His voice had changed.

"Even that Georg was taken from us?"

She got up slowly.

"Yes. That, too."

"I refuse to believe it," he said sharply. "If it makes any sense at all, it was the Devil's work, not God's!"

At that moment the maid entered from the library.

"I beg your pardon," she said. "Father Leo is here."

Falk's countenance brightened.

"My dear," Elisabeth said. "You know that I am beside you? That I love you?"

His eyes spoke his gratitude.

"Yes," he answered a little thickly. He turned to the maid. "Ask him to come in."

The maid disappeared.

"He'll have to excuse my appearance," he said.

Elisabeth went to the door leading to the living room. Falk's eyes followed her out. Then he went to the mirror, smoothed his hair and re-knotted his tie.

Father Leo entered.

28

"I JUST HAD to come to visit you," said the Dominican in his cheerful voice. "I prayed for Georg and for all of you when I said my Mass."

Falk shook hands, excused his dress and exchanged a few pleasantries with the priest.

"I won't stay long," said the Dominican. "I know that you must get a little rest after all you've been through. But there is one thing I want to ask you."

"What is that?"

"The day you gave me Georg's letter which you retrieved from the fireplace—since then you have refused to mention it. Well, I have it here. Do you absolutely refuse to read it?"

Falk nodded, but when the Dominican held it in his outstretched hand, he took it.

"I'll take a look at it," he said quietly. He began to read but was unable to continue.

"No," he said, his voice raw. "I can't. You read it!"

The Dominican took the letter:

"Dear Father: I imagine that you are waiting for an apology. Well, I want to ask your forgiveness, if I have hurt you. I've always respected and admired you. But I've come to a point where I have to make a decision—just as you, too, once had to choose your own life. I know where I'm going. Unfortunately it's a road that you don't think much of. That hurts me, but I can't help it. If you ask me why I don't follow *your* way, I have to answer that I don't believe in it. I don't believe in a man who talks democracy but is a dictator in his own home."

Falk raised his arm. "Why, that whelp!"

The Dominican continued reading aloud, ignoring Falk's outburst.

"I can understand your ideal, but your own life doesn't measure up to it. That's why you convince nobody, that's why you're driving your children away from you."

"Must I listen to that?" Falk said in sick despair.

"Yes," said the Dominican. He continued. "If I were a Christian I would pray for you. That I cannot do. I can't pray for you because I saw the way you pray . . ."

Falk's clenched fists were in the air.

"Stop," he shrieked. "Stop, I say!"

The Dominican paused. "You must hear this letter to the end." He continued to read:

"Father, I don't ask that you think the way I do in politics, or that you even understand me. But I wish for you the same thing that I wish for myself, to live in harmony with what I consider right and not to compromise my ideas and ideals by my actions. I know it isn't easy. You keep saying that you want to unify rather than rule. I believe you. But you should first unify your own family rather than rule over them, and do that before you try to rule the country! So far you haven't succeeded in either. Georg."

Falk was beside himself, and cried out almost in anguish, "Father Leo! Why are you tormenting me?"

"I'm not tormenting you," the Dominican answered. "I want to help you."

"But that's only words!" Falk shouted. "Say something! Say something concrete and sensible! What can I do for my son anyway, now that he's dead?"

Father Leo stood quietly and looked at the Prime Minister.

"You also have a daughter."

"Regina? She's a whore!"

"You should try to win her back and try to forgive her."

Falk pulled himself up rigidly.

"I should pardon her her shameless life, her impudence, her miserable . . ."

"You should forgive even more than that," the Dominican answered. "Above all, you should try to understand her."

"I'll never understand loose morals and degeneracy," Falk asserted righteously.

"I certainly don't ask that you should," said the priest. "But *why* has Regina become loose and degenerate? It didn't happen by chance."

Falk strode to the window.

"You mean it's my fault?" he roared. "This, too? Is everything my fault?"

"Don't waste time trying to figure out who's more to blame," said the priest. "Such bookkeeping never accomplished anything. Show her that you love her, that you want to help her. Show her that you want to help her exactly as she is now."

It seemed that Falk had not heard a word.

"At any moment," he said, "my secretary will be here.

There'll be reports, newspapers, telephone conversations. How could I find time?"

"Regina is sitting upstairs reading," the Dominican answered quickly. "I could see her at the window when I arrived. Go to her. Now!"

Falk turned. "But what can I do?"

Father Leo smiled.

"Go," he said. "Now! Go upstairs to your daughter. Win back the one child you still have left. Do it before it's too late!"

Falk hesitated.

"It's horrible," he said, trapped. "I'm so completely helpless, so alone."

The Dominican stepped closer to him.

"You are not alone," he said softly. He made the sign of the Cross on Falk's forehead.

Falk stood, his head bowed. Then his eyes met the priest's. He pressed his hand and went slowly toward the door. The Dominican watched him go. Then he went to a chair far in the rear of the library beneath a tall floor lamp, where he sat completely still with only his fingers playing over his rosary.

Christer Wendt entered, carrying the large attaché case. His step was rapid.

He put the case on the desk, looked through various papers, and then whistled softly to himself. The telephone rang and he reached for the receiver.

"This is the Prime Minister's secretary. He will be here in a few minutes. I'll have him call. No, I can't arrange an appointment with him today, he's going to be extremely busy. Thank you."

He hung up.

"Congratulations," said the Dominican softly. "Congratulations. You played your cards well."

Wendt looked at him boldly.

"Better than you, at any rate," he said.

"Perhaps," the Dominican answered. "The difference between you and me is that I make no secret of who gives me my orders."

Wendt's face remained unperturbed.

"I cannot see that we profit by talking with each other," Wendt answered. "I ask you not to disturb me at my work."

"The Prime Minister will be downstairs in a minute," said the Dominican. "I would like at that time to discuss with him, in your presence, who you really are. You have no objections to that? Or do you?"

"Not in the slightest! I have never made a secret of who I am. I only hope that you have some proof to back up your allegations. The Prime Minister is accustomed to insist on such formalities."

"Naturally," the Dominican answered. He crossed his arms and continued: "But first of all I'd like to say a few things to you myself. You are a very able man. You have helped to ruin Regina. You've had your revenge on her father. You've practically sent his son to his death. You have broken up this family. And if the entire state flounders it will be largely your doing. That's not a bad score."

Wendt turned his back.

"You overestimate me," he said. "States aren't toppled by insignificant private secretaries, but by economic laws that no one can ever alter."

"I recall that you stressed that point in your lecture," the Dominican said. "But that doesn't make it any more convincing."

Wendt pretended that he hadn't heard.

"You are completely misinformed," he said, "if you think that I hate the Prime Minister for having separated me from Regina. I must admit that I wasn't immediately drawn any

263

closer to him, but when I got to know him better I realized that he is approximately like all other mortals. Not any better, not any worse. You can believe me or not—during my years here I have learned to esteem him."

"One would never know it," said the priest.

"You would not," said Wendt, trying to puzzle out just how much the priest really knew. "You live in a society where all actions are interpreted on the basis of hurt pride and similar emotions. I see mighty forces determining history and life. These forces are unsentimental and dig in deep. I have put myself at their service. This state is going to perish because the laws will so have it. The House of Falk is going to perish, too, because the time has arrived when the bourgeois form it represents is about to perish. One can make such an affirmation in all calmness, without being driven by hate. I am almost sorry for the old man."

Wendt continued, now for the first time with hate modifying the inflection of his cutting tone:

"Or, if you don't like that interpretation, what about God? The Lord of the World! He Who guides the course of history —in love? Where does He fit in?"

Wendt stepped close to the Dominican.

"*Why* is Falk going under? Not because he's a criminal and a miscreant who must be punished. He's being defeated because he's an honorable man, a gentleman and an idealist who has burned his last ounce of energy for what he considers to be good and true. And God? What's He doing?"

Hate glowed in the depths of his eyes as Father Leo stood calmly before him.

"I know this family," the Dominican answered softly. "I know it just as well as you do. When you say I've failed here, you are completely right. I haven't been able to accomplish a thing."

Wendt smiled.

"At least you're honest enough to admit it!"

264

"I admit it readily. But the job I couldn't accomplish you have been able to do for me. God has brought it about through you."

"What sort of rubbish is this?" Wendt asked irritably.

"I saw from the begining," the priest replied, "that one thing had to happen here. Falk's pride had to be broken. He had to learn how to evaluate himself. I couldn't do it. Not with all my prayers, nor with proposing to him the whole calendar of saints."

"Possibly you got in the way of his vision."

The Dominican nodded. "Exactly. He judged Christianity according to me and for that reason remained unconvinced. But God didn't give up simply because I was an unsuitable instrument. He chose another one—you!"

Wendt laughed. "Me!" he said. "You're really quite a humorist."

The Dominican continued as though Wendt had not spoken.

"And the interesting thing is that you are convinced that you're the instrument of some law, some relationship or other; fate, perhaps. A fate that breaks pride and raises men from their degradation I cease to call fate. I call it God."

"Twaddle," said Wendt. "Monkish twaddle, for the very old and the very young."

The telephone rang and Wendt quickly reached for the receiver.

"Yes," he said. "Yes. No. I'd better come myself. I have the time. It will be much safer if I come myself. I'll take the car and be there in fifteen minutes. Thanks."

He hung up.

"Unfortunately I have to go on important business to the Executive Offices. I thank you for the arguments you have proposed. And I hope to have the opportunity to resume the discussion again."

"Yes," said the Dominican.

At that moment the Prime Minister entered from the living room. He had heard the last words.

"You have to leave?" he asked astonished.

"Yes," Wendt said and grasped the attaché case. "I dislike having to, but I think it would be better if I were personally to get those important papers at the Office. They wanted to send them out, but I said I'd come for them, if Your Excellency agrees."

"Of course," Falk said apathetically, almost absent-mindedly. "Of course."

Wendt left quickly.

He needs a quarter of an hour to get there, thought the Dominican. Thus, we have plenty of time to bring the Executive Offices into the picture . . .

He turned to the Prime Minister.

"Did you see Regina?"

Falk walked heavily to his desk, where he sat down and propped his head on his hands.

"Yes," he said in an almost inaudible whisper.

"Well?" the Dominican asked.

Falk sighed again. The Dominican went around the desk and put a hand on his shoulder. After awhile Falk looked up.

"Have you ever gone to someone with your hands outstretched and had him spit in your face?" he asked softly.

"What happened? Tell me."

"I went to Regina. I told her that I knew the kind of life she was living, scandals and so forth, her relationship with young Graber. Then I told her that I wanted a reconciliation, that I love her and forgive her."

"What did she say?"

"She went white, then she threw her head into that haughty angle. 'Forgiveness from *you*?' she screamed. 'I'll have none of your forgiveness. You're the one who should be begging me and the rest of us for pardon. But we'll never forgive you!' That's approximately it. What cheapness! What hate! I just can't understand it."

He looked at the priest.

"She's right of course," the priest said. "You shouldn't have offered her your forgiveness; you should have asked for hers."

Falk got up.

"I can't do any more," he said. "Pardon me, but I just can't."

"Well," said the Dominican. "You can at least listen, because out of everything that is now happening a voice is speaking that you have never wanted to hear."

"What do you think it's saying to me?" Falk asked with irony.

"Learn humility."

He made the sign of the Cross over the Prime Minister.

"I have another piece of news for you," he said. "You've been badly deceived by your secretary."

Falk looked up.

"Are you going to start on that line again?" he said wearily.

"Yes, I am," said the Dominican. "And you must pick up your telephone and order that he be arrested in ten minutes when he arrives at the Executive Offices."

Falk stood up in his amazement.

"What are you saying? Do you have any proof?"

"Yes, I think I have," answered Father Leo.

PART IV

Night Music

29

FALK had resigned as Prime Minister.

A storm of controversy had broken over him. The Communists represented him as the prototype of capitalistic brutality. The Catholic Party could not forgive him his campaign against Dr. Graber. He had quarrelled with his own party. And he was weary unto death.

Georg's escapade had not been underplayed; the newspapers for weeks on end had harped on the sensational nature of the boy's theft of the defense plans, his participation in the demonstration, and his infatuation with a Communist student.

The climax was the disappearance of Wendt. The Prime Minister's secretary had disappeared without leaving a trace behind him. Falk was politically dead.

One warm July day he was sitting in his library. He had had his law books brought out from the city and the shelves were quite well restocked. He had also bought a few artistic replacements after receiving the insurance settlement. Elisabeth had suggested that they travel abroad but he refused to consider it. The Villa was his last refuge.

He stood up to leaf through one of his legal works when his wife entered. Elisabeth smiled in surprise that he had been able to get almost all of the books set up so soon.

"It's already looking lovely here," she said.

He moved closer to her and awkwardly caressed her cheek.

"Yes," he said. "It's the original library I had as a professor. But in other respects—it has to be built up again."

He took from the table a volume of Montaigne which had been damaged in the fire, but which he had not yet been able to bring himself to throw away.

"Just imagine," he said in the soft, tired voice which was now habitual, "just imagine spending an entire life collecting first editions and special editions—now they're all gone."

He put the book down.

"It's exactly the way our culture will disappear, if the Communists ever attack or are attacked in earnest. Picture scientific expeditions in another age coming here to dig up our cities. Perhaps they won't even be able to read the few inscriptions and books that they find."

"It certainly could happen," she said.

He stood, arms hanging helplessly.

"It will be with a pitying smile that they'll grub about in our class struggles and wars. They'll look upon us as barbarians, irresponsible barbarians."

"They'll be quite right," said Elisabeth.

He remained standing, sunk in thought.

"And then they might come across the ruins of some cathedral, possibly only the crypt—like Chartres, say. Then they'll try to reconstruct our beliefs. What do you think will be their judgment of a culture that held out love as the highest ideal and at the same time used all its technical skill to rub itself out?"

"I don't know," she answered as she plucked a faded petal from a flower in the window display. "Perhaps they'll get to know their own nature—and realize that man by himself can do nothing."

"Yes," he continued. "And possibly the last Pope will have been driven from the Vatican with a small band of followers. Possibly the entire Church will have been swept away—only a handful of Christians survive—in China or Africa—a solitary negro Pope—the last Pope—why not?"

"No," said Elisabeth. "Why not?"

Falk went to a table where a bundle of books was lying. He took them in his hand.

"Can you imagine it? Almost all of Georg's books are still around. They were upstairs in his room at the Residence . . . I had them brought out here . . ."

"That was good of you," she said.

"I am begining to understand him a little. I have noticed what he underlined, in Ibsen and Schopenhauer and Heidegger. I was amazed to find that he had bought himself a copy of Catherine of Siena—of course, he wouldn't deign to use my copy. He made considerable annotations in her *Dialogues*. Can you understand how he could have become a Communist at the same time?"

"I don't believe he really became a Communist. He became . . . what we were not. He saw us—and for that reason thought he had to reject our faith."

Falk's face clouded over heavily.

"My faith!" he said. "Not yours."

Elisabeth went over to him. She tried now and again to go for a whole hour without using her cane.

"Oh, no, dear," she said. "My faith, too. I understood him. He was hungering for real love and we gave him now and then a bit of sentimentality, that was all. You know—I've gone through his clothes. Do you have any objections if I give them away?"

"No," he said. "Of course not. To whom were you thinking of giving them?"

"I'm not sure yet. I was thinking of giving them to the gardener's son. They were approximately the same age, and good friends."

"Isn't he a Communist, too?" asked Falk.

"Yes, I think so."

Falk thought for a moment and then nodded. There certainly would be no harm in giving them to him.

"How calm it is here," she said.

He turned.

"Yes," he answered. "Like a grave."

"It's wonderful, I think," said Elisabeth. "We have peace here. And you can use a bit of it."

The maid came in.

"Here are the papers and mail," she said. She put them on the desk and left.

Falk didn't turn. Elisabeth smiled.

"A short while ago you couldn't wait to read the papers," she remarked.

"Now they can stay where they are," he said. "I know exactly what's in them. Everyone is happy that the government has resigned, that the good-for-nothing Prime Minister has disappeared from public life. Everyone rejoices in my misfortune."

That's part of the game," Elisabeth rejoined quickly. "You shouldn't be surprised at it."

"No. I know it."

He walked across the room and sat down heavily in his old chair which he had brought out from the city. It was his "professor's chair," an ugly but comfortable old relic.

He laughed almost soundlessly.

"Bank Director Berwald in my own bank," he said. "Really a nice fellow! I was the one who made him Bank Director—he's forgotten it. I was the one who gave the nod for him to be admitted to party leadership—I was the one who got him his Order of Merit. What would he be without me? A president of a bank in the provinces! But now he sits in the party councils and lectures me as if I were a schoolboy. I'm a charlatan and a political dilettante—I've lost the confidence of the party, indeed the confidence, of the entire country.

The party must have new leadership—he means himself, of course. The party that I created, which without me . . ."

Elisabeth went to him, stood at his side and laid her finger on his lips.

"You're right, you're absolutely right," she said. "They are ridiculous—and ungrateful. Let Berwald do what he wants. His nonsense doesn't concern us any more. Not in the least!"

She went to the window and opened it.

"Have you noticed the continual peace? It's like God's breath. I'm constantly aware of it."

Falk had not listened. He sat, his eyes half closed, and spoke in agitated fragments:

"For fifteen years I haven't rested for a moment. My entire being has been attuned to activity, wakefulness and struggle."

Elisabeth looked at him.

"There is another activity that concerns us now," she said. "An inner activity. Yesterday I visited a convent of the Dominican Sisters. They live in complete isolation from the world. They never go out, they don't even perform charitable works, they seem to be completely passive. They sing all the hours of the Office and live in almost uninterrupted contemplation. Can you imagine anything more useless, or stupid in the eyes of the world? Yet I am convinced that no activity is stronger or more influential than theirs."

He smiled, something that happened so seldom nowadays that Elisabeth was deeply touched.

"I suppose you want to make me into a contemplative monk! Maybe a Trappist. They're never permitted to speak!"

It was wonderful to see his smile.

"No," Elisabeth said. "I want you exactly as you are. But perhaps listening a bit more with the inner ear."

His face became serious again.

"I almost believe that I can no longer hear anything—except through you."

"Well, then hear through me! That's what I'm here for."
Again he smiled.

"You're an unfathomable person," he said. "If I could only understand how you keep going. You realize that we can't rest easily at night, that anything at all could happen in the wake of the hate I've stirred up. I am sure there are some threatening letters lying there in my mail. It's only a matter of time before they come back to set my house on fire again. Do you realize that they hanged me in effigy in the dock area the day before yesterday, while a happy mob shouted itself hoarse with joy?"

He paused, then in a scarcely audible whisper:

"There is no man in the entire country more hated than I."

She looked at him; her tired, defeated husband.

"There is also no one who is more loved than you," she said.

Once more his thoughts had wandered and he hadn't heard.

"And Regina. She doesn't say a word. Sometimes I think that her eyes are on me—filled with hate. She barely answers when I speak to her."

"Pray for her," said Elisabeth, who had herself almost despaired of her daughter.

"I do!" he said passionately. "I hurl my prayer out into the room—it disappears into the void, rolls off and is sucked up."

He stood up and looked at his wife.

"Elisabeth, you believe, you know. Tell me, for God's sake, *what is faith?*"

After a moment she said slowly:

"Faith means to climb for years up an endless ladder, and when you finally reach the top rung exhausted, and are looking for a hand-hold so you can swing yourself over the top, you hear a voice. 'Let go. Let yourself fall.' You know how a person grabs hold when a ladder begins to wobble! To believe is to let yourself be hurled backwards giddily into the abyss and still know that down below a strong hand is going to catch you."

"I want to believe. But I can't. I've wished I had the will to believe . . . I can't do any more!"

She stepped closer to him.

"That's enough," she said. "No more than that is asked from any man, and we are not able to do more than that."

She looked at him. Should she risk asking her question? Would it torment him too much?

"How did your talk with Dr. Graber go?" she asked at last, fearfully. "Do you want to tell me about it?"

Falk shrugged bitterly.

"I went there," he said in a voice devoid of all tone. "I realized that I had to—that I had acted wrongly. He received me quite coldly."

"That's only natural," said Elisabeth. "He had been frightfully hurt."

"I said to him everything that I had vowed to say." Falk was now speaking with considerable effort. He had to exert himself enormously to control his voice.

"I said to him . . . I said to him that the existence of men like me explained all the tragedies of our society—even Communism. I said that I now recognize my mistakes . . . that I felt unsuited for my job and was going to resign."

Elisabeth folded her hands.

"What did he answer?" Her voice was soft, her tone apprehensive.

"He said that he understood me." Falk's voice had all but left him. "I told him that I had determined to make a clean breast of it, no matter what the cost. Then I said that I regretted my campaign against him, that I had been badly hurt by his attacks on me and had felt that I had the right to hit back . . . that throughout it all I had known that he had been

277

guilty in the Gloria affair only as regards the letter of the law—not in any moral or deeper interpretation . . . that I had violated justice both with regard to him and to his wife."

Falk's voice was now very indistinct. But he made a fresh effort and continued: "I asked him . . . to forgive me . . ."

Silence. Elisabeth was just able to get out her question.

"What was his answer?"

Falk hadn't heard. His eyes were closed and his chin had sunk to his breast.

"I prayed the whole time," he whispered. But as he turned around and brushed at his eyes, his face assumed some of its hard strength.

"Do you know what he answered?" he said loudly. "He said, 'Is that all you have to say?' I nodded. 'Then,' he said, 'I have only one thing to say to you. This is it: I never believed in your sincerity. I've always thought that you were rotten with pride, that you were dishonest to the marrow. And you're lying now. Stop this farce, and get out of my house!' "

Elisabeth rose quickly from the chair to take her husband's hand.

"I don't know how I got out of the room," he went on. "I was dying from shame. I don't remember how I found my hat . . . how I got out to my car . . ."

She stroked his hair, unable to speak.

"As the car was bringing me out here," he said, "I thought to myself: 'I'm dead . . . I've ceased to exist . . . I'm completely alone . . . And this aloneness is emptiness . . .'"

He straightened to his full height.

"Thanks be to God," Elisabeth said.

He wheeled to face her.

"What do you mean?"

Her face was radiant.

278

30

REGINA was standing in the doorway. Her parents' voices had been so quiet that she had heard nothing as she stood quietly watching them.

"Regina," Falk said in an attempt at composure, "have your heard anything from Wendt?"

"No," she answered, "but I know where he is."

"You know?" he asked, astonished.

"The whole country knows," she answered, and waved the latest newspaper at him. "The whole story is right here."

She snapped the paper open and read:

"New Mobilization Plan Stolen by Prime Minister's Secretary. Disappears Across Border. Will Hand Plans to Russia."

Falk's hand pressed heavily back across the top of his head.

"Wendt," he said. "The man I trusted! Why? Why?"

"Why?" snapped Regina. "Because he wanted revenge. Because he hated you for the pain you caused him. I understand him. He's finally become a man."

"Regina!" Elisabeth cried.

The daughter glanced at her mother.

"I mean what I say." The words came in a spate. "I'm glad to see him cutting loose, going his own way, daring to do something on his own instead of always bowing and scraping. I wish I had gone with him."

"You could have, for all I care!" Falk was scarcely able to restrain himself and Elisabeth had gone to his side and taken his hand. Regina looked on with scorn, then walked to the radio and turned it on.

"What are you doing?" Elisabeth asked.

"I'm going to listen to the King's address! The last act in this comedy is bound to be the funniest."

"No, we can get along without that," her mother said.

But Falk replied dully, "No, Regina's right. We should listen."

Regina was still leaning over the radio adjusting the volume and no one noticed that a car had drawn up in the driveway.

"Oh, it's too late," she said with her habitual irritation. "My watch is slow, as usual."

But suddenly the King's voice filled the room:

". . . one of the few important moments in which a constitutional monarch, as I see it, has both the right and the duty to interfere. Our country is facing the most difficult crisis of the twenty-five years of my reign. In the certainty that my intervention would be to the advantage of my people I have requested the resignation of the present Government. This afternoon the formation of the new Government will be announced. Fortunately, it has been possible to arrange a coalition. I want to urge the nation to exercise disciplined calm as we await the announcement of the Government's accession to authority. Nothing can be accomplished by acts of desperation. The entire nation is under martial law. I am confident, however, that this will be but a passing phase. The previous Government came to power against my wishes. It represented a minority of the population and proved itself in many respects immature in its dealing with the problems of the moment. In the wake of its failure, it has resigned. It represented precisely those egocentric, bourgeois, opinionated citizens with no thought of sacrifice, unity, or the surrender of class privileges, who have made possible in this country the prevailing opposition . . ."

Elisabeth had listened despairingly to the attack on her husband. Now she stepped up and turned the radio off.

280

"We can do without any more of that," she said.

"Why not?" Regina said coldly. "The King's right. He's a clear thinker and intends to hang on to his own privileges. But he'll sacrifice his ministers. He's tremendous."

"We are going to hear the rest of the speech," Falk said thickly.

Regina turned the radio on again.

". . . in complete confidence that the overwhelming majority of the population will approve of the steps I have taken I will, in conclusion, call upon the Almighty: God bless this ancient land. We commend ourselves to His guiding hand."

"Amen!" Regina shouted and broke out into peals of laughter. "That song-and-dance went over superbly. And the Dear Lord came in at the end. That was so certain I could have bet on it!"

A tall figure was standing in the doorway and when Falk looked up he saw that it was the King. Falk and Elisabeth rose to their feet; Regina recoiled in dismay.

The King nodded to Regina.

"Yes, indeed, Miss Falk," he said. "The finale was really good. Patriotic, paternal and heart-warming. Hello, my friend. Good day, Madame Falk. I couldn't resist stopping here to visit you since I go by every day. My aide-de-camp tried to dissuade me—he's standing outside now cursing his baronial mustache into a snarl."

The King had a package in his hand which he now began to unwrap.

"So many of your things were destroyed here," he said, "that I brought along this little trinket. You probably have a pedestal that you can place it on."

They all watched the agile hands in amazement as he produced a figurine of a youth.

"The noble youth is really ghastly from an artistic standpoint," he said. "But you see, this bauble is the only thing

281

I have ever earned entirely on my own. And now you must have it."

Falk tried to make objections but the King gestured him to silence.

"You must hear the story. It happened while I was still Crown Prince and was putting in some service on a destroyer. We had a bad fellow on board, an anarcho-syndicalist he was, continually shooting off his mouth. He fell overboard and I knew he could swim no better than he could talk, so I followed him over the rail."

The King placed the statuette on the desk, shook his head in disapproval and then tried it on a windowsill.

"If I am going to be completely honest," he continued, "I must probe some of the background a bit. At that time I still had the ability to fall in love. Yes, Miss Falk, really. And at my father's court there was a charming young Countess with whom I had had a few contacts. But my father and my mother, fine old-fashioned people that they were, would not consent to this business. I was consequently depressed. I wanted to marry her and renounce the crown, court life and the country itself—so I plunged overboard. But you can imagine what it was like when I hit the water. It was October. I became quite sober, clawed my way to the syndicalist, took him by the top lock. He resisted—these people are always trying to resist something—so I gave him a good uppercut that put him to sleep. And when the destroyer was able to come about to fish me out—it was the old *Integrity* that was always running aground—there I was happily treading water with an inactive syndicalist in my arms. Undoubtedly he was in the bunch recently that threw stones at my car. Well—that's how I got this horrible 'youth'!"

He walked up to Falk.

"Will you accept it?"

Falk bowed. The scene was more than grotesque.

"Your Majesty embarrasses me," he said.

"I had planned this evening to go to the Opera," the King said, wandering up and down the room, picking up various objects and inspecting books. "Everybody is warning me against it—there'll be demonstrations and one never knows what will happen, the initiates say. But little Miss de Wette is going to be the solo ballerina and she's charming."

He had gone over to Regina.

"Why so serious, young lady?" he asked.

"I'm not, Your Majesty," she stammered.

"Then I must have made a mistake," said the King. "I often do."

Once more he approached Falk.

"You know, Falk, yesterday I felt approximately the way I did the day I jumped from the old *Integrity*. It was conceivable that yesterday I might have done what many had seriously advised me to do. Abdicate. It was conceivable, I say. Then you came in with my speech prepared . . ."

Regina and Elisabeth looked at each other in amazement.

The King sank into a chair.

"At first I thought that you had gone completely mad," he said. "You had written for me the best speech I had ever delivered, while offering yourself as the sacrificial scapegoat. It would be *I* who would emerge as the far-seeing father-of-the-country. You're simply an old-fashioned medieval knight, freely sacrificing yourself for the Fatherland. It sounds almost romantic! Can you imagine it? I was touched. Really touched."

He rose again, to make the rounds of the library, rearranging slightly the furniture and some of the books.

"Miss Falk," he said. "Once we played 'theatre' at the Palace. It was a sort of pastoral. The girls bowed and scraped and warbled like berouged stable girls. I yawned, leaned back and looked out the window—perhaps you know that in my private box there is a window that overlooks the park. And do you know what I saw? I saw a real peasant girl, without rouge, alone and in full bloom. She stood there and saw neither the Palace, nor the theatre, nor the window in my private box. Do you know what she saw?"

He paused.

"She saw the sun! She was standing looking at the sun. I'm telling you the truth. She was utterly real and glowed in the sunshine. I forgot all the cheap music on the stage. 'Reality,' I thought. 'Blessed be ordinary, simple reality.' I wanted to jump out the window and take her in my arms —but of course I can't act like that."

Again he went close to Falk and gripped the sleeve of his coat.

"Falk," he said, "as you stood there, white in the face, and urged the speech upon me that has now evoked the heartfelt gratitude of the people, I thought to myself, 'Old Falk. I thought he was like all the rest. But no. He is absolutely real!' You will remember that I pinched your arm. Of course. I had to be sure that you were the real thing, that I wasn't dreaming. Then, when you had left after I had said a few stupid formalities as is my custom, I thought further. 'Falk is now making his exit into silence. He shall have my fine Youth to keep him company!' "

He picked up the figurine from the windowsill and handed it to Falk.

"Here it is," he said, his voice suddenly giving evidence of deep emotion. "It's atrocious—I never knew how I could get rid of it decently."

Falk took the statuette. There were tears in his eyes.

At that moment the aide-de-camp appeared in the doorway.

"Pardon me, Your Majesty, it is already quite late."

The King wheeled.

"Just look at him. What did I tell you? Yes, I'm coming. But I'll probably be back, Falk."

284

He grasped Falk's hand and turned to the ladies. He delayed a moment longer in the attitude of one listening.

"Strange," he said, "I have the feeling today as if something were going on behind the scenes . . ."

He turned to the aide-de-camp:

"Do you notice it, too?"

"I beg pardon, Your Majesty?" the aide answered, without understanding in the least.

"No," said the King. "You notice nothing. But I do."

Again he turned to Falk.

"You know—sometimes it's as if you see billows running through the scenery. You know that something's going on —*in behind*. Now I'm leaving, but before I go I'm going to say one thing more, Falk. You are . . ."

The King fell silent and shook his head. No one dared break that silence.

"Pardon me," he said softly. "I was reflecting whether what I want to say is absolutely true. It is. Yes, you are the only human being . . ."

His words now were very deliberate:

". . . the only human being whom I envy. A little bit. Goodbye!"

He raised his hand in greeting and sprang down the steps followed by the aide-de-camp. Falk followed while the two women remained behind in the library.

Steps could be heard on the gravel. Then the slamming of doors and the purring of the motor.

Falk re-entered the library.

Deeply moved and very pale Regina approached her father.

"Father," she said. "Father, is it true?"

He stopped and looked at her with tired eyes.

"Is what true, Regina?"

Regina shook her head and turned to her mother.

"But you, Mother—did you know it? Did you have any idea that he wrote the speech himself?"

"No, Regina," Elisabeth answered. "Your father said nothing about it."

Again Regina turned to her father, but dared say nothing more.

"We won't discuss it any more," he said wearily. "I think I shall go out into the garden. The sun is shining beautifully today."

He went past his daughter. Her eyes followed, then she went after him. At the doorway she kissed him.

"Father," she whispered. "Father . . ."

He patted her on the cheek as if she were a little girl.

Heavily he went out the door, crossed through the living room, and went out on the terrace.

The gravel could be heard grinding under his feet until he had reached the lawn.